One Last Stand

Whispers of Grace Series

Book One: One Woman Falling
Book Two: One Way Home
Book Three: One Last Stand

One Last Stand

Whispers of Grace Series

Melanie Campbell

Dedication

For my husband

Acknowledgments

I faced many obstacles in writing this book, but because of the people mentioned below and with God's great grace, I was finally able to type "The End" to *One Last Stand* in 2022.

As always, thank you to my family for bearing with me during the difficult times in my writing journey. My husband and youngest daughter took on extra home duties while I worked frantically toward a deadline. Those extra hours in the evening helped me finish on time.

My heart swells with gratitude when I think of my three daughters. Katie, Natalie, and Sarah have encouraged me throughout the writing of this series. Their belief in me and hope for my success meant more to me than any five-star review or award I've received.

Thank you to my mom who brags to everyone she meets, from bus drivers to doctors, about her daughter being a published author of "three books." I couldn't make a liar out of her by not finishing the third book in the *Whispers of Grace* series.

My critique group, The Fictitious Five, helped make this story far better than anything I could have done alone. The members of this group have changed over time, but I want to say a special thank you to Patricia Lee, our faithful leader. She encourages us and pushes us to be better. She holds us accountable but also gives us grace. She prays for us and makes us laugh. Pat, you are priceless. Also, a special thanks to the newest Fictitious Five member, Becky Harwood, for reading and critiquing far above the call of duty. Becky, I can't wait to see your book reach publication! Amanda Bird, Dorcas Smucker and Kathy Lee Sheldon—your input was invaluable. Thank you!

I know little to nothing about horses, but thanks to Sara

Scott and my stepmom, Candy Maidens, I was able to bring an important scene to life in this book. I appreciate your willingness to answer all my equine questions!

Dani Crowley, I can't thank you enough for your willingness to read and give me feedback on this story, not to mention your eagerness to share my books with others.

I'm deeply grateful for Miralee Ferrell of Mountain Brook Ink for not only giving the Whispers of Grace series a publishing home, but also being patient and supportive while I wrote these stories.

I almost gave up on *One Last Stand* because I couldn't see how it should end. Once I truly trusted God to lead me through this story, the words flowed. Some of them surprised me. That's what He does, though, isn't it? He leads us on adventures better than we could ever imagine.

Chapter One

Cassie

I BEELINED THROUGH THE WALKWAYS THAT connected the brick and stone buildings of the University of Oregon. The campus was beautiful—luscious green landscaping surrounded a mix of old and new buildings. An atmosphere of both history and academia pulsed from the brick structures, making my heart zing. If only I could shake the feeling of standing out like a sore thumb. How many of my classes would have other single moms in their thirties? Though it was summer term and not as busy as it would be in the fall, most of the people who traversed the campus looked to be in their late teens or early twenties. Only a few appeared to be my age or older. Not to mention the majority were dressed casually in shorts and t-shirts, while I wore my gray pants and a short-sleeve rayon blouse.

I glanced at my phone. In ten minutes, my parking meter would run out of time, and no doubt I'd end up with a ticket. Picking up my pace, I forced myself to ignore the text notification on my screen. Other people might be able to jog-walk and text at the same time. I wasn't that coordinated.

I had used my lunch break from Wardwood, Rosen, et al. to see an academic advisor before I registered for fall term classes. The advisor, who was, thankfully, a kind and middle-aged woman, had helped me figure out my schedule for the entire school year. Returning to college at the age of thirty-two was daunting, especially as a single mom working full-time, but the pleasant woman assured me it wasn't impossible.

Breathless by the time I made it to my Explorer, I checked my phone again and smiled. The text was from my boyfriend, Matt. He wanted me to let him know all about my appointment. Knowing he'd been watching the time of day with me in mind and was eager to hear about what happened made my chest flutter with delight. I only had ten minutes to drive back to work, park, and stuff food in my face. I quickly pecked out a message letting him know it'd gone great and promised to fill him in on the details later. My boss, Cynthia, was supportive of my back-to-school endeavors. She'd even said I could decrease my hours a little if I kept up with my work—but she was a stickler about being on time. Returning late from my lunch break was not an option.

I chomped down a protein bar while I weaved my Explorer through the parking garage. My mind was swirling with the information the advisor had given me. I sighed, wishing I had time to talk to someone before I had to be back at the keyboard. Once parked, I speed walked to the Park Place building. On the eighth floor, I used my key card to get in the back door of the office, thankful to avoid Lana, the official purveyor of office gossip. I checked my phone again. I had a few minutes to spare. Maybe I could shoot Matt another quick text, but first, I needed something to wash down the protein bar. I popped into the nearly empty break room.

"What's the scoop, College Girl?" Missy's familiar voice made me smile. Her tanned arms were full of two cases of Snapple tea. It reminded me of our fist conversation in this exact place, over two years ago. It was amazing how much my life had changed since then. How much I had changed.

"I think it's something I can handle, and if I stay on track, I could have my degree in Human Services in three years instead of four."

Missy set the cases of tea down and lifted her hand for a

high-five. I met her hand with mine, and my heart soared. My life was all high-fives these days.

I opened the fridge and grabbed a peach iced tea, popped off the cap and gulped half of it down.

Missy laughed. "Thirsty much?"

I exhaled, shaking my head. "Protein bars make a dry lunch."

"Well, don't let yourself starve. I've heard those pastor types like the curvy girls." Missy winked. Though I knew she was joking, heat ran up my cheeks. She liked to tease me, in a good-natured way, about having a youth pastor for a boyfriend. I figured at this point the fun-making was a habit. Matt and I had been officially dating for nearly a year.

"Funny." I chuckled. "You know I'm not giving up on getting you into a church building one of these days." If I could get Missy to go to church, that would make exactly two churchgoers at the law firm where we worked—me and Missy.

Missy tilted her head, her eyes holding their typical mischievous twinkle. "Oh, I'm sure I'll be in one for your wedding."

I rolled my eyes, but my heart lurched. "I hope you don't wait that long." I held up my ringless left hand. "No ring. No proposal. I think we have a way to go before the wedding bells."

Missy puckered her lips. "I've seen the way Matt looks at you." She lifted her eyebrows. "He is head-over-heels."

I bit my bottom lip but couldn't suppress a smile. Matt and I had talked about marriage, but there were no plans in the works. I knew lots of couples talked about and planned their wedding and marriage before there was even a proposal, but Matt wasn't like that. He was so old-fashioned he had even asked my mom for permission to date me before he broached the subject with me. It was one of the many things

I loved about him—and another example of how incredibly good God had been to me since my divorce from Derrick.

I glanced at the clock on the wall and jumped. It was after 1 p.m. "I need to get to my desk."

Instead of sending Matt another short text, I decided to wait until I got off work and call. I didn't have to worry about picking up my seven-year-old daughter, Renee. Mom always got off work by 3:00 p.m. to pick her up from daycare, and this afternoon Renee had swimming lessons. The five o'clock traffic would afford me plenty of time to talk before getting home, and Matt didn't have any church responsibilities on Tuesday nights. Thankfully, the busy afternoon flew by, and before I knew it, I was heading to my car to go home. Once out of the parking garage, I pushed Matt's number on my phone and waited for the Bluetooth to pick up.

"So, it went well?" His voice was calm yet inquisitive. The sound of someone who genuinely cared.

"Yes. Oh, my goodness. Better than I expected." I excitedly poured out all the details. My first term would have two online classes and one early morning class. Cynthia had already okayed me coming in late on Mondays, Wednesdays and Fridays so I could take the class. We still needed to run it by her boss, Brian, but he'd likely be fine with it. My stomach burned when I said Brian's name. I'd forgiven him for how he'd lied to me and used me when I first started working at Wardwood, Rosen, et al. Knowing how I had fled my abusive marriage, he had seen me as an easy, vulnerable conquest. In the end, Brian helped me get custody of Renee, so it would seem the strikes against him were even. But the truth was, seeing him every day was a regular reminder of how naïve and foolish I had once been.

"That's wonderful, Cassie. I'm so happy to see you following your dreams." Matt's voice was so tender, it brought tears to my eyes. He treated me with the kind of love I'd longed for all my life but never believed I'd have.

"Thank you. I can't even put into words how excited I am about going back to school. I'm so glad I have my mom living with me to help with Renee. If I was totally on my own, I don't know how I'd do it."

"You'd find a way, with God's help."

Matt was right, God had been taking care of me. When I left Derrick, the last person who I would've seen myself having as a roommate was my mom. After all, who in their right mind would leave one alcoholic to go to another? But Mom had really changed after my sweet Nannie—her mom—had passed away. She'd given up drinking and was now even regularly attending church with me. Sometimes I wondered how one person could change so much, while another kept on the same destructive path.

I took the exit to Springfield. If my mom hadn't gotten sober and devoted herself to being here for Renee and me, we would've still found a way, with God's help. But it undoubtedly would have been much harder.

"How was your day?" I asked. Our entire conversation had been focused on me, and I longed to hear more of Matt's voice. His job as a youth pastor kept him busy.

"It was good, really good." Matt's voice trailed off.

"Are you sure?" His "goods" didn't sound convincing.

"Positive. It was a typical day. But I wanted to ask you if you're free Saturday? I thought maybe we could grab an early dinner and then go see a waterfall."

"Since I don't start classes until the fall, I'm pretty sure I can do an outing on Saturday." I chuckled, but my stomach knotted. When I did start school, my time with Matt would have to be cut back. We'd already talked about the time issue, though, and Matt assured me that the quality of time—and who you spent it with—was more important than the amount.

"Good! How does four o'clock sound? I know that's early to eat, but I'm hoping we can time our hike to catch the sunset."

I smiled and warmth washed over me. How did I end up with such a great guy? "Works for me. Where are we going to go eat?" Matt was a total foodie. I usually let him pick the restaurants we dined at because he knew what was good. Of course, with him on a youth pastor's salary and me being a single mom, we didn't go out to eat very often. It was always a treat.

"Hmm. I'll have to think about it." Matt chuckled. "I don't want to ruin my winning streak on restaurant choices."

I laughed. "That would definitely be tragic." In all honesty, I didn't care where we ate. Spending time with Matt was better than the most gourmet meal.

I parked my Explorer in the driveway of the duplex I shared with my mom and told Matt I'd Facetime him before I went to bed. It was our routine, and I always looked forward to seeing his face, even it if was by screen. Mom's old Buick was parked on the street, and she and Renee were getting out of the car. I headed toward them.

Renee sprinted to me, still in her swimsuit. Mom carried Renee's backpack, swim bag, and towel. Suppressing a laugh, I bent down to give Renee a big hug. Her chlorine scented hair was wet and left a patch of moisture on my shirt. I put my hand on my hip, mustering a stern voice. "Renee, why is Grammy carrying all of your stuff?"

Renee's eyes widened and she looked behind her. "Oh, sorry!" She ran back to Mom and grabbed her backpack, but Mom held on to the rest.

"I've got it Sweet Pea. Let's get you inside and washed up." Mom ushered Renee toward the house.

Mom turned to me. "She did great today. I think she has the backstroke down pat."

"And her Grammy wrapped around her finger." I lifted an eyebrow at Mom.

Mom waved her hand dismissively at me. "That's what grandmas are for."

I sighed. Mom spoiled Renee. My own grandma, Nannie, had always said you couldn't spoil a child with love. I hoped she was right. One thing I did know was that Renee was a happy girl and her confidence had increased immensely since Derrick's and my divorce.

We made our way into the house. Mom got Renee set up in the bathroom while I headed to the kitchen to start dinner. I couldn't complain about Mom spoiling Renee. I benefited from her being here to help as much as Renee did. My heart swelled with thankfulness. Mom had changed so much over the last year. She'd not only conquered her alcoholism but walked in a freedom and light I'd never seen before. Her devotion to Renee and me was unshakable. She had made some new friends at church. Mom even attended a small group, and they had her bring her guitar a few times to lead them in worship songs before their bible study time.

While Renee showered, Mom joined me in the kitchen and got right to work unloading the dishwasher. I told her about my visit to the University of Oregon, and she told me about an obnoxious guest at the hotel where she worked. Mom had started out there as a maid but was now the head housekeeper and was in training to work the front desk.

"Oh, before I forget, can you watch Renee Saturday evening?"

"Hot date with Matt?"

I stopped chopping vegetables. "How'd you know?"

Mom turned away and shrugged her shoulders. "What

else would it be?"

"I don't know. A church thing. A girl's night out with Missy. A support group meeting." I squinted at Mom, whose back was still turned toward me. Did she know something I didn't know? "But you jumped right to 'hot date'."

Mom grabbed the silverware holder out of the dishwasher and passed me on the way to the utensil drawer. "Mother's intuition." She murmured, not looking at me.

I sighed. Mom and I didn't keep secrets from each other anymore. We'd broken that family curse. I'd have to trust her, but butterflies erupted in my chest. If Mom knew about mine and Matt's date before I did, there was only one reason why...

Chapter Two

Sharon

I PULLED INTO THE DAY AND Night Inn and eased my old Buick into one of the employee parking spaces far from the building. The sun was peeking over the hills, promising another hot day. The laundry room would be sweltering. Even though I was now the housecleaning supervisor, I knew what it was like to be overworked and unappreciated, so I'd wind up helping in the laundry room. I took a deep breath and closed my eyes, the question I'd posed to myself last night still nagging me.

Is a white lie still a lie?

It'd been over a year since the last time I lied to my daughter. Back then my lies were to cover up my shame and bad decisions. The lie I told her last night was different. Kind of the same as pretending you don't know about a surprise party or what Santa is putting under the tree for Christmas.

Surely, God must make exceptions for these untruths. At least, that's what I told myself.

Cassie would know the truth soon enough. Matt approached me weeks ago. The poor guy was so nervous when he came by the house on my day off, while Cassie was at work and Renee was on a playdate. I wasn't stunned when he asked my permission to marry Cassie. Him wanting to marry Cassie was no surprise. A person would have to be in a coma not to see that coming. Many men wouldn't have bothered asking their girlfriend's mom for permission, but that was Matt, and I admired him for it. To tell the truth, I was honored to the point of tears that he asked *my* permission. Granted, there's no one else to ask. Still, my past is murky and I'm not a prim and proper lady. I guess it's that little bit of leftover shame I can't seem to get rid of.

I exited my car and made my way into the hotel. My crew would be arriving soon, including Janice. Happy-Feet, as I liked to call her. I shook my head. It was weird that I was her supervisor. She seemed fine with it though. The woman was as easy going as anyone could be and a solid friend. Another blessing to count among many.

"Hey, Marissa, I need the room list for today." I spoke to the eyes-half-closed front desk attendant when I entered the lobby.

Marissa gave me a nod and typed a few keystrokes on the computer. "We had a busy night. Some late check-ins." She yawned as she handed me the piece of paper the printer spit out. "We have a few people who already said they'll be checking out late."

I smiled and nodded. Poor girl. Working the front desk on the graveyard shift had to be one of the most boring jobs in the entire world. It gave her lots of time to sneak in some studying for the college classes she was enrolled in. Too bad Cassie's job didn't allow her time to work on the classes she'd be taking.

I took the room list to the break room and made a pot of coffee. As it brewed, I looked over the list and sighed. There was an unusual amount of room check-outs for midweek. I'd need to call in another housekeeper to get all the rooms cleaned before check-in. While I waited for the coffee to finish brewing, my mind wandered again to Matt's visit to me.

The man was good-hearted. He'd assured me, without even one bit of prompting from me, that I would be welcome to live in their home after they were married. He said he knew how important I was in Cassie and Renee's lives and that he already loved me like a second mother. Talk about tugging at an old woman's heart strings. Still, it seemed wrong for me to live with them. A mother-in-law living with you from day one of matrimony couldn't be part of any man's idea of happily-ever-after. Cassie and Matt needed to start their home and lives together, just the two of them and Renee. They didn't need me in the mix to complicate things.

The coffee machine beeped, indicating the brewing cycle was done. I got up and poured myself a cup of coffee and looked at the clock on the wall. I'd give it a few more minutes before I called anyone. Many of the women who worked here would still be sleeping this time of day if they weren't scheduled for work.

I sat down with my coffee and perused the list of people I could call. Juanita was probably my best bet for a yes. She was trying to get her parents to the U.S. from Mexico and worked every extra shift she could pick up, unless one of her kids was sick.

Taking a sip of coffee, I picked up my phone to check my email, but found myself on Facebook instead. I rarely posted anything to the social media app other than pictures of Renee, but the updates from people on my friends list was better than any soap opera. Not to mention the memes were good for a laugh. I scanned through my newsfeed, disappointed by its lack of excitement. Without even thinking, and with an uptick in my heart rate, I went to the search bar and typed in the name I'd entered in it more times than I cared to admit— Johnny Beckett.

Johnny's profile came up. I looked at the top of his page and noted he still hadn't added anything new. At least not anything he'd made public. Johnny and I weren't friends on Facebook. In fact, I hadn't heard a word from him since I turned down his offer to move with him to California. The frustrating thing was I still thought about him every single day. He'd made a Facebook profile shortly after moving to the bay area. I'd found him when I'd looked him up on Facebook but couldn't bring myself to send him a friend request. Sometimes I wondered if he'd made that profile just for me. He had posted so much stuff that he'd made public, I guessed he'd either not figured out how to change it to friends only, or he wanted the "public" to see what he was up to. Johnny was smart, so I figured the latter was the most likely option. I didn't see Johnny as a social media kind of guy, so the fact he had an account was interesting. Also, he never posted pictures of any girlfriends, and his relationship status had remained single. As wrong as it was, this made me happy. How selfish was that? I'd repented in my prayers and asked God to bless Johnny and keep him safe. I was still in love with that man, no matter how hard I tried not to be.

The fact that he hadn't posted anything new in over two weeks worried me. Did he have a girlfriend and all his new posts were for friends only? Yet his status was still single...could that little detail be an oversight? Had something happened to him? My stomach clenched with dread. *Please Lord, let Johnny be healthy and safe.* If something did happen, I didn't really have a way to know...unless I contacted him. I grunted in frustration. I needed to stop obsessing over that man. I was too old for this. I closed my Facebook app and dialed Juanita's number. Time to focus on work.

"What night of the week is your small group?"

Janice worked beside me as we made a bed. Juanita hadn't been able to come in because she had a doctor's appointment she couldn't miss. I hoped it was nothing serious.

"It's Thursday nights, which is kind of a bummer because my favorite AA group meets on Thursday nights, but this small group is important, too. Why do you ask?"

Janice happy-feeted across the room to empty the trash.

"I was hoping it's not tonight, because I'm afraid you're gonna be bone-tired, Girlfriend."

I chuckled. *Ain't that the truth.* "Nope, and hopefully tomorrow isn't this busy at work."

"I hear you." Janice's deep brown eyes looked at me with concern. "You never really talk about your church group."

"I don't?"

Janice shook her head emphatically. "I wasn't even sure if you were still going, but I didn't want to bring it up. Because. . . you know." Janice shrugged sheepishly.

Because of Samantha. That's what Janice left unsaid. After the drama that ensued with my first visit to Cascade Christian Church, I wasn't sure I could ever return to the building. How often does someone run into the one woman whose home they had essentially wrecked? Even after nearly thirty years, we'd both recognized each other and the venom that shot from Samantha's death glare was probably not fitting for the women's ministry leader. If it hadn't been for Cassie, I would've never gone back.

I nodded. "Yeah, that's all water under the bridge. Samantha has ended up being one of my best friends at church." I smiled wistfully. "Who would've thought?"

Janice sprayed the vanity with disinfectant. "God can do *anything.*" She shrugged her shoulders. "Never say never, that's my motto."

My mind leapt to Johnny faster than a dog to a bone. I grunted, purely irritated with myself. Never say never. He'd said those words to me once.

Janice turned to me with a lifted eyebrow. "You okay?"

"I'm fine."

"Do we really want to go down this road again? You know what fine stands for. It's—"

"Yeah, yeah, I know. Let's finish up this room so we can clock out before midnight." I took one of the "THIS ROOM HAS

BEEN CLEANED AND DISINFECTED" post cards off the utility cart and put it on the dresser.

Janice sighed. "You're the onion of my life." A whimsical smile lifted the corners of her mouth.

I wasn't sure what that meant, but I was thankful that Janice understood when I wasn't ready to talk about something.

The mystery of what Johnny was up to plagued me. What could I do about it? I could pray, of course, and focus on other things. Like Matt's upcoming proposal, and how happy Cassie would be. Or Renee's swim lessons and how she was almost fish-like in her water abilities. I smiled, thankful for my family.

If my heart could only forget about Johnny, all would be well.

Chapter Three

Cassie

MATT WAS SECRETIVE AFTER HE PICKED me up Saturday afternoon. When I asked him where he was taking me to dinner, his response was playful. "Dinner? I thought we were going ice skating?"

I didn't have the heart to tell him that his secretness reminded me of the time Brian had taken me to Silver Falls. My stomach turned at the memory. Young, desperate and gullible. That's what I'd been. Not anymore. Still, as soon as I saw we were heading north, the déjà vu of the memory sent a cold shiver down my spine. Matt wasn't Brian. They were as different as night and day—and we weren't on I-5. Matt was driving down an old section of Highway 99. A beautiful, meandering two lane highway through small towns and farmland.

"What's troubling you?" The lines edging Matt's eyes deepened with obvious concern.

"Oh, nothing. Really." I fidgeted in my seat. "I guess I'm not good at waiting...not knowing what's going to happen."

Matt frowned. "Understandable, considering all you've been through."

I knew he was talking about everything that happened in Derrick's and my divorce and custody battle. Maybe that was really the source of my uneasiness, more than the memory of Brian. Matt had a spiritual wisdom that far surpassed mine. I always felt a little bit like a Christian newbie next to him. Compared to Matt, I was a new Christian. My shoulders sank. I should be happy. Excited. Why did negative thoughts creep into my mind like tiny fire ants?

I reached for Matt's hand. "At least now I know I'm with someone I can trust."

Matt squeezed my hand. "I'd never hurt you, Cassie. I love you too much."

I swallowed the emotion that constricted my throat and threatened to bring tears to my eyes. "I love you, too." I raised my eyebrows. "Plus, I'm starving. I sure hope you're taking us somewhere good."

Matt looked at the clock on the dashboard. "You'll know in about thirty minutes."

Time flew as our conversation continued. The next thing I knew, we were taking a left into Albany. "Wait...we aren't going to Silver Falls, are we?" If we were, a stop in this area would make sense for dinner. I'd avoided Silver Falls since the time Brian had taken me. With Matt by my side, it would be a completely different hike, but there wasn't enough time left in the day to do the ten-mile loop.

Matt winked at me. "I'm not answering any more questions. You're going to have to trust me."

After a few turns we were in historic downtown Albany. I'd never been to the area before, but I immediately fell in love. The charm of old buildings tugged at my heart and piqued my interest. Matt pulled the car into a parking spot near some restaurants and shops, then hopped out of the car. I waited patiently. Matt always wanted to open my door for me, like a gentleman. One of the many things I adored about him.

After taking my arm, Matt led me to the doorway of a restaurant called "Sweet Red."

The warm and lively sound of Italian folk music greeted us as we walked in the door. A hostess greeted us warmly, but I was so engulfed by the beauty of the building, I barely heard what she said as she led us to our table. The old red brick walls and well-worn wood floors were obviously original to the building. Tall windows lined the wall by the sidewalk, allowing diffuse light in the charming room. A wine case lined another wall. The hostess seated us at a small square wood table flanked by two black lounge chairs. This would be a nice restaurant to get engaged in. I pushed that thought away. That was obviously *not* happening today.

"I feel underdressed." I glanced down at my yoga pants and short-sleeved shirt. At least my shirt had a feminine cut to it and bunched sleeves.

Matt's periwinkle blue eyes held a sparkle that made my heart do a double beat. "You look beautiful, as always." He glanced at his watch and then the menu. "What looks good to you?"

I scanned the menu. *Oh. My. Word.* Everything sounded delicious. I sucked in my lip. "What are you going to have?"

"The prime rib. I've heard it's to die for. I bet they cook it in a rock salt so it's especially tender and flavorful. Plus, they have homemade horseradish."

"I think you should get a side job as a food critic." I teased, gently kicking Matt under the table.

Matt shook his head. "The pay might be better than pastoring, but I'd have to buy a whole new wardrobe."

I cocked my head. "You have plenty of suits."

The dimples in Matt's cheeks deepened with his widening smile. "Yeah, but I'd need everything in a triple x size if I made my living eating food." He shook his head. "My metabolism isn't what it used to be."

I rolled my eyes. Matt was only a few years older than me, but he often talked lately about how being around teenagers all the time made him realize how old he really was. "Okay, old man. You've talked me into the prime rib." I set the menu down and leaned forward. "My metabolism is still pretty good."

Matt reached across the table and squeezed my hand. "How can it not be? You go nonstop."

He had a point. Like a snowball rolling down a hill, my mood slid, collecting weight. How would I ever have time to see Matt once school started? I barely had time for him now between work and Renee. We walked a fine line of having Matt part of Renee's life but not too much. If we were married, that part would change. But we weren't.

Our meals arrived. Everything was perfect. The food, the atmosphere, the handsome man sitting across from me. There was obviously no marriage proposal coming today, but I assured myself that was okay. After all, I mused, Missy would have to go to church now.

Chapter Four

Sharon

RENEE SQUEALED WHEN SHE SAW HER friend walk in the door of our home. That granddaughter of mine was shy with strangers but a total ham with anyone she felt comfortable with. Isabella fit the latter category. The sweet, freckle-faced little girl greeted Renee with a big hug.

Samantha followed her granddaughter inside the house. She was dressed in her usual feminine way, all florals and flow and pastel colors. Quite the opposite look of my faded blue jeans and well-worn Old Navy t-shirt. Who would picture us as friends? Especially with the history between us. God really does work in mysterious ways, I could testify to that.

If someone would have told me a year and a half ago that Samantha and I would end up friends, I would have either laughed until I peed my pants or slapped them silly for being stupid. When I'd gone to Cassie's new church with her and ran into the woman whose home I had wrecked nearly thirty years ago, I'd never planned on going back. I couldn't face my past or the disdain I saw in her eyes. But God had worked on my heart, and then on Samantha's. A sincere apology from me had led to an olive branch from her. That branch created a tender bridge we'd managed to build a friendship on.

Isabella and Renee immediately took off to Renee's bedroom down the hall, and I motioned Samantha to the dining table. I'd cleared it of the dinner dishes, but the smell of chicken nuggets and French fries still lingered in the air. The room was warm and stuffy from the late summer heat, despite the fan in the corner and the opened kitchen window. I grabbed a couple of glasses and poured us both ice water.

"What time do you need to leave?" Samantha flashed me a smile and made herself comfortable in one of the chairs.

I set the glasses of water on the table and took a seat. "I just got a text from Matt. If I leave in half an hour the timing should work out right. I'm on pins and needles." I shook my head. "Don't ask me why. I know she's going to say yes, and she's going to be over the moon happy about the whole thing."

Samantha nodded. "I'm sure." She paused as if considering her words. "Lots of changes in store."

My stomach tightened, the increasing unease about my future triggered by Samantha's words. "Yeah. One bridge at a time, that's what I keep telling myself."

"Very true." Samantha took a sip of her water. The sound of the girls' laughter echoed through the walls. They were obviously having fun. "Isabella was so excited about being able to come play with Renee, even if briefly. With school starting soon, there'll be less time for playdates."

I nodded. With Cassie starting school, too, Renee's extracurricular activities would require my time more than ever. I didn't mind. Being a grandma was the best thing that had ever happened to me.

"I appreciate you coming by. This waiting is killing me." I laughed, but I was earnest. What I wanted to say was that I also appreciated Samantha's friendship and her willingness to forgive me after everything that happened in our past. Not to mention everything she did to nurture the friendship between our granddaughters. Isabella was Renee's only real friend from church. It was hard to establish friendships on a Sunday-only basis. I wasn't one of those sentimental types, and I was fairly certain Samantha understood my feelings.

"There's actually something I wanted to talk to you about, Sharon. Something that doesn't have anything to do with pending engagements."

The seriousness of Samantha's tone made me sit upright.

Had something happened at church? Had I done something wrong? "Is everything okay?"

Samantha blinked a few times. "I'm sorry, that came off too serious." She laughed. "But it is important, and I really feel like God has been speaking to me about you and a need we have in our church."

I sucked in my bottom lip, both unease and anticipation washing over me. As the women's ministry leader at our church, it wasn't unusual for Samantha to feel that God was prompting her to reach out to other women about specific needs. But this was the first time I'd personally been the object of her ministry attention. "So, what's the big guy telling ya?"

Samantha chuckled and shook her head. We had different spiritual styles, but she never seemed to hold it against me. "I think He has a job for you."

"I kind of already have one. Two, actually." Between my job at the hotel and helping with Renee, my days were booked. Or at least as busy as I wanted them to be.

"I'm sure you've noticed that there is a lack of outreach in our church for those affected by addiction." Samantha's expression turned serious.

Yes, I had noticed. My AA group was my support for my recovery from alcoholism. Our church had a group for single parents, divorced parents, people who were grieving, lonely seniors, and even parents who were raising children with special needs. The closest group they had to address addiction was the adult children of alcoholics group, which Cassie attended. Nothing to help the alcoholics themselves. "I figured the church didn't see a need for it among the people who attend." I shrugged my shoulders and looked away.

"There is a need. We have two services and a total of almost four hundred people in our church." Samantha tapped the table with her index finger, as if amplifying her point. "I've read that over fifteen million people in the United States struggle with alcoholism. It'd be ignorant to think that a segment of our congregation doesn't suffer with addiction."

"You have a point." I'd wondered the same thing myself as I'd scanned the faces in the sanctuary. In so many of them I saw the secretness and shame I was all too familiar with. Who knew what lay beneath it?

"There's a national, Christian organization that equips people to lead small groups for those in recovery. It has a step-by-step program. Something like AA, I believe."

I nodded. "Yeah, I've heard of a few of them."

"We just need someone to lead the group. Someone who understands the struggle and has overcome it. Someone with compassion and a sense of humor." Samantha lifted her eyebrows at me.

"Maybe you can put an ad on Craigslist." I joked, but my heart hammered like a jack-rabbit's free leg when it was partially caught in a trap.

Samantha tilted her head. "I think we already have what we need, right here." Her index finger tapped on the table again, accentuating her point.

"I'm flattered. But I'm not a leader. Trust me." I gulped down the rest of my water, suddenly parched.

"Maybe your definition of leader needs to be . . . refined."

I shook my head. "Look, I'm not qualified for that kind of thing. I mean, I'd love to help people, but I don't see myself running a group."

"You manage the cleaning team for the hotel you work for."

"Well, yeah, but—"

"You practically manage this household."

I shook my head. "I just help Cassie out."

Samantha rolled her eyes. "You've led worship at our small group."

"I play my guitar and sing. I don't really lead anything."

"And you're not stubborn *at all*." Samantha laughed. "Which, by the way, is an ill-gotten side effect of a strong will. Another good trait in a leader, when properly applied."

I blew air through my teeth as the emotions swirled inside of me. I was honored. And horrified. Excited about the possibility. Terrified of failing. Most of all I was in awe of what God can do in a person's life. Especially someone like me. How could I not share that hope with others? Still, I had no idea how to go about it.

"Maybe I could co-lead a group." My own words surprised me. I'd expected myself to say *sorry, find another guinea pig* or, at most, *maybe later.*

Samantha's eyes shimmered, and her face shown with hopeful expectation. "So, if I find someone to co-lead with you, you'll do it?"

I shrugged. "I mean, sure, if you can find someone in our church who's game." I had no idea who that could be.

"I know the perfect person." Samantha beamed. "His name is Frank."

Chapter Five

Cassie

DESPITE MY NUDGING, MATT DIDN'T PROVIDE any information about where we were going after dinner. My mind searched for possibilities as we drove east through rolling farmlands and don't-blink-or-you'll-miss-it towns. No mountains in sight. It didn't feel like we were on our way to a hike. It felt like we were on our way to Nanny's old place at the Resthaven Retirement Home, which we could have been, geographically speaking. An aching hollowness filled me, a reminder of the empty place Nanny's passing had left in my heart. Finding out the secret about Grandpa she'd spent her entire life keeping from me had angered and hurt me at first, but those hard feelings had mellowed and softened with understanding and time. Her life had not been an easy one and she had made some tough choices. I knew what that was like.

A brown sign along the road was the tell-tale of where we were headed. McDowell Creek Falls. It was one of the few waterfalls I had not yet visited within driving distance of Eugene. "We're going to a waterfall?" I smiled at Matt, who was trying to keep a poker face.

"What makes you think that?"

"Uhm, the sign on the road."

Matt leaned over the steering wheel and squinted his eyes, looking from left to right with exaggerated movements. "I don't see a sign."

I laughed but shook my head. "Funny."

"I thought you'd be happy." Matt's dimples accentuated his wide smile.

"I haven't been to many waterfalls lately." I stared

straight ahead, surprised by the pain in my chest. If I was too busy to see waterfalls and go hiking now, what did the next three to four years hold for me? But it would be worth it, in the end.

"I'm going to make sure you see some before the rainy season hits."

I knew Matt meant well but wondered if he could keep such a promise. It was already late August. He'd been busy with youth group activities all summer. Between camps and special outings, his weekends had been booked. I'd worked beside him during most of them. Partly out of a sense of service, but also because of my own desire to spend time with the man I loved.

After a few more miles, Matt steered his car into a small parking lot. Only a few other cars were in sight. I didn't see any signs noting directions to the waterfall at the trailhead in the parking lot, but I knew Matt wouldn't lead us on a wild goose chase.

"This must not be a very popular waterfall." Based on the pictures I'd seen of McDowell Creek waterfalls during my waterfall searches, I was surprised more people weren't here. From what I remembered of the fall's location, we had taken quite the detour and added about an hour to our drive by stopping for dinner in Albany, but I didn't say anything about it to Matt. No doubt he'd put a lot of thought into choosing the restaurant, and the food had been delicious.

"I think this is just one of two parking lots for the trail." Matt offered as he killed the ignition and stepped out of the car.

We walked hand-in-hand at a casual pace as we started on the trail, crossing a bridge over a slow-moving creek, then moved to single file as we made our way up a forested hill. Ferns and other greenery lined the path. Light from the slanting sun dappled through the broad leaves of the trees overhead, creating soft spotlights that shone on various parts of the path ahead and the forest surrounding us. We came to a trail sign that pointed to Royal Terrace Falls in one direction and Majestic Falls in another.

"Which one should we see first," I asked.

Matt slanted his head toward the trail leading to Royal Terrace Falls, then grabbed my hand and led me down the path. We came to a long bridge over the creek. We were only a fourth of the way across the bridge when we saw the falls. I sucked in my breath in surprise. I had expected to hear it before I saw it, but the fall was a quiet one as it flowed over the smooth rocked terrace before us.

"I've never seen one like this." My entire body tingled with delight at the sight before me. The water flowed over three solid rock terraces that were so smooth they almost looked man-made. One waterfall, but three streams. Beautiful and magical.

We stood at the rail of the bridge in silence. Matt wrapped his arm around me, pulling me close. "You know what this makes me think of?"

"A waterpark ride?" I teased. That's what Renee would see if she were here. But despite his youthful heart, Matt wasn't a kid.

Matt gently turned me, so we were face to face. He brushed a strand of hair off my cheek, his eyes full of emotion. "It makes me think of us."

"How so?"

Matt's gaze shifted to the waterfall. "It's three streams, but one waterfall. Really, it's one creek and on the way down the rocks divide it into three separate channels, but they are still one. They join back together at the bottom." Matt turned his focus back to me. "The three become one."

My eyes watered at the emotion in his voice. "But we are only two."

"God makes us three. 'Though one may be overpowered, two can defend themselves. A cord of three strands is not quickly broken.'" Matt's eyes held mine as he dropped to one knee on the wooden bridge.

Goosebumps erupted on my arms and a lightness filled my body. I'd heard of people saying their feet left the ground, but never personally experienced it—until now.

Matt reached in the pocket of his cargo shorts and pulled out a small black velvet box. He opened it, revealing a diamond solitaire ring. The stone wasn't large, but the angle of the sun made it sparkle in every direction.

Was I dreaming? A man could not have proposed to me in a more meaningful way. Even the sun was in perfect position, shining its light on us in the opening through the trees as the soft rushing of the waterfall filled the air.

Matt took my left hand in his. "Cassie, will you marry me?"

Tears filled my eyes. I'd found God at a waterfall. Now the love of my life was proposing to me at one. "Yes." I laughed, brushing tears away with my free hand. "How could I say no after a proposal like that?"

Matt smiled and slipped the ring on my finger. It fit perfectly.

I heard squeals and looked up. Across the bridge, Renee ran toward me, my mom walking at a fast pace behind her to keep up.

My jaw dropped. "What?"

Matt stood, keeping my hand in his. Perspiration dotted his hairline, but his eyes sparkled. "I didn't want to leave the rest of the family out."

I searched for words but came up empty. Renee stopped right before barreling into me and gazed up in wonder. "Mommy, did you really say yes?"

Reaching down, I pulled Renee into a tight hug. "Yes, I did sweetie. What do you think about that?"

Renee pushed back from me, her eyes dancing. "I think it's the best thing ever!"

My mom reached us. The love and happiness that shown in her eyes spoke more than any words.

"You were in on this, weren't you?" I narrowed my eyes at her but couldn't hide my playful smile.

"It was hard to keep it secret, but Matt made me promise." Mom rocked on her heels. "Sure would've been awkward if we showed up here and you'd said no, though. I think I would have quietly walked down another trail."

"I would have followed you, with my tail between my legs and a broken heart." Matt shook his head.

"Mommy, wouldn't say no. She's *crazy* in love with you." Renee looked at Matt seriously.

We all burst into laughter. Renee's brow furrowed. "She is! I heard Grammy say so." Renee put her hand on her hip and turned to Mom. "You did say that, Grammy."

Heat ran up my neck and into my cheeks. *Good heavens, leave me a little pride.*

Mom looked guilty for a moment, but then a sadness washed over her face. "Being crazy in love is a good thing, I think." Her voice was unusually soft.

Matt pulled me close and planted a kiss on my cheek. "I wholeheartedly agree."

Renee giggled.

Mom cleared her throat and held up her phone. "I managed to snap some pictures of the proposal from our hiding place at the end of the bridge. Now I can take some closeups."

Matt and I posed for several pictures, including one that involved a kiss.

"Eeew!" Renee made gagging sounds from her spot next to my mom.

Matt chuckled. "Renee, I think you should join your mom and me for some of these pictures." He turned to me, his eyes searching mine. "After all, we're going to be a family soon."

I swallowed the ball of emotion in my throat and motioned Renee toward me. She quickly joined us and posed with gusto. My heart wanted to burst with joy. We were going to be a family. Renee would finally have a father in her life. A good one.

"How about we see the other waterfall that's here? It's only a short hike away." Matt motioned toward the opposite end of the bridge.

We continued across the bridge and down the trail, toward the direction of Majestic Falls. Renee led the way, skipping along. Mom followed behind her, and Matt and I lingered back, holding hands. The dirt path rounded the creek, and then we came to the roadway. I saw that the trail continued across the road. Mom called for Renee to stop and wait for her before crossing, then they traversed the road together. Matt held me back, letting them gain some distance on us.

"There's something I want to run by you. Please understand you don't have to say yes. Or you can say you want to think about it."

I cocked my head. "Is everything okay?"

Matt nodded. "This is a big day. For us. But I want Renee to know that…it's a big day for her, also. I mean, I want her to know I love her. That I'm choosing *her* to be in my life, too."

"She loves you, too, you know."

Matt tilted his head and looked at me with a whimsical smile. "Yeah, she's an open book, just like her mom."

"What did you want to ask me?" Someday I'd get used to

the fact I couldn't hide my feelings. At least with Matt, I knew my heart was safe.

"I bought this little heart necklace for Renee. I was hoping to give it to her today as a token of my promise to love her like a dad loves a daughter." Matt shrugged. "I know it might seem like a little much for today, but I really wanted to make sure she doesn't feel left out or cast aside."

Gratitude mixed with amazement filled my already overflowing heart. How did I get so lucky? *Blessed.* Yes, blessed. I could almost hear Nannie's voice. She'd felt closer today than she had in a long time.

"I think that's a wonderful idea. She'll be tickled pink."

Matt exhaled and I realized he'd been holding back nervousness over asking me. The poor guy. He always strived to do the right thing. It was one of the many things I loved about him.

We crossed the road and started down the trail on the other side, picking up our pace to catch up with Renee and Mom. We walked in silence, but thoughts filled my mind. Not about how to plan the wedding, but about how we would be a family together. We had talked some about the what ifs of our future, but never about specifics. I guessed we would work out the details before the wedding.

We caught up to Mom and Renee at a wooden viewing platform and joined them at the edge of it. Below us was the top of the next waterfall. It was a different way to view one, from the top. To see the water flowing along, and then disappear over a rocky precipice. Looking over the edge of the platform, I could see what must be an unofficial path off the trail and to the creek's edge. It was possible to stand on the ledge where the water dropped and look straight down at the fall. Longing to stand on that edge and be closer to moving water filled me. Now was not a good time for venture taking.

Renee would want to join me, and it was too dangerous for a seven-year-old.

Matt pulled Renee aside and got down on his knees, so they were at eye level. From the opposite pocket in which he'd carried the ring, he pulled out another velvet jewelry box. With the rushing water, I couldn't hear the words he said to her, but the emotion on his face was evident. When he opened the box, Renee's mouth shaped into a huge "O", and she brought a hand to each cheek. I nudged Mom and whispered, "Hurry and take a picture."

Matt took the gold necklace out of the box and wrapped it around Renee's neck. Like a little lady, she held her hair up so he could clasp it in the back. As soon as it was secured, she ran up to me, her face lit with joy.

"Mommy, look at what Matt got me!" She held up the little golden heart from the chain around her neck.

"That's beautiful!" I blinked back a fresh wave of happy tears.

Renee nodded. "He said he already loves me like I'm his daughter, and now he'll get to be my daddy for real." Her eyebrows came together, and she stepped closer, motioning for me to bend down to her level.

I leaned over so my face was near hers. "Yes?"

Renee whispered. "Can I call him daddy now?"

Hopeful, pleading emerald-colored eyes met mine. I wanted to tell her yes, but a little warning flag was waving itself in my head as thoughts tumbled together into a thousand scenarios of everything that could go wrong. While I appreciated Matt's heart, maybe this was too much, too soon. I cupped Renee's sweet face in my hands. "Let's wait until the wedding when it's officially official. That will make it even more special."

Renee frowned but nodded her acquiescence. "Okay.

When's the wedding?"

I shook my head and laughed. "One thing at time, Sweet Pea. We need to figure out all those details."

Renee sighed and walked off to show Mom an up-close view of her necklace.

Matt joined me back at the railing. I smiled and opened my arms to him for a big hug, but the questions in my mind were rushing through my head, overpowering the sound of the water falling beside the platform we stood on.

Chapter Six

Sharon

"GRAMMY, DO YOU THINK I'LL BE a flower princess?" Renee grabbed a soapy plate from me and rinsed it in lukewarm water, carefully balancing it in the dish drainer when she was done. I could've done the dishes ten times faster alone, but having Renee stand on a dining chair and help was a good way for her to learn responsibility. Cassie had her church small group tonight, so it was just Renee and me.

"For Halloween?" I wasn't sure if Renee was planning way ahead or if there was some new Disney princess I didn't know about.

Renee's face scrunched up. "No, Grammy." She exhaled in exasperation. "At Mommy's wedding!"

"Oh..." I chortled at my misunderstanding. "A flower girl. Yes, I think your mommy is counting on it." Cassie and I hadn't talked in too much detail about any wedding plans since Matt's proposal on Saturday, but one thing she had mentioned was a flower girl dress for Renee. Even though she planned a low budget wedding, my poor daughter was already stressed about how to make that work.

Renee beamed, forgetting the task at hand. "I want to wear a flower crown and a pink dress with lots of little flowers on it and sparkly shoes with heels."

"I'm sure your mommy will go over all of the details of your dress with you, when the time is right." Hopefully Renee's heart didn't get too set on what *she* had in mind. I shook my head. The girl could be a bit stubborn when her mind was set. I guessed it ran in the family.

I handed the last soapy dish—a water glass—to Renee

and then held my breath while she rinsed it. Most kids had dishwashers, but the duplex we lived in was old and the owners never installed one. It was an inconvenience, but the dishwashing was therapeutic. I dreaded the day Renee realized her disadvantage and rebelled against the handwashing. Then again, maybe once Cassie and Matt were married, they could afford a newer, nicer place. The thoughts of the future caused a pit in my stomach. Though Matt and Cassie had both said I was welcome to stay in their home after the wedding, I wasn't sure that was the best thing to do. Ideally, I'd have my own place but still be available to pick Renee up from school or daycare and take her to activities while Cassie worked and went to school. Figuring out how to make that happen financially was another story.

I helped Renee off the dining chair. "You can go play for a bit while I finish up, Sweet Pea." I wiped the counters and dried the dishes, humming to myself as I worked. The muggy warmth of late summer surrounded me, making my t-shirt stick to my back. When the kitchen was tidied up, I poured myself a glass of iced tea and sat at the kitchen table, staring out the window into the backyard. The leaves on the tree outside waved in the slight breeze, their undersides dappling in the sun. My phone buzzed. I picked it up and saw Samantha had texted—about the group she wanted me to co-lead, no doubt.

Frank is available this Sunday after the 10:30 am service to talk about the group. g?

My shoulders slumped and I looked at the ceiling, the awkward combination of movements causing a kink in my neck. I rubbed the sore spot as my mind whirled. My daughter was getting married. I needed to find a place I could afford to live on my own or find a roommate. Samantha wanted me to throw leading a group of recovering addicts into the mix. The old rebellious, run-from-my-problems-or-die part of me wanted to flat out tell her no. To tell her I'd given it some thought, and it was not for me. But...after all God had done for me, wasn't it time for me to pay it forward? Even if it meant stretching myself a little. Samantha had made this Frank guy sound like someone I could get along with and who knew what he was doing. Apparently, he'd led some group at another church.

Sure, I can make that work. See you then.

I sighed and dropped my phone back on the table. *Lord, I'm trying. Help me do what you want me to do.* Peace settled on me for a moment, washing away the edgy uncertainty that was crushing me.

After I got Renee in bed, I grabbed my guitar and the chord sheets to a new song I was trying to learn. I worked at the chords, humming and singing as my fingers worked across the strings. The song was Christian, but also a song about a couple who had been waiting for God to bring them the perfect partner. It was both romantic and spiritual, though honestly leaning more on the romantic side if you asked me. I liked the sound of it, as well as the achy longing in the voice of the singer when I heard it on the radio. It resonated with my own heart.

As I hummed the song, a lightning bolt of realization ran through me. This would be a great song for Cassie and Matt's wedding. I set the guitar down so I could text Cassie, too excited about my discovery to wait until she got home. Maybe I could even play and sing it for them at the wedding. After sending the text I stared at my phone as if I was waiting for her to reply instantly. That was dumb. She was in group. Loneliness settled on me, heavy and hollow all at once. The next thing I knew, I was opening my Facebook app. I scrolled through my newsfeed, looking for something exciting, but it was all the same old stuff. I went to the search bar and typed in the familiar name—Johnny Beckett.

Johnny's page came up and my heart stopped. For the first time in weeks, there was something new posted. There was no picture, just one single sentence typed in all capital letters: HEADING HOME.

I scrolled down his page, looking for anything else new. Nothing. I checked his About page, looking for a new job listed or a new relationship status. Still truck driver at the company in California. Still single.

By heading home, did he mean Oregon? Was he going to his parents' house outside Junction City, or his sister's house in Springfield? Or was there someplace I didn't know about that Johnny considered home? I scanned his most recent post again, noting the date and time. The day before yesterday at 9:00 p.m.

Was he in Oregon *now?*

My heart took off like a racehorse on steroids.

As I expected, Matt and Cassie's engagement was all the buzz at church on Sunday. Though Cassie wasn't one for being in the spotlight, I could tell she was basking in the glow of love and excitement each time someone came up and congratulated her on the engagement. I lost count of how many people said to me, "I heard you're gaining a son," or "you must be so excited about the engagement," or some variation of the two.

Only a few knew me well enough to ask how I felt about it, and only one knew that I'd known about the upcoming engagement before most of them. "Did everything go as Matt planned?" Samantha pulled me close to a large potted tree that offered a smidgen of privacy as people filtered out of the auditorium and into the foyer after the service.

"Yes, it was pretty much perfect. Renee and I found the spot without a problem and were well hidden by the time Matt and Cassie got to the bridge. His timing was right on the nose." I laughed at the memory. "Renee was quiet as a mouse until her mom had that ring on her finger."

"How precious is that." Samantha tilted her head. "It's like a fairy tale."

I nodded in agreement.

Samantha scanned the foyer. "Oh, there's Frank." She waved her arm at someone in the crowd.

I turned and searched the sea of faces, looking for whoever this Frank guy was. Based on what Samantha had told me about him, I'd already created a picture of him in my mind. He was a former opiate addict, about my age, who now worked as a tax accountant and loved bird watching. He sounded about as exciting as a Saturday night TV dinner. A man approached us with a hesitant smile. "Hi, Samantha."

This couldn't be Frank. The lean man was about 5'11" and wore a button down short-sleeved shirt and dark blue, well-fitting jeans. His tanned arms were not muscular but sported some old, faded tattoos, and his narrow face was topped by a full head of thick, wavy, salt and pepper hair. While he was not movie-star handsome by any means, he was definitely more attractive than a cardboard dinner.

Samantha introduced us. I shook Frank's hand. My dad always said you could tell a lot by a person's handshake. Frank's hand was warm, dry and soft. His grip was gentle but solid. I decided he was probably a decent enough guy.

"Nice to meet you." Frank offered me a genuine smile that expressed his friendliness. The heavy bags under his eyes and the deep lines surrounding them were the biggest tell of his age. Other than that, he looked young and in great shape.

"Samantha's told me you've had some experience in leading groups. I haven't. At all." I shifted my feet, suddenly feeling self-conscious. "Just so you know up front, I don't know how much help I'd be in the beginning."

"Your life experience and your heart are what's going to be the most help to anyone there." Samantha interjected. She gave me a pointed look, like she suspected I was trying to bow out of the commitment.

Frank nodded. "She's right. I know it sounds intimidating when you haven't done it before, but there's a program we can follow that really sets everything out and makes it easier." His golden-brown eyes held mine.

I looked away, my heart stammering. Why couldn't he be the short, badling man with bad breath that I was expecting him to be?

Frank cleared his throat. "Maybe the three of us could meet for coffee this week and I could show you both the program I've used before."

"Well, um…" my work schedule shifted through my mind. "I could make Friday work?"

Samantha nodded. "Friday is great. I want to have time to put something together to present at the staff meeting next week for approval."

My stomach knotted in apprehension. I didn't know Samantha hadn't sought the staff's approval yet. I didn't even know the staff had to approve. I didn't pay that much attention to church politics. What was I getting myself into?

After we set a place and time for our meeting, I excused myself, grateful to have the meeting over with. I found Cassie and Renee near the doors to the foyer. Usually Cassie was at Matt's side, but he was nowhere in sight.

"Where's Matt?"

Cassie stepped closer, within inches of my ear, and spoke barely above a whisper. "James, I mean Pastor Reynolds, and Mark Schmidt said they needed to have a brief meeting with him right after service."

Mark Schmidt? Who was that? I rolled through the rolodex of church people in my mind. Oh, yes. Mark assisted

Ben Wescott in overseeing personnel stuff. I studied my daughter's face. The lines between her eyes and the way she chewed on her bottom lip told me she was more than a little concerned about the surprise meeting.

I touched her arm and motioned Renee toward the door. "I'm sure it's nothing serious and Matt will fill you in later."

"I hope so." Cassie exhaled. I could almost see the weight easing off her shoulders as we walked away from the building.

We crossed the parking lot, now almost empty. The outside air was hot and humid, causing beads of perspiration on my forehead before I even reached Cassie's vehicle.

"I saw Samantha and you talking to someone, and I'm assuming it was Frank." Cassie unlocked the doors to her Explorer, and we all piled into the hot vehicle.

I immediately rolled down my window even as Cassie turned the air conditioner on high.

"Does Frank seem like a nice enough guy to co-lead a group with?" Cassie raised her voice over the hum of the AC on full force.

"Yeah, he seems okay. I'll know more after our meeting on Friday."

Cassie lifted an eyebrow at me. "He's not bad looking, and I heard he's single."

I rolled my eyes. That daughter of mine. Was she trying to get me married and sent off before her own wedding? I laughed out loud at the idea. "That ship sailed long ago."

"Mom, maybe it's a *new* boat."

It might be new, but it was no Johnny Beckett.

Chapter Seven

Cassie

IT WAS LATE WHEN I GOT home from my small group bible study Tuesday night. I'd felt only half present during the entire meeting. Matt never told me why James, or Pastor Reynolds as he was known to the congregation, had called him into his office on Sunday. All Matt told me was that it was a sensitive church matter, so he couldn't discuss it, but that after the board meeting, which was tonight, he'd give me all the details. The secrecy irked me. Would I be privy to these matters once I was his wife? Or would I need to become used to having a husband who had to keep things confidential? I would have loved to bring my concerns up during bible study, but how could I without giving anything away? Soon enough, I'd know. I couldn't wait to get home and have our nightly Facetime call.

I was almost to the front door when I remembered the mail. I paused, momentarily debating whether it was worth turning around and walking back to the curb. Given the less-than-stellar criminal rating of my neighborhood, I decided to make the trek back. The mail undoubtedly held little more than bills and junk, but I didn't want to chance someone using a piece of my personal information to steal my identity.

Walking on the dried grass of my front lawn, I made it to our rusty mailbox. There was still a soft, deep orange light from the sun setting on the horizon, so I shuffled through the envelopes as I ambled back to the house. An offer for satellite radio. Free return address labels from a charity wanting donations. Ugh. Now I'd feel bad if I didn't send them money to at least cover the costs of the mailing labels. My power bill. I really needed to sign up for online statements. The next envelope stopped me in my tracks. Neat, block handwriting addressed to Renee. My eyes went to the return address and my pulse exploded as adrenaline surged through me.

No. It couldn't be.

Why now?

"Well, are you going to open it?"

I sat across the dining table from my mom, the envelope from Derrick sitting like a stick of dynamite between us. Renee was tucked into bed for the night, unaware of the letter. I sighed, shaking my head. "I don't know. Maybe I should talk to an attorney first."

My mom raised her eyebrows. "You need to talk to an attorney before you *open* a letter addressed to your child?" A hint of chiding was in Mom's voice, but she remained calm.

I looked into my mom's eyes. They were full of love, understanding. Comfort. All proof of what God could do in one person's life in a short period of time. I smiled. "I guess that does sound pretty ridiculous." I shrugged. "Side effect of working for attorneys, I guess. I look at the possible legal consequences of everything." It was also a testament to the tentacle of fear insidiously trying to work its way into my heart.

Mom returned my smile. "Maybe...a tiny bit." She chuckled and looked away, her eyes seeming to see something beyond my vision. She turned back to me. "You know what Nannie would say, don't you?"

What would my sweet grandma say, if she was still with us? "Do not fear. You're not in this alone. You're stronger than you think." Or she might simply say, "Don't keep us waiting for goodness-sake, open the darn thing." I grabbed the envelope and tore it open, careful not to tear the corner with the return address. A fleeting thought crossed my mind. What if Derrick had put poison in the envelope and my mom and I would soon fall to our deaths? I brushed the thought away. Ridiculous. He wouldn't do that...at least not in a letter addressed to Renee.

I pulled the letter out while my heart hammered my sternum, fear claiming its ground. I closed my eyes for a moment, sending up a silent prayer. Peace flowed, slowing my heartrate. I gazed at the handwritten letter on lined notebook paper. The words appeared evenly spaced, carefully penned for easy readability by a seven-year-old.

Knowing that my mom was waiting with bated breath, I read the letter out loud, my voice barely above a whisper in the quiet room.

Dear Renee,

I know it's been a long time since we've seen each other. I'm really sorry about that. There was rules Daddy had to follow to see you and things I needed to work on to be a better person. I've missed you so much, Pumpkin. I can't believe you're going into 2nd grade! I bet you're the smartest girl in your whole class.

Daddy is doing much better than I was when I last saw you. I'm working at a good job and have a new house. I got remarried to a nice lady named Brooke. You would love her. Another exciting thing is that you now have a baby brother!

I'm hoping to see you soon. I'm working on making that happen. I know this is probably a lot to hear at one time. Just remember I love you and not one day has gone by that I haven't thought about you. If you want to write me back, that would be great. I'm sure your mom can help you.

Love, Daddy

A hurricane of emotions swirled in my chest. Fear. Uncertainty. Disbelief. Anger. Sorrow. My head pounded as my pulse throbbed in my temples.

"That man is a piece of work." Mom shook her head, the

lines between her eyes deepening.

"What? I don't know, Mom. I mean..." I shook my head and tried to calm my breathing. "I guess he's gotten his act together?" What did this mean for Renee? Was he working on setting up a supervised visit? Questions whirled in my head.

Mom took the letter from my hands and scanned it, shaking her head again. "Look at how he's putting things. There were rules he had to follow." Mom rolled her eyes. "Poor guy, all held back by a restraining order and court order supervised parenting time and all." She put the letter down, her pointer finger tapping on it as she continued. "This is all about him. How great he's doing. How much Renee would *love* his new wife! And to top it off, "Oh hey, guess what, you're a big sister...aka...I have another child." Mom exhaled loudly. "It's almost like he's bragging. And then he ends it with "I'm sure your mom can help you write me." She pushed the letter away, disgust on her face. "This was as much—or more—for your eyes than Renee's."

I studied Mom's face. This was the most riled up I'd seen her in quite some time. Not long ago I would've worried the stress of this would send her back to the bottle. Now, though, I knew she'd be reading her Bible or playing a worship song on her guitar later tonight.

"Yeah...now that you say it, I have to admit it kind of felt like it was for me the entire time I was reading it, but I thought I was seeing it through my own fear and hurt." I twisted my mouth, frustrated by both the circumstances and my reactions.

"It can be both, you know."

"What do you mean?"

"You can *feel* something, and it can be *true*. Sometimes it seems like you dismiss your feelings because you don't trust them." Mom held my gaze, conviction deepening the brown in her eyes.

I swallowed, unwilling to admit the truth of Mom's statement. Instead, I turned my attention to the opened letter on the table.

"This wasn't exactly how I expected the day to go." I shook my head. "I don't know what to do."

"You don't have to do anything right now. Pray. Sleep. See what the morning brings." Mom's voice was soft and full of wisdom, reminding me of Nannie.

A question begged for an answer in the whirlwind of thoughts in my mind: If Mom could change so dramatically and be free of an addiction that had ruled her life for nearly thirty years, could Derrick have also changed?

After getting ready for bed, I settled in my room and Facetimed Matt. It was our nightly routine, and proof of how comfortable we'd become with each other. Me, sitting against my headboard with no makeup on and my hair a mess. Matt, propped up on pillows in his own bed, wearing a t-shirt, the beginnings of stubble darkening his lower face, looking at me with tired but happy eyes. I loved ending my day hearing his voice, seeing his face. Tonight, though, the thought of the phone call only filled me with dread. My stomach was in a million knots.

When I thought of telling Matt about the letter, the memory of him putting the heart necklace on Renee filled my mind. She'd been so delighted and longed to call him Daddy. Would that change if Derrick was back in our lives?

"So, now that the board has convened, I can fill you in on what's going on."

With the letter from Derrick, I'd almost forgotten about the church business. It felt trivial now, about as relevant to my survival as who won *The Voice.* But I knew it was important to Matt, and it bought me a few minutes to break the news about Derrick.

"What's the scoop? I hope it's nothing horrible." Really, though, how bad could it be? Was there a disagreement about the budget? Adding a new service time? Studying Matt's face on my phone, though, I noticed for the first time the dark circles under his eyes.

Matt took a deep breath. When he spoke, there was an unusual graveness to his voice. "Ben is resigning."

I sat up straight in bed. "What? Why?" I wasn't close to Ben Wescott, the associate pastor, but I knew Matt had looked up to him as a mentor.

"He..." Matt closed his eyes for a moment. When he opened them, the graveness they carried shot straight to my chest. "He's been having an affair."

"Ben? I don't believe it." My heart sank to the bottom of my stomach. Ben and his wife Evie had been married for thirty years. They had four grown children and even a couple of grandkids. They always seemed so happy. Holy. Perfect. How could it be?

"Yeah, I was shocked, too. Trust me." Matt shook his head. "They are stepping down from leadership and moving to Tempe so they can go to the home church there. He said they are going to try counseling but...it doesn't look like Evie is fully invested in it."

"I can't say I blame her." I blurted out. I knew what it was like to be hurt. My hurt had been in the form of abuse, though Derrick's quick remarriage after our divorce made me highly suspicious that he had been seeing someone else while we were still married.

"It's not a road I'd want to walk down, that's for sure." Matt's face drooped. He looked exhausted. "I'm hoping they can find healing at Risen Son Church in Tempe."

Risen Son was the main church in the He is Risen network of churches, which Cascade Christian Church was a member of. Even with all I had been through, I couldn't imagine the combined humiliation and devastation of infidelity, losing your job, moving, and then starting over. The Wescott's were in their mid-fifties. They should be getting ready for their golden years, not having everything they knew shattered. All because of Ben's marriage destroying choice. How many lives would it affect?

"How are you?" My heart broke for my fiancé. His mentor had just dealt him a gut punch.

"I'm hanging in there. Trying to absorb everything." Matt shifted the pillow he was leaning up against. "James said He is Risen is sending one of their leaders here to guide our church through this whole thing, and basically assess if there was some systemic thing that led to this happening." Matt took a deep breath and paused. "They'll discuss Pastor Wescott's replacement after that."

Pastor Wescott. Not Ben. Was that Matt's way of emotionally distancing himself from his mentor? My chest tightened. "Do they have anyone in mind?"

Matt pursed his lips together and shifted again. "Well James said among the current staff, he'd recommend me for the position."

My breath in my throat. "Is that what you want?"

Matt shrugged a shoulder, the hint of a smile bringing a glimmer to his eyes. "I am getting a bit old to be a youth pastor. Plus...it's one step closer to getting back to what I believe God's call is on my life. To pastor a church." Even through the limits of the phone screen, I could feel the yearning in his voice.

I nodded, unable to find words. I wanted Matt to follow his dreams. While I'd become accustomed to the idea of a being a youth pastor's wife, the increased responsibilities of running a church brought with it a whole new arena of expectations for both Matt and his family. His future family. Could I live up to those? I pushed away the uncertainty. I shouldn't think of myself and my own insecurities.

"Anyway, we can talk more about that—if and when the time comes. How was your day?"

My day seemed like a lifetime ago already. I wished I had something good to share with Matt after all he'd been through. "My day didn't end too well...even before finding out about . . . Pastor Westcott." I followed Matt's lead in how to refer to Ben Wescott.

Matt cocked his head, his brow pinched together. "Why's that?"

"Unwanted mail." In a blur of run on sentences I told Matt about Derrick's letter and gave him a summary of what it had said.

Matt sat up straight on his bed, his eyes wide. "Wow. Cassie. I'm so sorry. That had to be a kick in the gut."

I swallowed, touched by his emotion. "I don't even know what to think. Or do. I guess I'd written him off as gone forever. Now..." I shrugged.

Matt nodded and rubbed the stubble on his chin. "Yeah...me too."

Silence fell between us. The dream of happily ever after as a family of three looking like a ship sailing off to a distant, unreachable land.

"When are you going to give the letter to Renee?"

My stomach flip-flopped. I didn't want to think about it. Part of me wondered if I had to, but what I already knew about parental rights, gave me the answer. "I don't know. Maybe this weekend."

"How do you think she's going to react?"

Good question. She seldom, if ever, asked about her dad these days. Matt was one of her favorite people on the planet, already primed to take on the role of a dad in her life. The last time she'd seen Derrick, he'd been in an auto wreck with her in the backseat and then was arrested. My chest tightened at the memory. I thought those days were past. The fear of subjecting my daughter to the erratic, abusive behavior of her father was supposed to be behind me. Behind *us*.

The tentacle in my chest sank deeper into my heart, claiming its place.

"I'm afraid to find out."

Chapter Eight

Sharon

THE WELCOMING AROMA OF BREWING COFFEE and fresh baked pastries enveloped me as I entered the Good Perks Coffee Shop. I spotted Frank and Samantha at a bar height wooden table in the corner, flanked by glass windows on one side. I hated being the last one to a meeting, but it was one of those Murphy's Law mornings. Between going back home to retrieve Renee's forgotten water bottle and then encountering an accident on the freeway, I was fortunate to only be ten minutes behind schedule.

"Sorry I'm late." I slid onto one of the two stools left at the table.

Samantha reached over and touched my arm. "No worries. Go ahead and order a drink."

I shook my head. "I'm good. You two have already been waiting."

Frank cleared his throat. "What do you like to drink?"

You're a Jack and Coke kind of girl. Johnny's voice from a year ago echoed in my head. I exhaled, pushing the image of his face out of my mind.

"Nothing fancy. Just decaf, no sugar, maybe a touch of cream. But, really, I'm good. Let's get to business." My tone came out harsher than I intended.

Frank got up and smiled kindly. "I'll get you some. That'll give Samantha time to go over what you missed."

I knew his gesture was meant to be helpful, but I felt like the slow kid at school getting special treatment.

Samantha pushed a navy-blue folder in front of me with the words "Higher Focus" printed across the middle in a fancy font. "This is the program that Frank mentioned. It sounds really good to me, but I'd love to know your thoughts."

The folder was thick. I opened it and saw what looked like a summary sheet with bullet points. "I'm not a fast reader..."

Samantha laughed. "I don't expect you to read it all right now." She tapped the summary sheet. "This lays out the basics. It starts out as a sixteen-week course that focuses on the different challenges in overcoming an addiction. From my understanding, it's similar to AA in the steps it goes through. The difference is the focus isn't on a..." Samantha raised her fingers in air quotes, "'higher power,' but on the one true God. It delves into more theology focused things. After the sixteen-week course, which includes time for prayer and support, there are smaller support groups for daily struggles faced during recovery."

"It's specifically for Christians?"

"Well, it is a church program, so those are the ones it would reach, yes."

I chewed on my bottom lip. On the one hand I liked the idea. Even before I started going to church again, I'd never been too keen on the open-ended higher power of Alcoholics Anonymous. However, the availability and openness of the meetings, along with the acceptance I had found there, were pivotal in my recovery. "Are people who don't go to church welcome?"

"Certainly. It would be like all the other small groups we offer." Samantha smiled, "There's no membership requirement... of course, we'd hope coming to the meetings would encourage them to join us on Sundays."

I smelled Frank's cologne before I saw him set a cup of coffee down in front of me. "I hope I got the amount of cream right."

I glanced at the cup of coffee. It was the perfect shade of brown. I looked up at Frank as he slid back onto the stool opposite of me. The sun coming through the window brought out the golden in his brown eyes. He was kind of cute, in an almost peculiar way. "It's perfect. Thank you." I cupped the warm mug in my hands. "Samantha was starting to tell me a little bit about," I glanced down at the folder to make sure I got the name right, "Higher Focus."

Frank took a sip of his drink, which looked like some fancy latte. He put the cup down and nodded toward the folder on the table. "I attended the group for about five years at my old church, then ran a group for two years before I moved."

I'd wondered how and when Frank had ended up at our church but didn't want to pry. Now that door was opened. "Where'd you move from?"

"San Diego." Frank smiled, displaying his perfect teeth.

"Why in the world did you move here?" Summers were beautiful in Oregon, but rain and clouds dominated the rest of the year, as well as much cooler temperatures than southern California. I'd envied Johnny when he'd moved to central California. The idea of warmer weather and sandy beaches sounded like a dream come true to me.

Frank laughed. "Well, let's see." He held up the pointer finger of his ringless left hand. "Let's start with the exorbitant cost of living in Southern Cal." He lifted a new finger with each fault of the sunshine state. "Traffic. Excessive tourism." He raised an eyebrow. "Bad government. Crime."

I wondered if those were the same reasons Johnny had changed his Facebook status to "going home" and apparently left California. "How long have you been in Eugene?" And why couldn't I stop thinking about Johnny?

"A year now, and I've been attending Cascade Christian Church the entire time." Frank glanced toward Samantha. "I'm curious if your leadership is really okay with a couple of newbies leading a group."

"I've mentioned it to Jeremiah, our outreach Pastor,"

Samantha flitted her eyes toward me. "He thought it was a great idea." She spread her hands out in front of her. "He said to talk to you both, get some more information and present it to the leadership team." She smiled and lifted her shoulders. "So here I am."

A knot looped in my stomach. What would the leadership team say? I could see them approving Frank—he'd obviously been sober for quite some time and he had experience—I was still fairly new in my recovery and had absolutely no leadership experience. At least not at church.

Frank nodded, seemingly unaffected by the mention of the leadership team. He raised his eyebrows as if a new thought had occurred to him, then turned his focus to Samantha. "You've been kind of spearheading this whole thing. I think it would be good to continue to have your involvement as Sharon and I work on getting it up and going."

Did that mean he was also worried about the church approval process? Or was he unsure about my ability to help him get the program going? "I don't know." I blurted out.

"What don't you know about?" Frank asked.

I hated being put on the spot and was certainly not going to admit my insecurities to some stranger. Especially when that stranger was a single, not-too-bad looking man. I focused on Samantha, avoiding Frank's questioning eyes. "I know there's a need, I just don't know if there is enough of a need among the people who attend our church to justify a group. That's one reason why I was wondering about outsiders being welcome." I sighed. "I'd want to reach the community, somehow."

"We can do that." Frank's voice held confidence. "And you might be surprised by the need in the church."

Samantha nodded. "Sharon, I really think this would be good for the church, and I can't think of any other woman in our congregation who is a better fit to co-lead this group." She dropped her chin and gave me a pointed look.

Was that a compliment or an insult? I shifted uncomfortably in my seat. "Thanks, I guess." I lifted my coffee to my lips, welcoming its distraction.

Frank chuckled, and I couldn't help but look his way. His warm, golden eyes held a new sparkle to them as he studied me. "I never asked...how do you and Samantha know each other? I kind of get the feeling you two go way back."

I tried not to choke as I swallowed my coffee. "You could say that."

"It's a long, complicated story." Samantha offered.

Most of the leadership in church knew that 'long, complicated' story. It wouldn't be long until Frank did, too. Would he still look at me with such warmth then? Better to get it all out in the open. "I slept with her ex-husband, you know, while they were still married." When it came to confessions, I'd learned it was best to just cut to the quick.

There was dead silence at the table. Samantha cleared her throat, then gave a little laugh. "Well, that is how we met, true story."

Frank's expression did change, but not to disgust. It was the gentle, knowing look of someone who could understand the pain of the person that sat across from him. "I guess it's safe to say you two didn't start off as friends."

Samantha laughed lightly "Certainly not."

"It was a long time ago, back when I was at the beginning of my battle with alcoholism. I honestly didn't know he was married." I swallowed, the memory from my past still left a bitter taste in my mouth. "I was too drunk to know anything, really." I shrugged. "Samantha found out and tracked me down. Luckily, she wasn't the kind to carry a gun." I gave Frank a half-smile.

"We didn't see each other again for about thirty years." Samantha piped in. "Then one day Sharon shows up at church."

"I almost didn't come back." I said, taking another sip of my coffee. It seemed like a lifetime ago that Cassie basically dragged me to her new church. So much had changed since then. I'd found my father, though in his state I wasn't able to get the answers I longed for. I'd learned I had a brother. I'd let go of the guilt I'd carried for decades over my husband's death. Most importantly, I'd realized God still loved me.

Frank looked back and forth between Samantha and me. "How'd you go from that to"—he spread his hands, as if balancing us on opposite sides of an invisible scale—"this? That has to be a story in itself."

Samantha nodded. "It really was God at work. I didn't think I could ever truly be okay with her being in my vicinity, but then one day she came up and apologized to me and something in me broke." She shook her head. "God really changed my heart. I not only forgave her but began to understand what *she* had been through." Samantha looked at me, the telltale shimmer of tears in her eyes.

A heaviness weighed on my chest. I waved my hand, attempting to brush the topic away from the table like a fly trying to buzz into our coffee. "Let's just say it. You're a saint." This conversation was going much deeper than I wanted, and there sat Frank, taking it all in. *Good grief.*

"Hardly." Samantha chuckled. "But it's definitely been a growing experience."

"You can say that again." I checked the time on my phone. It was my day off, but I had a lot I wanted to do.

Samantha turned to Frank. "Some time passed, and I felt the nudge to invite Sharon to a women's Bible study I was leading." Sharon smiled, a faraway look in her eyes. "Also, I have to admit . . . my granddaughter and Sharon's granddaughter quickly became friends and were inseparable at church. Children can be the best peacemakers." Samantha gave a little laugh as she shook her head. "Everything just lined up. Sharon accepted my offer to come to the Bible study and the next thing I knew, we were going out for coffee afterwards."

Frank nodded, the crease on his brow telling me he was processing the information. "Now here we are." He turned his focus to me.

Silence once again fell between the three of us. I shifted in my seat, avoiding eye contact with Frank. Why did I care what he thought, anyway?

"Sharon."

Frank's voice made me lift my gaze from the table. He studied me with a knowing that made me want to look away again, but I held my ground.

"So what do you say? Are you up to co-leading?" The hopeful expectation in Frank's eyes also came through in his tone.

Why did I feel like I was embarking on an uphill battle, when I hadn't even started the journey? *You never know if you don't try. See what happens.* Mom's voice. Always calm. Always reassuring—and sometimes just a little annoying. I turned my focus to my coffee, as if the answer would show up in swirling letters at the top of the cup. "I'd like to read over the information you have, before I agree to anything."

Frank nodded. "Of course."

It looked like I'd be spending the next few days reading and praying. Who knew—maybe I'd be too preoccupied to think about Johnny.

The agony in Cassie's eyes made them a darker shade of blue. She sat across from me at the dining table, sipping a cup of coffee from her favorite mug. Her hair was askew, and the skin around her eyes was puffy. I doubted she'd slept more than a few hours the night before.

"I've prayed about it." She took a deep breath and held my gaze across the dining table in our little duplex. "And I talked it over with Matt, then ran it by Brian." The way she said Brian's name held a hint of venom. "I'm going to show Renee the letter Derrick sent."

I nodded slowly, taking in her words. Right or wrong, if it were me, I'd toss that letter from her ex in the trash. I guessed God hadn't quite quelled that rebellious, stubborn streak in me yet. As far as I was concerned, Derrick didn't deserve a place in Renee's life. Then again, one could say I didn't, either. My ruffled feathers shifted down a notch. "If you think that's the right thing to do, I'll support you." I sighed. "I hope Renee isn't set back by it. She's a sensitive girl."

"I know." Cassie shook her head. "There's no good answer." She lifted her hands. "I'm praying she takes it well, though I'm not sure what that'll mean, really."

"When are you going to give it to her?"

"Sometime today . . ."

I supposed Saturday was a good day for big news. It was only two Saturdays ago Cassie got engaged. My heart pinched, remembering Renee's excitement over the engagement and the necklace Matt had given her. All I wanted for my family were those happy moments. Hadn't we had our fair share of bad ones?

"Do you want me to be with you?" I hoped beyond measure Cassie would say yes, but I wanted to give her whatever space she needed with her daughter.

"Yes, I was hoping you would." Cassie blinked and looked away. "I thought about having Matt here, too, but that just doesn't seem right. . . not yet, anyway."

Why did life have to be so complicated?

We spent the rest of the day doing Saturday chores, then took Renee to the park. When we got home, Cassie had Renee sit by her in the living room so we could have a family meeting. Of course, Renee happily obliged. Family meetings were where she usually got to air her own grievances about things, like too many chores or not enough snack food in the house. The girl cracked me up every time. Tonight, though, was going to be different.

Renee sat next to her mom with her hands folded in her lap, all prim and proper and expectant. Normally, Cassie would talk about plans for the future, like a family outing, or about how "someone" kept leaving their dirty towel on the floor and we needed to all be better about picking up after ourselves. We'd never had these kinds of meetings when Cassie was a kid, but she'd heard about it in one of those parenting books she was always reading.

"Sweetie, I have something I need to show you." Cassie got up and walked to the shelf over the television and pulled an envelope out from between two books. She set the letter on the coffee table in front of Renee.

Renee cocked her head. "What's that?"

Cassie sat back on the couch, next to Renee, and put her arm around her. "It's a letter from your...dad."

I watched Renee's face. The frown and draining of color from her cheeks told me all I needed to know about what was going on inside her heart. "Is he writing to tell me good-bye?"

Cassie and I both looked at each other at the same time. I shrugged to her scrunched eyebrows. We were both surprised.

"No . . . he's just writing to tell you what he's been up to." Cassie picked up the letter gently. "Do you want me to read it to you?"

"But you said Matt was going to be my daddy now."

Cassie closed her eyes. I could almost hear the silent prayer she must've been sending up. "Yes, Matt is going to be your step-dad." Cassie wrapped her arm around Renee and pulled her close. "I know this is so confusing."

Renee turned her head toward Cassie. "Mommy, I don't even remember what Daddy sounds like." Her voice cracked. "I hardly remember what he looks like." Her frown deepened and she buried her face in her mom's chest.

Could Renee have forgotten so much of her dad that quickly? It'd only been a couple of years. Then again, Renee was barely five years old the last time she saw him, and it hadn't been under the best of circumstances. I'd heard more than one story about children blocking memories out—both good and bad—because of traumatic events.

I scooted closer to Renee and put my hand on her shoulder. "Sweet Pea, if you don't want to read the letter right now, you don't have to." I was overstepping my bounds by my offer, but the mother in me knew Renee needed a chance to take this all in. A knowing nod and glance from Cassie told me she agreed.

"Grammy's right. If you want to wait, we can." Cassie gently lifted Renee's chin with her hand. "I'm not making you read it if you don't want to."

Renee sucked on her lips, intently studying her mom's face. What was she thinking? My chest ached, wanting to pull them both into a bear hug and protect them from Derrick. Protect them from the storm that seemed intent on raining on their happily ever after.

"I guess it's okay if you read it now, Mommy." Renee's voice was strained with emotion.

Cassie closed her eyes and kissed Renee's forehead before picking the letter up. She pulled the paper out of the envelope and held it where Renee could see it while she read, like a mother would with a bedtime story. My skin crawled at the sight of Derrick's block-style handwriting.

Cassie read the letter out loud, almost devoid of emotion. I couldn't imagine what was going on inside her heart, but knew it had to be torture. Nausea filled me when Cassie reached the part of the letter about the new baby. I couldn't even look at my granddaughter to see how those words might be affecting her. When Cassie was finished, she set the letter down on the coffee table and looked at Renee. Silence filled the room, broken only by the tick-tocking of the grandfather clock.

"Do I have to write him back?" Renee's voice held a quiver.

Cassie shook her head. "No. If you want to write him, you can. But if you don't, then you don't have to." She lowered her head to Renee's eye level. "*Whatever* choice you make is a good one."

Renee nodded once. "Can I have the letter?"

My breath caught in my throat. Did this mean Renee wanted to write Derrick back?

"Uhm...yes." Cassie looked at me, a hint of fear in her eyes. "Of course. It's yours." She handed the letter to Renee, who jumped up and walked away and down the hall, toward her room, her tiny footsteps echoing in the quiet house. Cassie looked at me and shrugged, the lines around her eyes deepening. The clock ticked.

A moment later the sound of ripping paper broke through the silence of the house.

Chapter Nine

Cassie

So much for happily ever after.

As soon as I heard the ripping paper, I beat myself up for sharing Derrick's letter with Renee. Obviously, it was the wrong choice—but what was the right one? I hadn't checked with a custody attorney, but my experience so far told me how the eyes of the law regarded these things. Any attempt to thwart a relationship between Renee and her father would be looked down upon by a judge. Derrick was within the bounds of our custody agreement to write Renee a letter. It was my duty to relay the letter to her.

When did my maternal duty to protect my daughter's heart ever get a say? Did genetics give a man a right to inflict emotional pain on his offspring, over and over and over again?

Mom and I both zipped to Renee's bedroom after we heard the paper ripping, only to find the letter in shreds on her floor and Renee in her bed, face down in her pillow. I sat on the edge of her bed and stroked her hair, but she didn't respond. She didn't seem to be crying. Her body was stiff as a board, resisting my gentle tug on her shoulder, trying to coax her to flip over. She wouldn't budge. I eventually kissed the back of her head and left her alone. In my mind I screamed at God. "Why?"

God didn't answer.

After assuring Mom I was all right, I called Matt and told him what happened.

"That poor kid." He sounded nearly as pained as I felt.

"I feel horrible." The tears fell now, hot streaks down my face. To the world, it probably seemed like an overreaction.

Anyone who understood what Renee and I had been through with Derrick though...to them, the tears would be appropriate. Matt was one of the understanding ones.

"It's not your fault, Cassie. You did what you had to do." Matt sighed loudly. "Derrick didn't put much thought into what he wrote in that letter."

"I think he knew exactly what he was doing." My mom's words replayed in my head.... *This was as much—or more—for your eyes than Renee's.*

Matt was silent a moment. "Perhaps. More likely, though, he didn't know his words would cause the reaction it did in Renee. What would be the point of that? What good would it do him?"

"Causing me pain. That's all he cares about! Even if Renee gets hurt in the process." My voice rose as my grip on the phone tightened.

"Cassie..." Matt's voice was barely above a whisper. "I know this is hard and brings back bad memories. You might be right, maybe Derrick wanted to poke a thorn in your side with the news about the baby. But do you think maybe he really does want to reconnect with his daughter and out of ignorance didn't choose the best things to share in his first letter to her in two years?"

I raked my free hand through my hair. The hammering in my heart slowed to a gentle thud. "I don't know. Maybe."

"Renee probably needs time to process this. I'm sure this coming on the heels of our engagement has her on an emotional roller coaster."

"That makes two of us." I plopped down on my bed, suddenly exhausted.

"Two? Let's make it three." Matt gave a short laugh.

Oh, Matt. He'd been stoic and pastor-like. I'd almost forgotten about what he must be feeling and assumed his emotions matched his calm counsel. "I'm sorry." I closed my eyes and searched for words. "How are you feeling about the whole thing?"

Matt cleared his throat. "I hate seeing you and Renee hurt. But...also...I don't know."

Was he having second thoughts about a blended family? Did having Derrick back in the picture make things too complicated, even for him?

Before another frantic question could form in my head, Matt continued. "I'm kind of sad for me, too. I know this sounds selfish, probably, but *I* want to be Renee's dad. I was hoping I wouldn't have to share her with Derrick." He sighed. "Now that I've said it, I sound pretty childish." He laughed hollowly.

I shook my head. "I feel the same way. I was hoping—expecting—for it to be the three of us starting a new life together, free from the past." I bit my bottom lip, willing the emotions down. "You're everything Renee *should* have in a dad."

"Lord knows I want to be, but we're going to have to trust that God knows what He's doing. In all of this, He has a plan, even if we can't see it yet."

God had a plan. I knew it had to be true. When I closed my eyes though, all I saw was a forlorn path zigzagging through dark mountains, its destination uncertain. The vision reminded me of the recurring dream I'd had about Grandpa near the end of mine and Derrick's marriage. A cold shiver ran through me, one that was oblivious to the late summer heat.

The fallout from the letter reminded me of a wintertime dusting of snow in the Willamette Valley. More often than not, the promise of a snow-day was gone in the morning when the moisture from the sky turned back to rain, washing away any evidence of a winter storm. So it was with Renee. By Sunday morning she was back to herself, the letter forgotten. I decided I wouldn't mention it, leaving the ball in her court if she wanted to talk about it. Despite Renee's good mood, I couldn't shake the sense of foreboding while I got ready for church. Would Derrick try contacting Renee again? And was something brewing under the surface of Renee's calm? A storm quietly gaining momentum, ready to show us its destructive force with another mention of her father?

The church foyer was packed when we got there. Mom had to work because one of the housekeepers was sick and she couldn't find anyone to cover the shift. Usually we attended the second service, as that was the one that had children's services, so Renee and I arrived a little later than I would have liked. I longed to be near Matt, and the first service was the only one he could attend with me because the youth met during the second service.

"Have you met Pastor Ferguson and his wife, Myrtle, yet?" Trish, the wife of the children's pastor, barely uttered a hello before asking me the question. Her eyes were bright with excitement. Pastor Thomas Ferguson was the leader He is Risen had sent to help guide the church and assist in filling the associate pastor position.

"No, not yet." My emotional hangover from the events of the night made it hard to focus. I looked around for Matt but couldn't find him in the sea of people around me.

Trish's enthusiasm about meeting the Fergusons echoed what I'd seen in most everyone else when it came to the visiting leaders. I couldn't understand why there wasn't more outward mourning over Pastor Wescott and his family, who had been hushed and ushered off like an unwed pregnant teen in the 1950s. Matt had told me the Fergusons had flown into town from Tempe, Arizona, this weekend to meet with staff and begin their search for housing. To me, their presence was only a reminder of what had happened with Pastor

Wescott and the uncertainly of my own future if Matt was promoted to the position of associate pastor.

"Oh, let me introduce you." Trish stood on her tiptoes, scanning the crowd. Seeming to find what she was looking for, she turned toward me and gently pulled on my arm. "Come on, they're over near the middle door to the sanctuary."

Reluctantly, and wishing beyond reason that Matt was with me, I followed Trish to the doors and pulled a frowning Renee along with me. A group of people stood around a well-dressed couple who looked to be in their early sixties. We stood outside the group, waiting for our turn to get a face-to-face with the new people. Something about the commotion rubbed me the wrong way, but I couldn't exactly say why. Finally, the people in front of us drifted away and we were in front of a couple who had to be Pastor Ferguson and his wife, Myrtle.

They both smiled benevolently. The man's face was tanned and deeply weathered. His dark brown eyes shined from underneath bushy black eyebrows. His ebony hair was speckled with gray. Mrs. Ferguson's hands were clasped behind her back. Pastor Ferguson was the first one to hold out his hand for an introduction, which Trish breezed through with continued exuberance. "Nice to meet you, Pastor Ferguson." I said, hoping I sounded sincere.

"Nice to meet you also, Ms. Peterson." He motioned to the woman beside him. "This is my wife, Myrtle."

Myrtle held out her hand to me. Her cool fingers were manicured and slender. A diamond bracelet graced her wrist, touching the sleeve of her cream colored and expensive looking blazer. "Pleased to meet you." Her blue eyes sparkled, but I couldn't tell if they were the sparkle of welcoming tropical Ocean waves or the gleam of an ice-capped peak.

I cleared my throat. "Nice to meet you." I glanced around, desperately hoping Matt would be nearby. He was not. I focused on the woman in front of me. "What do you think of Eugene?"

"Oh my. Well, we haven't seen much of it yet, I'm afraid." Myrtle sighed. "But the glimpses I've caught during house-hunting," Myrle put her hand on her chest and shook her head, making her perfect platinum bobbed hair swing, "Such beauty. So much green!" Her smile widened, accentuating the lines in her face that makeup couldn't hide.

I nodded in agreement. "You should see the waterfalls." My smile turned genuine, remembering the last one I'd visited with Matt.

Myrtle raised an eyebrow. "Oh…yes, of course! You must be Pastor Armstrong's fiancée." Myrtle's voice dropped an octave. "He's told us so much about you."

Pastor Armstrong? No one called Matt "Pastor Armstrong". They called him Matt or Pastor Matt. For the most part, only our lead pastor and the associate pastor were typically referred to by their last names. Why were these people so formal? When had Matt talked to them? It must've been this morning, because he made no mention of it during our conversation on the phone last night.

"Yes, that's me."

Myrtle nodded, her smile fading away.

I glanced down at Renee, who was looking up expectantly. "And this is—"

Music poured out the doors of the sanctuary, signaling the beginning of worship.

"I'm sure we'll be talking more soon. Looks like it's time for service." Myrtle looked beyond me toward the few people who were obviously waiting to meet the new couple before joining worship.

I moved aside, pulling Renee, who had remained silent, with me. My daughter tugged on my hand, demanding my attention. I glanced down at her. Squinted, emerald eyes stared up at me. Her mouth moved, but I couldn't hear her above the rising sound of the band. Leaning closer, I put my ear near her mouth.

"Yes, sweetie."

"Mommy, those people didn't even look at me."

I felt my chin drop, realizing Renee was right. In all the hubbub of the quick interaction, I didn't get to introduce Renee. The Fergusons had also not acknowledged her standing beside me. Myrtle even seemed to usher me off as soon as she realized who I was.

I patted Renee's shoulder. "They were just really busy meeting everyone. I'm sure they'll love to be introduced to you later when things calm down." I steered Renee through the line of people pouring into the crowded sanctuary. Despite the warmth of the building and being amongst people I'd been going to church with for two years, cold goosebumps washed over my body.

Chapter Ten

Sharon

FROM EVERYONE WHO HAS BEEN GIVEN much, much will be demanded.

I tucked the corners of the sheets snuggly into the hotel bed, mildly amused that the scripture from Luke had popped into my head as I did so. Being the maid supervisor who ended up working the rooms when others didn't show up on Sunday probably wasn't exactly what Jesus had in mind when he was talking to his disciples, but I was sure feeling the weight of being in demand.

My heart ached to be with Cassie and Renee at church. My sweet granddaughter had seemingly bounced back from the shock of the letter from her father, but something in the pit of my stomach told me there was trouble brewing in that little soul. To top it off, Cassie had texted me from church, saying she'd met Pastor Ferguson and his wife and didn't know what to think of them. It was unusual of Cassie to text during church. She usually put her phone on silent and slipped it in her purse before she walked through the doors. Plus, she rarely had anything negative to say about members of our church. I found myself biting my tongue on a regular basis, keeping my opinions to myself, but that girl never seemed to struggle much with judgment or suspicion. Kind of drove me crazy, to be quite honest. She saw the best in people, especially fellow church members. Then again, I guess it was her seeing the best in me that accounted for our relationship surviving the lowest of my lows. Maybe it was time for me to start doing the same.

From everyone who has been given much, much will be demanded.

I chuckled to myself as I pushed the cleaning cart out of the room. Lord, you're always working on me, aren't you? As I promised Samantha, I'd spent time praying about whether or not I was up to the challenge of co-leading the Higher Focus small group at church. I wish I could say I'd received a clear answer from above, but so far, I was as empty handed as a fisherman without bait.

It was past noon and Maria and I were less than halfway through cleaning all of the rooms. We'd decided to divide and conquer instead of working as a team, since we were short-handed. My neck and shoulders ached, and my lower back was tightening up into what would soon be a nice hard knot. Time for lunch and a little rest.

Instead of heading to the breakroom, I grabbed a bottle of water and exited the hotel, making my way to a short trail behind the parking lot. While I longed to sit down, I knew getting back up would be painful. Better to keep moving and get some fresh air. I made my way down the trail that cut through a landscaped area and ended up on a residential street lined with tall trees. The heat of the late summer afternoon was nothing compared to the humid heat of the hotel laundry room, not to mention outdoors smelled much sweeter.

While I knew Cassie's text wasn't meant to discourage me from taking on any kind of leadership role, I felt a nagging uncertainty rising in my chest. Derrick making a surprise appearance in our lives via his letter to Renee probably was partly to blame for my general unease, too. Then, there was the mysterious Facebook post by Johnny...who I shouldn't even be thinking about. The thing was, I couldn't stop thinking about him. What I needed was a sign. In my small group, we'd been studying the story of Gideon and his fleece. Nora, who led the group discussion, said sometimes we needed to lay a fleece down for God to give us a sign. There was some debate in our group about that, but I liked the idea. What "fleece" could I lay down? I stopped walking and closed my eyes.

What's most on your heart?

It wasn't like I could lie to God. Johnny was taking up way too much space in my heart and mind lately. I needed to either lay that burden to rest or pursue it.

An idea hit me like a shock from an ungrounded outlet. It was so simple. I pulled my phone out of my back pocket and opened my Facebook app, then searched for Johnny Beckett. His page came up. Nothing had changed since his last post. The "add friend" button stood out like a shining spark of light through a cloudy sky—or a blaring stop light, I wasn't sure which. I took a deep breath. "Lord, if he accepts my Facebook request by the end of the day, then I'll say no to leading the group now and instead maybe . . . *maybe* . . . reconnect with Johnny. If he doesn't accept it by the end of the day, then I'll know you're telling me to say yes to the Higher Focus group thing."

I tapped the blue button. The wording immediately changed from "add friend" to "cancel request." My finger hovered over the button. No, I couldn't cancel it. I had just prayed about it. I sighed and stared at Johnny's profile picture. Would he respond?

I slid my phone back into my pocket and turned around. Time to head back to work in time to grab a little something to eat. The vending machine had just been restocked on Friday, and the Snickers bar was calling my name. I didn't usually eat candy that much anymore. I'd found that sweets were a crutch for my addiction to alcohol. Despite my prayers, the edgy feeling of uncertainty wouldn't leave me be. The comfort of chocolate was a guilty indulgence I could afford.

When I got home, Cassie and Renee were in the backyard. The sprinkler was on and Renee was running through it in her bathing suit, enjoying the last days of summer. Ringlets of hair had fallen out of the ponytail at the back of her head and stuck to her water covered face. My chest swelled with love. Coming home to this would never get old. I had missed so much of Cassie growing up, and now, through the undeserving grace of God and my daughter's forgiveness, I was getting a second chance to enjoy treasures like this, as a grandma. When Renee saw me, she ran straight at me and hugged me tight, soaking my pants. The cold water was refreshing, and I'd soon be changing my clothes anyway.

"Renee, it's time to get dried off and dressed for dinner." Cassie spoke from a lawn chair under the shade of the Oak tree that bordered our backyard.

Renee looked back at her mom and then up to me, her eyes hinting she wanted to say something. Instead, she nodded and walked to the back door without a fight. I walked over to the faucet and turned it off, relieving the overwatered grass of the sprinkler's deluge.

"How was your day?" Cassie still sat in the lawn chair. I couldn't see her eyes through the shade. The tone of her voice, though, told me she wasn't doing good. I grabbed the other lawn chair and dragged it over to the shade. Changing my uniform could wait a bit.

"My day was good." I positioned the chair by Cassie and eased myself into it, my wet pants tugging on the skin of my thigh. "How was yours?"

Cassie turned her head toward me and the redness of her

eyes and puffiness underneath spoke a thousand words.

"Oh, baby girl, what's wrong?" I reached for Cassie's hand.

Cassie looked away. "Nothing major . . . I mean . . . it's just me, I think."

"Did something happen at church? I know it sounded like your interaction with the Fergusons was less than fun." Bitterness crept into my voice, despite my efforts to squelch it. No matter how old my girl was, if someone hurt her, my mama bear instinct kicked in.

"Yeah, the rest of the day didn't really get better, I guess."

I leaned forward in my seat. "It's not Derrick, is it?"

Cassie shook her head. "No, thank God."

I sighed with relief.

"It was more church stuff." Cassie looked at me and blinked several times, as if trying to fight off the urge to cry again. "The whole thing with the Fergusons just hit me the wrong way. Then Matt was so busy and distracted. When I finally got to talk to him after church and told him about my impression of the Fergusons, he was not supportive, to say the least."

"What? That's not like him."

"I know." Cassie sucked in on her lip and stared at the ground.

My mind raced. Something was off. "What did he say?"

"Well, he kind of got mad at me. He said I was acting insecure. I guess all his interactions with them have been great and he thinks I read the entire thing all wrong."

"He said you were being insecure?" My voice echoed in the backyard, louder than I intended. Such a remark didn't sound like the Matt I knew. Or at least, thought I knew.

Cassie's mouth opened, then closed. She pursed her lips. "I guess he didn't say that *exactly*...he more or less alluded to it."

I exhaled loudly. I didn't know what to make of this. On one hand, if I was honest with myself, I could see how my daughter was feeling a bit insecure. There was a good chance the couple she had talked to today was distracted and she simply read them wrong. On the other hand, the last thing I wanted to do was give any inkling that I didn't trust Cassie's intuition. I knew firsthand how disastrous not listening to the guiding voice of your conscience could be.

"That doesn't sound like Matt. Was he having a bad day?"

Cassie shrugged and looked away. "I think church stuff has him kind of on edge."

"I see."

My daughter turned to me, her eyes caverns of desperation. "Mom, I'm so afraid I don't have what it takes to be a pastor's wife. What if Matt realizes that, too, and he changes his mind?"

"Then that would be *his* loss." I raised my eyebrows, emphasizing my point. "Stop doubting yourself." I paused, searching my heart for words to comfort Cassie. "What do you think Nannie would say?"

"Nannie?" Cassie's expression turned soft, full of reminiscence.

I nodded, urging her on.

"She loved Matt." Cassie smiled.

"She had good taste, don't you think?" I tilted my head, knowing the answer.

"Yes, she did." Cassie sighed and sat back in the lawn chair, staring at the sky. "She would tell me I was more than enough." Her voice was barely above a whisper.

"She was a wise woman." My own voice cracked.

I would never stop missing my mom.

It was bedtime before I got around to checking Facebook. Or maybe I put it off to the last minute, giving Johnny every second available to respond to my request. As I sat in pajamas in my bed, I tapped the Facebook icon. I had a few notifications. One was a friend liking a recent picture I'd posted of Renee. The other was someone else inviting me to like some page for a new hair salon in town. The third was a friend request from some guy I'd never heard of and who lived in Nigeria. My heart fell to my stomach. I closed the app, uninterested in looking at anything else.

It looked like God had answered my fleece prayer, though not in the way my heart had hoped.

Chapter Eleven

Cassie

I COULDN'T REMEMBER THE LAST TIME I'd looked forward to going to work on a Monday. My morning class at the University had kept me distracted from my problems, but now I was rushing to work, trying to beat the clock and avoid intrusive thoughts.

The last time I'd found such reprieve in work and busyness was when I was divorcing Derrick. Back then, I needed every possible distraction possible to thwart the worries in my mind and the agony in my heart. I'd found more than one way to distract myself at the office. Images of Brian and my schoolgirl-like naivete about his intentions flitted through my mind, almost as fast as the yellow traffic light in front of me turned to red. I slammed on my brakes, barely stopping in time to miss the rear bumper of the car in front of me. My heart jack-rabbited as my seat belt tightened like a battle-field tourniquet across my chest.

What was wrong with me?

I knew the answer. Church. Between meeting the Fergusons and Matt's unusual behavior, I was doubting myself more than I had in a long time, battling feelings of inadequacy. Did I have what it took to be a pastor's wife? Mom's reassurance from the night before should have comforted me, but I couldn't help but wonder if God was trying to show me I wasn't up to the task.

The memory of my conversation with Matt ran through my head for the thousandth time as I finished my commute to work.

Worship had been well underway by the time he made it to his seat next to me. I knew I wouldn't have a chance to talk to him until after service. Then, during the altar call he'd disappeared toward the back of the sanctuary. When I looked back, I saw him talking to a young couple I didn't recognize. After service, I tracked him down in the foyer, but he was in the middle of a conversation with the Fergusons. I waited around, making small talk with people I knew and trying to keep Renee entertained at the same time. No easy task. Finally, Matt was free, and I made my way toward him. Instead of looking at me with his usual warmth and big smile, he looked surprised.

"Cassie, I thought you'd have headed home by now."

That stung. I almost never left without saying goodbye to Matt. It wasn't often I joined him for the first service, and I hoped we'd at least get a chance to visit for a brief amount of time before he got ready for the youth group gathering during second service. "I was waiting to see if you'd be coming by later. I made a chicken salad for Sunday dinner and was planning on saving you some."

Matt's eyes warmed, putting me at ease. "Of course! I should be able to make it there by four or so." He glanced down at Renee. "Maybe I can bring my bike and we can go for a ride. It's not too hot today."

Renee nodded enthusiastically.

I should've waited for him to come over to talk to him about the Fergusons. That would have been the smart thing to do, but the interaction had been eating at me. "Can I talk to you a second—alone?"

"Uhm...yeah." Matt glanced around the foyer, his brow furrowed. "I need to get things ready for second service, but let's go sit for a minute." He motioned toward the youth room, which was currently empty.

I grabbed Renee's hand, and we walked in silence. Once inside the room, Matt quickly found a Jenga game and set it on a table for Renee, encouraging her to see how tall she could build a tower in five minutes, clearly marking our time limit for conversation.

"What's up?" Instead of sitting, he stood close to me, his head cocked.

I exhaled, relieved to have him close, to feel his concern. "I met the Fergusons this morning."

Matt smiled. "They are a great couple, aren't they?"

I raised my eyebrows. "I guess...I mean they weren't exactly friendly toward me. Or, at least, the wife wasn't."

"Myrtle? How so? I know she comes across a little formal."

"And cold."

"Cassie . . ." Matt's eyes narrowed. "You don't usually judge someone so quickly."

"I'm not. It was the way she reacted when I told her who I was, and the way she completely ignored Renee . . . it was like . . ." I lowered my voice to make sure Renee wouldn't hear. "It was like she was looking down on us." I shrugged my shoulders. "Maybe because I'm divorced."

Matt shook his head. "I think you're reading something into this that's not there."

"I misread her?" Irritation added a hardness to my voice.

"Maybe you assume people think things of you because you're worried about them yourself, even though you shouldn't be." Matt spoke tenderly, but his words still stung.

I exhaled loudly and looked away. Was Matt right? The queasy feeling in my stomach told me otherwise. "You weren't there. You didn't see the look on her face or hear the tone of her voice."

Matt put his hand on my cheek and gently turned my face toward his. Love burned in his beautiful blue eyes. "Hopefully, next time, I will be." The corners of his mouth lifted into a smile. "It won't be long until you're introduced as Cassie Armstrong, instead of Cassie Peterson."

My heart lifted. I liked the sound of my soon-to-be name. Cassie Armstrong. Mrs. Matt Armstrong. I'd never changed my name back to my maiden one after my divorce from Derrick. From one married name to another, my birth name remained in the past. A tiny wave of unease splashed my insides, making me pause. "I'm looking forward to that day." I forced a smile, telling myself I was worrying too much about nothing.

"Me too." Matt kissed my forehead lightly, then gave me a long hug. The warmth of his embrace chased the shadows away. Maybe I was making the entire Ferguson interaction into more than it truly had been.

Matt pulled away and looked at his watch. I then ushered Renee out of the building so he could get ready for the teenagers that would soon fill the room. With each step toward my car, the reassurance I'd briefly felt dissipated, and Matt's words weighed on me.

I think you're reading something into this that's not there. He didn't trust my perceptions.

Perhaps you assume people think things of you because you're worried about them yourself, even though you shouldn't be. He thought I had a low self-esteem.

It won't be long until you're introduced as Cassie Armstrong, instead of Cassie Peterson. A phrase that should have brought me joy, but now made me pause.

By the time I pulled on the door handle of my Explorer, hot tears threatened to spill. It took all I had to make it to the road before letting them fall silently down my cheeks, streaking my makeup.

And now here I was on my way to work, fighting back those same tears.

"Mondays are worse than a horse that's eaten hot hay."

Missy showed up at my desk with a mug of coffee and her signature playful grin. Her demeanor brought a smile to my lips, even though my heart was still heavy. "That sounds pretty bad."

"It sure is." Missy took a long sip of her coffee and gave a little nod. "How was your weekend? Were you busy making wedding plans?"

The mention of the wedding made my shoulders feel heavy. "No, not yet. I don't even know where to start."

"Well, dang, don't look so happy about it." Missy gave a little laugh and took another sip of coffee.

I shrugged. "I don't really have that much time to think about it, honestly."

"Hmm." Missy sucked in her cheeks. "Okay, girlie, what's up?"

I turned toward my computer screen. Time to work, not talk. Cynthia was gone for the day, but she'd left me enough work to keep me hopping. "Nothing." I waved my hand. "I'm just getting nervous, I think."

"That doesn't usually happen until closer to the big day, from what I've heard."

I lifted a shoulder, unable to meet Missy's gaze. "That whole letter from Derrick threw me for a loop. I'm kind of emotional, you know." There was probably more truth in that than I wanted to admit.

"Everything good with you and the Pastor Man?"

The Pastor Man. Missy's choice of words was a good reminder of who I was talking to. I loved my friend, but she wasn't a follower of Jesus and definitely not a fan of church. What would she think if I told her my misgivings about the Fergusons, or what Matt had said? She'd be quick to take my side, as always—which meant the church people would be the bad guys. I couldn't risk that. Some things were more important than my feelings.

I turned back to face my friend. "Oh yes, things are fine. He's been especially busy with some stuff at church." Sighing, I motioned to my inbox. "Speaking of busy, I better get back to work."

Missy studied me in the calculating, way-too-knowing way she'd done since the day I'd met her. In that moment, I knew *she knew* I wasn't telling her everything, but I also knew she wouldn't pry, at least not yet.

Hopefully, by the time she did come at me like a mother trying to comb a rebellious toddler's hair, the situation with Matt and church would be better.

It had to be.

Since Cynthia was gone, all her calls were rerouted to me, so a good part of my transcription time was interrupted by answering the phone. I assumed when Kylie, our new receptionist, buzzed me, it was another call for my boss.

"This is Cynthia Steeleborne's assistant. How may I help you?"

"Cassie, sorry." Kylie's voice was higher pitched than normal and apologetic. "It's not a call for Cynthia. There's someone here for you."

Someone to see me? Matt immediately came to my mind. Who else could it be? Maybe he'd realized he hadn't been as supportive as usual yesterday and was making a surprise appearance to brighten my day. He'd come by the office unannounced a couple of times in the past, and both times he'd brought flowers. My heart pounded as I hurried to the front desk with a smile I couldn't hide if my life depended on it.

Matt wasn't in the lobby. The only person there was a stranger—a short, hipster-looking young man with nearly shoulder length hair. He held a clipboard and a small stack of papers in his hands.

"Here she is." Kylie motioned toward me, her glasses making her eyes look especially wide.

The hipster took a step toward me. "Cassie Peterson?"

I felt the smile vanish from my face as my heart dropped to the pit of my stomach.

"Yes."

He handed the stack of papers to me. "I'm serving you these papers on behalf of Derrick Peterson."

I took the papers from him. He nonchalantly looked at his electronic watch and made a note on his clipboard. "Have a good day." He sauntered out the door without another word.

I swallowed, willing my heart to be still. *Lord, I know you're with me. Please give me strength to read this.* Nodding toward Kylie, whose mouth was now agape, I turned on my heel and walked away.

It was like I was moving through water as I made my way back to my desk and sat down. The feeling of being pulled back in time was overwhelming, making it hard to see straight. It was a lifetime ago that Derrick had served me divorce papers in this exact same office, and yet in some ways it felt like yesterday. In reality, three years had passed since that day and now. It had seemed his purpose then was to destroy me, yet in the end he only destroyed himself. He lost much of what he owned and ended up in jail. Once he was released, he'd disappeared. Remarried. Acted like Renee and I had never existed. The only reminder of him were the small monthly child support and alimony payments deposited to my checking account each month. A payment I knew he wouldn't make if not for the consequence of possibly ending up in court and jail if he was delinquent. Payments that could have been increased if I'd gone back to fight for more child support, but I hadn't wanted to rock the boat. Didn't want to give him reason to remember us. To harm us.

I looked at the papers, forcing myself to focus on the words. As I suspected, it was a petition for a change in custody and parenting time. Once again, Derrick was filing his case without an attorney. I scanned through the details, feeling my throat tighten as I read the words.

Shared custody. Every other week parenting schedule. Alternating holidays.

Derrick was back.

Chapter Twelve

Sharon

THE GRASS AT THE PARK WAS green, unlike the underwatered and sun-weary lawn in Cassie's backyard. My daughter had tightened her wallet like never before since getting served the papers from Derrick. Which made perfect sense to me, though if I was honest, the thought of buying a baseball bat occurred to me before the gumption to find money for an attorney.

Frank and I found a picnic table under the shade of a large tree. The table was long enough for Renee to sit at one end and work on the puzzle she'd brought along while Frank and I talked. I couldn't believe she would start second grade the next morning. Where had time gone?

"I'm glad today worked out for us to go over the curriculum." Frank pulled a binder out of the backpack he carried, and then set down some notebooks and pens, tucking them under the binder. The slight breeze in the air rustled the leaves over our heads.

"Yeah, me too. Especially if we aim to start this thing in October." I took a sip of my Diet Coke and then placed it on the table, away from all the papers. With the temperature in the eighties, the bottle was already sweating. And so was I.

I'd gotten the call from Samantha about the group being approved by the church leadership just two days after getting the text from Cassie about Derrick serving her papers for custody and parenting time. I'd almost backed out of the group. The uncertainty of what Cassie and Renee would be going through seemed like enough of an unknown in my life. Then I'd remembered my fleece prayer about whether I should help lead the group or not. God had answered. I couldn't very well back out.

The fact that Johnny still hadn't accepted my Facebook friend request—or updated his status—helped solidify the matter.

"The upside of being a tax accountant is I have a pretty flexible schedule for most of the summer." Frank sat at the bench across from me, dressed casually in a nice t-shirt and khaki shorts. His dark tan was evidence he spent a lot of time outdoors.

"What's the downside?"

"The downside is I work sixty to eighty hours a week from January through April."

"That's not much of downside, if you ask me." I brushed a stray tendril of hair away from my eyes. "I'd take that over working forty hours in a hotel any day."

"Hmm." Frank pursed his lips and opened the binder. "You're obviously intelligent and hardworking. Have you thought about going into a different line of work?"

"At my age?" My voice rose in exasperation. I couldn't even imagine what that would be. I'd worked at dive bars, greasy diners and cheap hotels all my life. What'd he think, I could go apply for some fancy office job and know what I was doing? My odds were much better if I worked my way up the food chain at the Day and Night Inn, thank you very much.

Frank chuckled "You're not old."

"I'm too old for *that*." Mid-fifties and seeking a new career path. *Good grief.*

The edges of Frank's mouth lifted in a sly smile. He opened his mouth as if to say something and then seemed to change his mind and shook his head.

"What?"

"Nothing."

"You wanted to say something." Why had my irritation turned into the feeling of little wings beating in my chest?

The smile lines around Frank's eyes deepened. "You're right. But then I realized it may sound . . ." He shot a glance Renee's way. She was engrossed in her Disney castle puzzle. "Let's just say I thought better of it, but it wasn't anything bad." He shrugged one shoulder.

My stomach did a little flip-flop as my mind tried to guess what words he held back. Something about my age. Or my profession. Or both—but not something for Renee to hear. Then there was the twinkle in his eyes like he was amused, but something else was there also. Something that reminded me of the way Johnny used to look at me.

As if picking up on the tension in the moment, Renee looked up from her puzzle. "Grammy, can I go play on the slide? I've done this puzzle like one million times. It's boring." She frowned, her bottom lip protruding.

I laughed. "Yes, just put the pieces back in the box first and don't go anywhere outside the playground." I'd planned for Renee's inevitable change of focus and had taken a seat at the picnic table on the side that allowed me to watch the playground area.

Renee quickly put the pieces of the puzzle away and ran off without looking back.

"How long have you been an accountant?" The question was enough of a change of subject to get the attention off me but not so much it felt dumb.

"Thirty years, pretty much my entire life." Frank opened the Higher Focus binder and smoothed its pages.

"Even when you were using?"

Frank nodded. "I was what you'd call a functional addict."

I snorted. "Then why give it up?" My face heated, realizing Frank might take me seriously. "I'm joking, of course. I just mean . . ." I searched for words. For me, functional and addiction didn't go hand-in-hand. I'd lost everything because of my drinking. Would I have given it up if I had somehow managed to keep my life going with a Jim Beam bottle in hand?

Frank threaded his fingers together and rested his hands on the table. "I managed to keep my head above water financially, but my wife left me and took our son with her. I lost friends. Other family members didn't want anything to do with me. I was a complete jerk when I was using."

He had been married—and had a son. "I'm sorry. I can relate." I offered a smile, hoping it both encouraged him and hid my own pain. So many years lost.

Frank patted the booklet that sat on the table between us. "I can't change the past, but I can do something to help others." He swallowed, and his voice lowered. "To maybe help them get healed sooner, before it's too late."

I nodded. Not everyone gets a second chance. I silently thanked God, once again, for mine.

"Are things better with your son, and uhm, your ex-wife?" My questions felt personal, but if we were going to work together on this, knowing each other's stories was going to be part of it. Never mind my own yearning to know about his ex.

Frank inhaled, his lips pursed. "My son and I are on fairly good terms. Not as close as I'd like, but it's something I'm working on. As for my ex . . ." He looked me in the eyes, his gaze holding an earnestness that made my heart skip a beat. "She remarried long ago."

"Oh." I searched for more to say, hating the uneasiness I felt. "My husband died when I was young. That's why I started drinking." I shrugged a shoulder. "I never remarried." *But I was offered a ring.* The memory of Johnny's wanting me to move with him to California surfaced but the offer felt more distant than it ever had before. I shifted my gaze to the playground, keeping my focus there long after I'd spotted Renee spinning on a tire swing.

Frank cleared his throat. "I think it would be really good for us to know more of each other's stories before we have our first group meeting. Maybe we could have dinner sometime next week?"

Was he asking me on a date? Or was it purely for the purposes of leading the group? When I dated Johnny last year, it had been the first time since my husband died that I'd had any kind of a romantic encounter with a man since I quit drinking. Then again, maybe it didn't count because I'd first known Johnny over a decade ago, when I'd been drinking so much that sober wasn't even on the menu. But this wasn't a date. It was ministry. It had to be. "Sure, that'd be great."

Frank smiled. "All right. Good." He nodded. "Let's get to work."

By the time we'd wrapped up our first planning meeting, Renee had made her way back to the picnic table and restarted the puzzle. I could tell by her fidgeting that she was bored, but she didn't complain. She really was a good kid, even if she did have me wrapped around her finger.

We gathered up our things and made our way to the parking lot, Frank walking comfortably beside me. "I feel like we accomplished a lot today." We reached the hot black pavement. "I'll give you a call about setting up a time next week."

"Sounds good." I smiled. So that was it. I glanced down at Renee, who seemed to be distracted by something in the parking lot. I grabbed her hand. Better safe than sorry.

"And about dinner." He added, the sparkle in his golden eyes accentuated by the bright, early September sun.

I nodded. "Yep. Dinner." *It's not a date. It's not a date.*

"Grammy! Let's go!" Renee's voice cut through the uneasy moment as she yanked on my hand, startling me.

"Renee!" I gave her a stern look. It wasn't like her to yell at me, and she'd learned not to interrupt adult conversations. "What's going on?"

"I want to go. Now." Her big emerald eyes shimmered with tears.

I turned to Frank, who looked as surprised as I felt. "Sorry. I'll talk to you later." I waved good-bye, grabbed Renee's hand and headed for my car before Frank could respond. I glanced over my shoulder when I got to my Buick, but he'd already headed toward his own vehicle.

"Renee, why are you so upset?"

My granddaughter's face had turned to stone. She didn't respond. What was going on with her? Was it something to do with Frank?

"Sugar Bug, you need to tell Grammy what's going on." I helped her into the back and buckled her into the booster seat. The car was suffocatingly hot. "I'll get the car on and the AC going." I closed the door and walked over to the driver's seat, scanning the parking lot and edge of the park as I went. I didn't see anything unusual. Families with children. Kids running and playing. A few teenagers hanging out near the basketball court. Once the car was started, I rolled down the window while I waited for the AC to kick in.

I turned in my seat to face Renee. Tears streamed down her cheeks.

"Sweetie. What is eating at you?" My heart ached. This was so unlike Renee. When Cassie and Derrick had been going through the divorce, she had acted up quite a bit, but not anymore. Well, other than when she read the letter from Derrick. A coldness settled on me. Did this have to do with Derrick? I looked out my car window, searching more critically. Walking away from the parking lot and toward the playground was a man wearing a baseball cap, holding the hand of a red-headed woman pushing a stroller. Something about the way the man walked seemed familiar. I squinted, trying to see more. His free hand was clenched in a fist. Just like Derrick used to do. The telltale sign I'd picked up on all those years ago. My jaw tensed.

"Renee, honey, what did you see that scared you?"

Renee's face scrunched into a scowl. She looked away, but a tear streamed down her cheek.

I reached to the back seat, resting my hand on her knee. "Sugar Bug, it's okay. You're safe with Grammy. Talk to me."

She turned back to me, her eyes filled with tears. "I thought I forgot what Daddy looked like. But I didn't." Her bottom lip quivered.

"You saw your daddy." I tried to hide my anger. Why was he at the same park at the same time? Had he followed us the way he used to stalk Cassie?

Renee nodded. "He . . . he . . . waved at me. He was with a woman and a . . . a . . . little baby." She hiccupped, her tears turning into sobs.

I rubbed my granddaughter's knee, wishing I could take the pain away. What had been more upsetting for her? Seeing her absentee father? Or seeing the child who she probably thought of as her replacement? "I'm so sorry, honey. Let's head home. Everything will be better once we get home."

If only I believed my own words.

Chapter Thirteen

Cassie

THE RUSHING SOUND OF THE RIVER was barely noticeable over the buzz of rush hour traffic on the nearby freeway. My soul longed for the soothing hum of moving water and rustling sounds of the forest, but a walk along the bike path that ran between the river and highway was the closest I could get on a weekday evening. Guilt nipped at me, telling me I should be home with Renee, sharing in her excitement over starting second grade the following day. But after meeting with Zane Morray, the custody attorney Brian had referred me to, I needed to clear my head before going home.

After getting served with the modification papers at work, Brian was the first person I talked to. It was an eerie moment, as if I'd been sucked back in time. The feelings of self-doubt and insecurity that had plagued me during the divorce threatened to reduce me to a sniffling, teary and terror-filled mess. Back then, running to Brian had been my modus operandi, and today I'd found myself back in his office with legal paperwork in hand. The irony of it made my blood turn cold. Above my misgivings and fears, though, was the primal need to protect Renee. That need would make me do anything, no matter how uncomfortable or degrading.

This time, though, I had money. The divorce settlement had left me with a small savings account, all of which I'd held onto to help pay my way through college and provide a margin of financial security for my little family. I didn't need Brian to represent me. I just needed his wisdom in choosing the best attorney for the fight ahead.

To his credit, Brian's brown eyes had held genuine

compassion when I told him what was going on. He'd paced his office, hands behind his back, head down, apparently deep in thought. After a few moments he'd given me the name of Zane Morray. "He's a bulldog of an attorney, but not hot-headed. He has a lot of experience with complex custody cases. Probably half of the cases he represents are men and women like your lovely ex. Even if you don't go with him, I'd set up an appointment, just to make sure Derrick can't end up hiring him due to a conflict of interest."

That's what I'd done. I thought maybe talking with him would be enough to settle my worries about Derrick's odds of getting shared custody of Renee or even him having unsupervised parenting time. I'd been terribly wrong.

Zane had sat at his black desk, looking anything but bulldog like. He was young. His dark hair, square jaw and glasses reminded me of Clark Kent in the Superman movies, but without the geekiness. His calm confidence immediately made me feel like I was in good hands. The advice he gave me, though, sent me reeling.

"Based on what you've told me, he'll get what he's asking for." Zane didn't flinch when delivering his opinion.

"What? How?" My hands gripped the edge of my chair as my heart crashed into my stomach.

Zane sighed. "He's presenting himself as reformed. He's served his time, done the work. According to the papers he filed, he's sought treatment for his alcoholism. He has a good job, is remarried and has even started a family." He tipped his head toward an uplifted shoulder, looking almost apologetic. "If he was my client, I'd tell him he has a winning case."

"For custody?" My voice cracked.

"Not for full custody, no. Maybe not even for fifty-fifty . . . yet. However, I don't see any judge denying him generous parenting time, including the plan he's proposed here." Zane tapped the stack of paper in front of him.

"Renee doesn't even remember him. She doesn't want to see him." Tears welled in my eyes.

Zane nodded and looked at his desk. "I understand, but she's young. What she wants doesn't hold much weight in court."

"I think it will be horrible for her. You should have seen the way she behaved when he did have time with her." Memories of my daughter's haunted eyes and anguished face flooded my head. "There has to be something we can do."

Zane inhaled and looked away, seeming to consider his next words. "Unless he does something to weaken his case, I'm afraid all you can do is ask that the parenting time start out slowly and work its way up to what he's proposed."

"Will a judge grant that request?" A tiny spark of hope lifted my chin.

Zane shrugged. "It depends on the judge. If I represented you, I would push for it, especially if Renee doesn't remember him, or the memories she does have are bad. With this case, there are valid reasons for her to have misgivings and fears."

"Can you represent me?" I'd come looking only for advice, reassurance. Now I knew going forward without help was foolish.

"Yes. I'll need a retainer, of course, but I'd be happy to take your case."

My savings. Our safety net. My education and future career. It all came tumbling down with my next question. "How much of a retainer?"

"Five thousand. But be prepared to go beyond that."

I swallowed. I had fifteen thousand in savings. I'd gladly give it all to keep Renee safe. "How much more?"

"There's no way to know. It depends on if he hires an attorney, how far he wants to take this. It could be ten thousand. I have custody cases that have racked up bills of twenty thousand and beyond."

As I wrote the check for the retainer, my gut told me I'd be writing more checks to Zane Morray. I sent up a prayer that the amount wouldn't go beyond what I had in the bank.

Now here I was at the river, looking for answers from God the way I'd searched for answers at waterfalls not so long ago. Where was the justice in this situation with Derrick? What kind of system allowed him to do the things he'd done and then come waltzing back into Renee's life like nothing had happened? Why did Renee have to go through this emotional rollercoaster because of his mistakes?

If I had been in the forest, facing the power of a thundering waterfall, I would have screamed, knowing my voice would be lost in the roar. Here, with homeless encampments in the bushes and people riding bikes past me, that wasn't an option. I stopped and stared at the river. The sun created little diamonds on its surface as it flowed through the town and under the bridges. I waited for God to speak to me, to tell me everything would be okay.

God was silent.

I wanted to call Matt on my way home, but a quick look at the clock told me it wasn't a good time. Wednesdays were youth group nights, and he'd be busy coordinating the carpool and church van to pick kids up, as well as preparing the youth room for the night's activities. I tried to help him on Wednesday nights, but with my school starting soon, I'd already cut back my volunteer time at the church. Now I wasn't sure if finishing school was in my future.

I got home ready to hug Renee and talk to my mom. My stomach growled for dinner, and knowing my mom was probably already at work in the kitchen brought comfort to my soul. The love of my family would get me through the rest of this day. When I walked in, I stood frozen at the sight in front of me. My mom sat on the couch with Renee in her lap. Renee's little arms were wrapped tightly around Mom's neck. The look on my mom's face was somewhere between rage and heartbreak.

"What's going on?" I hung my purse on the coat rack hook and rushed to the couch. "Renee," I whispered, putting my hand on my daughter's back. "Are you okay?"

Renee's face remained buried in Mom's shoulder. Mom shook her head, jaw clenched. "We had a little surprise at the park."

The muscles in Renee's back tightened with my mom's words.

"What kind of surprise?"

Mom glanced down at Renee, then met my gaze, her eyebrows high in wordless communication. What was she trying to tell me?

Little pitchers have big ears. The phrase used by Bonnie, the daycare person who had first watched Renee after I left Derrick, rang through my head. Though Renee wouldn't be eavesdropping, Mom obviously didn't want to talk about what had happened at the park in front of her . . . or Mom had more to say about the incident than she wanted Renee to know.

I gently pulled Renee away from her grandma and set her on my lap. She willingly obliged, wrapping her arms around me tight. "Tomorrow is a big day. Second grade! Do you want to go choose an outfit yourself for the first day? We can lay it out and have it all ready with your backpack."

Renee tilted her head up. The whites of her eyes were red, and the skin around them puffy. "I can pick whatever I want?" Hopeful expectation cut through the hoarseness in Renee's voice.

I smiled. "You can pick whatever you want, *but* I'll need to make sure it's good for the first day. Remember, tomorrow will be hot."

Renee jumped out of my lap and headed for her room. A moment later I heard her door close.

"Well, that should buy us a few minutes." Knowing Renee, she would put great thought into picking her outfit, holding different shirts up against various pants, and even choosing the perfect pair of socks. We could very well end up with plenty of time to talk.

Mom exhaled loudly and leaned back on the couch. "What an afternoon." She shook her head.

"What happened?" The look on Mom's face made my stomach burn. Whatever it was, she was as upset by it as Renee.

"We saw Derrick."

I sank down on the couch beside Mom. "At the park?"

Mom nodded. "I guess it's not a big deal. I mean, he lives in the area, it's bound to happen at some point. But it was odd that he showed up right as we were leaving. Then the way Renee reacted." She closed her eyes. "My heart broke."

Renee's tear-stained eyes. Her clinginess. It made sense. But . . . "She said she doesn't even remember what he looks like." My words came out barely above whisper level.

Mom looked at me. "Yeah, well, she does. Plus, I think it was hard for her to see him with his new baby and wife." Mom blinked several times. She was fighting off tears herself. "When I put myself in her shoes, I can understand why she acted the way she did."

My heart lurched. I'd long ago adjusted to the idea of Derrick being remarried. Him having another child was another hit to my heart. It wasn't that I wished he'd had the child with me. It wasn't that I begrudged him becoming a father again, though I wondered how well that child would do in life with him as a father. It was the unfairness of it. I'd wanted more children. Little brothers or sisters for Renee. A big family. Now that I'd found Matt, maybe that day would still come, but I was getting older. Meanwhile, Derrick went on happily with his life, seeming to pay few consequences or suffer any pain from what he'd done to me, and to Renee. I pushed the thoughts away. "It definitely explains her tears," I said.

Mom's eyes met mine. "The tears came later. Her first reaction was . . . fear . . . anger."

I nodded, understanding all too well.

Mom patted my leg. "I'm so glad you saw an attorney today. The idea of sending Renee to see Derrick is unthinkable. I can't even imagine what it would do to her."

Mom's words echoed my own fears, putting a weight on my heart and sinking my stomach to the floor. I'd told Mom I was certain Derrick's case was beatable. Now, it was time to share my bad news for the day.

How much more could our family take?

By bedtime, I was physically and emotionally exhausted. The news from the attorney had upset Mom as much as me. Pacing the living room with venom in her eyes, the familiar unease I'd lived with before rose in me. Would this send her back to drinking? The fear was put to rest when she said, "We are going to pray, and have others pray with us. God has more authority than any judge."

When I tucked Renee in, the telltale signs of her crying earlier were replaced by the wide-eyed excitement of a new beginning. She'd picked out a cute outfit for her first day and talked nonstop about seeing her friends. Though I was bone tired, I indulged her in an extra fifteen minutes of bedtime chatter before insisting she go to sleep.

Now it was time to Facetime Matt and let him know what had happened.

I fluffed pillows up against my headboard and pushed the

Facetime button on my phone. While waiting for Matt to answer, I switched to a filter that added a little light to my tired face. I fussed with my hair as the ringing continued. The next thing I knew the ring tone ended and the screen prompted me to call back, cancel or leave a message. Before I could respond, a text message came through from Matt.

Sorry busy night hold on

I noted the time on my phone. It was already late. Another text came through.

Might be past your bedtime before I can talk. How'd appointment go?

Why was he running so late? Was he telling me to forget our usual Facetiming for the evening? I put down my phone and sank into the pillow. Matt had been acting so strange lately. Distant. Distracted. I told myself it was because of everything going on with the church and a possible promotion in front of him. Was it more than that? Even if it was only being busy, shouldn't I be important enough to make time for? Didn't he care what was happening with Renee's future? I swallowed the lump of pain in my throat, but it only turned into burning in my chest. I picked my phone back up.

It went fine. Good night.

I put my phone on do not disturb, turned off my bedside lamp, and covered my pillow with silent tears.

Chapter Fourteen

Sharon

I DOUBLE-CHECKED MY CAR WAS locked before walking away from it. The parking lot by the railroad tracks was free and right across from the 5th Street Market eateries but the people panhandling on the corner made me uneasy. The Market District was quintessential Eugene and boasted some eclectic shops. Frank had suggested meeting at the food court for our dinner date. I supposed that officially disqualified it as a romantic date and put it firmly in the friend zone get-together. Fine by me. At least that's what I told myself as I walked across the train tracks and down the sidewalk to cross the street.

I had to admit this area was quaint. The old buildings had been added onto and painted in such a way that held a certain charm. Frank was standing on the platform under the "Eateries" sign, waving at me. The savory aromas made my stomach growl as I walked up the steps. I hadn't eaten at the market in years. Decades, actually. Hopefully it wasn't all vegan and strange food I couldn't pronounce.

Frank motioned for us to go inside. "How's your day been?"

I shrugged. "It's been good." The truth was that ever since hearing about Cassie's visit to the attorney, no day had felt *good*. But that was another story.

Frank walked beside me as we entered the eatery. Several restaurant counters circled a large area with plank floors and a high, red-beamed ceiling. Sturdy black tables of various sizes filled the space and more than half of them were occupied. Frank turned to me with a hesitant smile. "Are you sure?"

What was this, therapy? "Yeah, sorry if I seem distracted, or . . . whatever. I don't come to this area of Eugene much. Had to find parking." I offered him a half-hearted smile.

"Well, thank you for coming here to meet me. This is one of my favorite casual places to eat. Lots of choices." Frank waved his arm across the area. "What sounds good?"

I scanned the selection. Greek. Thai. Fish. Barbeque. Coffee. Seemed like only one logical choice to me. "Barbeque sounds good."

Frank looked over at the barbeque counter and nodded. "I've heard their brisket is pretty good." He shifted from one foot to the other. Putting his hands in his pockets, he turned back to me. "I'm going for Thai myself." He glanced around the room. "I see a booth available on the far wall. Let's meet there after we place our orders."

I nodded but felt lost. Good thing this *wasn't* a date. I'd walk out. I ordered a sandwich at the overpriced barbeque joint and was given a table number thing so the server could find me with my food. Frank hadn't made it back to the booth by the time I got there. The Thai place was busier than the barbeque one. I slid onto the seat, feeling small in the high-backed booth that seemed built for giants. Frank was ordering his food at the Thai counter. He was slim and well-built for his age and dressed in nice khaki shorts and a striped polo shirt. His shoes were sandals I could almost see a woman wearing. Very much the preppy look. Definitely not my type.

What was my type?

A vision of Johnny filled my head, wearing flannel over a t-shirt. Beard trimmed but not overly combed. A sparkle of humor lighting his blue eyes. Laugh lines adding more character than age. My chest ached. I scanned the food court, looking for something to take my mind off the man who still walked around in my head, popping up when I didn't need him to. Disappointment sank my shoulders, feeling as heavy as the ceiling was high. The only thing I thought when I gazed at the room was, "Johnny wouldn't like this much."

"Sorry that took so long." Frank's voice pulled me out of my reverie. He sat across from me, putting a buzzer on the table. Apparently, the Thai place was a little more high tech than the barbeque joint.

"Must be a popular spot." I nodded toward the buzzer.

Frank chuckled. "It is good. Plus, it aligns with my dietary needs."

"Your dietary needs?"

"I'm vegetarian." Frank lifted a shoulder, an almost sheepish look on his face.

"Oh." Well, that explained him not wanting barbeque. It also was another check in the box for "not my type." I exhaled, relieved, in a way, that all romantic notions were clearly off the table. A meat lover and a grass-eater would make a terrible couple.

"Not your thing, right?" Frank smiled wryly, accentuating the lines under his eyes.

Heat ran up my neck, and I worried for a moment I'd voiced my thought about there being no chance at love between herbivores and omnivores. "Well . . . no."

"I like that about you. You know who you are." He shook his head. "Honestly, if it wasn't for a near death experience via a heart attack, I'd be joining you at the barbeque place."

A strange mixture of compassion, curiosity and self-scolding washed over me. I'd placed Frank in a box without getting the full story. Exactly the opposite of what I'd want someone to do to me. *Good grief, Sharon, way to go.* I'd expected that he was a little older than me, but it was scary to imagine needing to be worried about my heart health. Then again, I supposed I was at that age myself. I suddenly felt old. In my mind, heart trouble was something people in their seventies dealt with. Like my mom. A wave of grief—the gift that kept on giving—washed over me.

"When did that happen? I imagine that'd kick anyone right into lots of life-style changes." I knew all about those kick-in-the-pants moments, though I hadn't had any health-related ones.

"A couple of years ago. Just before I moved up here."

"You look healthy." Frank looked in far better shape than me, or most people our age for that matter.

"I exercise more now than I used to, and I eat better. I wasn't overweight or anything. I just had some predisposition to high cholesterol and all that." Frank waved his hand. "Enough about my health history. That's boring stuff. I can tell you I'm doing great now and trying my best to keep it that way. I'd like to live long enough to be a grandpa, at least." The warmth in his smile seemed to reach across the table and wrap around me.

A grandpa. My curiosity piqued again. I was certain Frank was older than me by about five years, but he didn't have grandkids yet. "Your son hasn't had kids yet?"

Frank shook his head. "Nope. He's very career-oriented, as is his wife. They don't want to have children . . . yet." He smiled, and I recognized the hopeful musing in his eyes. "I'm sure they will change their minds. Sooner rather than later. I hope." His smile faded, and he looked off in the distance, as if visiting a long-gone memory.

A server arrived with my barbeque sandwich and placed the platter in front of Frank. She grabbed my number thing and walked away. Frank pushed the platter toward me. "See, even the server could tell I'd rather be eating beef."

I met his gaze and my heart fluttered at the twinkle in his eyes. "I'm sorry. I feel kinda bad eating this in front of you now." The beef spilled out of the bread, juicy and sauce covered. The aroma made my mouth water. "But not that bad." I lifted my eyebrows playfully.

Frank laughed. "No worries. Go ahead and dig in. My tofu curry should be ready any moment."

As if on cue, Frank's buzzer went off. "I'll be right back." He picked it up and headed to the Thai counter.

I stared at my sandwich, debating whether to dig in or wait until Frank arrived with his tofu. Courtesy said to wait, but my stomach didn't care about manners. I compromised by nibbling on a French fry. Frank returned with a steaming bowl of yellow looking vegetables and a small bowl of rice.

"I'll say grace." He offered as soon as he was seated.

Oh yeah, praying before you eat. A Christian tradition Cassie and I didn't practice often enough. A tradition I was raised on.

If Mom and Dad were still alive, would they like Frank? Though my head was bowed, I opened one eye to look at him while he prayed. His face was sincere as he blessed our food and time together. I closed my eyes just before Amen.

Yes, Mom and Dad would approve.

It didn't matter. This wasn't a date. And Frank wasn't my type.

"Sunday fun day!" Cassie announced as we pulled into the church parking lot. I lifted an eyebrow at her and tried to hide my annoyance at her overly cheery, not-like-her-at-all demeanor. She'd been acting strange all morning. When I asked her what was going on she'd been too quick to say "nothing." It irked me that she wasn't talking with me about whatever it was, and I wondered if something had developed in the court case with Derrick.

It didn't help that my own nerves were on edge. Frank and I hadn't talked or texted since our dinner, and today would be the first time I'd see him since. This week we would meet to go over our plan for the first Higher Focus meeting. It was no big deal, really, but for some reason my stomach was doing little flip-flops at the thought of seeing him again. Maybe because I'd shared too much of my past when we had dinner. Maybe because I'd heard more of his than I thought he would tell me. Maybe I'd had too much coffee this morning, even if it was decaf.

The sky was dark and threatening rain. We quickly exited the car and scurried into the church building. "Grammy, will you take me to get a donut?" Renee reached for my hand.

"Of course, Sweet Pea." Not only was the donut thing mine and Renee's Sunday routine, but I was pretty sure the pastries weren't vegan. Hopefully it'd be a Frank-free zone.

We made it through the pastry line without incident, including no sighting of Frank. Relief and something else washed over me. The only problem was I was pretty sure that something else was disappointment.

While Renee and I sat on a bench in the foyer eating our donuts, I spotted Cassie talking with Matt. Something in her body language put my mom senses on high alert. She was too stiff. Her smile was small and tight. The distance between Cassie and Matt was friendly, but not intimate.

Was something wrong between them?

I thought about the last week. Cassie had started her classes. She'd spent yesterday doing homework and housework. She hadn't seen Matt all week. I supposed it was to be expected but seemed odd for an engaged couple. Cassie had said Matt was especially busy with church stuff. I wasn't sure what that church stuff was, but my daughter didn't seem so happy about it.

"Hi, Sharon."

I looked up at the familiar voice, my concern for my daughter trumping the wings that wanted to beat against my chest. "Hi, Frank. How are you?"

Frank smiled and took a seat beside me on the bench. "I'm looking forward to this week."

"Oh?" I swallowed the last piece of donut in my mouth and shot a glance at Renee. She still had a few bites to go.

"It'll be great to get the program started here. Are you still able to meet Tuesday night to get ready for Wednesday?"

I nodded. "As long as you're still good with coming to my place so I can watch Renee while Cassie does her online class."

"Of course. I was thinking I could bring dinner."

"You don't have to do that."

"I want to." Frank leaned forward and craned his head toward Renee, who sat on the other side of me. "You like pizza Renee?"

Renee's eyes widened as she bobbed her head up and down.

Frank chuckled and then sat up straight. "Pizza it is."

I puckered my mouth. "Does that fit into your diet?"

"I'll bring salad, too." He was still smiling.

The wings in my chest beat harder. "I might eat some salad myself."

"I'll make sure to bring enough to share." Frank looked at me a long moment, but I couldn't read the expression in his eyes.

"Ready to grab a seat?" The tone in Cassie's voice surprised me. She stood before me with a red face and furrowed brow.

Frank stood. "I'll see you ladies on Tuesday." He turned to Cassie. "I hope you all have a wonderful Sunday." He nodded toward her before walking away.

"What is wrong?" The edge in my voice left no room for denying an answer.

"I don't want to talk about it. Not right now." She reached for Renee. "Worship is starting. Let's go."

Renee diligently took her mom's hand but gave me a wary look.

The good news was Cassie was at least admitting there was something wrong. The bad news was I was afraid to find out what it was.

Chapter Fifteen

Cassie

I DIDN'T WANT TO TELL MY mom what was wrong because I wasn't even sure I could explain it.

Every time I reassured myself I was blowing things out of proportion, something new would happen. Or not happen. Like this morning. Matt had said Renee and I could join him and some church leaders for lunch after the service. I'd been looking forward to it. I knew it'd be a late lunch. Time enough for me to run Mom home and get Renee a snack to tide her over. But at last, I'd get to finally spend some time with my *fiancé* after our busy week.

Then I talked to him when I got to church. He'd looked uncomfortable, hesitant even, when telling me the change of plans. "I was talking to the Fergusons about lunch, and they said it's for staff only." He'd looked away a moment, either afraid or ashamed to look me in the eye.

"Is it another church meeting then, and not only lunch?" I'd joined Matt on many lunches with church elders. It had never mattered that I wasn't one of the paid staff or the head of any ministry. What was different now?

"No, just lunch, as far as I know. I guess church business could come up." Matt shrugged. "Thomas does things a little differently than we are used to. With everything going on, I don't think anyone wants to rock the boat." He'd met my gaze then, his blue-as-heaven eyes searching mine. "I could come over later."

At that moment Myrtle Ferguson walked up. "Looking forward to visiting with you at lunch, Matt. Maybe afterward you can show us that beautiful park you mentioned before."

The woman breezed on her way, not waiting for a response or acknowledging my existence.

"She's going to be there too? Is she on staff now?" The tightness in my throat gave my voice a harsh sound.

Matt's mouth opened, but it took a moment for words to come out. "Well, actually, yes. She's the new promotions director."

"The church has a promotions director?" The superfluous title rankled with me.

Matt gave a dry laugh. "Well, we do now."

I rolled my eyes. "Doesn't that seem a little odd to you?"

"No . . . yes. But no. She's used to being busy and wants to help." Matt held out his hands. "She's not paid, it's a volunteer position."

"Must be nice to have that much time on your hands." The bitterness oozing from my words surprised me.

"I think we all make choices about how to spend our free time."

What was that supposed to mean? I bit down on my lower lip and clenched my hands. Was Matt implying I was choosing attending school over serving in the church?

Matt looked around, then took a step closer to me. "Look, I think you and I are both making a lot of sacrifices right now. It's hard. But it won't be forever."

Making sacrifices? I was working full time, raising a child, and going to school. I was short on sleep and already running out of energy, and the term had barely begun. Plus, I was trying to find time for Matt in any way I could.

Music blared from the sanctuary, signaling the start of service. "I need to go." I turned to walk away.

He called after me. "I'll see you tonight." I pushed down the confusing mix of thoughts and feelings circling like a tornado inside me. Turning around, I gave Matt the largest smile I could muster. "See you tonight."

As Mom, Renee, and I drove home after church, I debated on how much I should share. I didn't want to say anything in front of Renee, so whatever I told Mom would have to be while Renee was distracted. Mom had always tended to be quick to anger, but in the last year or so she had mellowed out quite a bit. The last thing I needed was for her to have a beef against Matt. If this all blew over, which I was almost certain it would, I wanted Mom to keep thinking highly of him. Yet I also needed someone to talk to about the entire thing.

After an easy lunch of tuna sandwiches and fruit, I set up a movie for Renee in the living room, then joined Mom back at the dining table.

"Hey, kiddo, are you ready to talk?" Mom's voice held a gentle inquisitiveness to it, encouraging me to open up.

I sighed. Where to start? "Things with Matt have felt kind of tense lately."

Mom nodded. "I picked up on a bit of that this morning. Is it because Derrick's back in the picture and all of the court stuff?"

Derrick. It seemed logical he would be the cause of all my problems, but he was only one of them. The situation with Matt was completely separate. In fact, Matt and I had hardly discussed the court case since I'd met with the attorney. Matt didn't even know that mediation had already been scheduled. That was how little we'd been talking recently.

"No. It's not that." I rubbed my temples. How much should I tell Mom about the church situation? "You know how Matt is being considered for the associate pastor position?'

Mom nodded but remained silent.

"Well, it seems like ever since that became an option, he's been so focused on church, it's like he doesn't have time for me or Renee."

"And now you've started school, so you have less time too."

"Yeah . . . which was to be expected, I guess. It just seems like he's not really trying, you know?" I twirled a strand of hair around my finger, words leaving my mouth as my thoughts tumulted. "We used to always Facetime at night, no matter what. There's been a few times he's too busy for even that. Then today I thought Renee and I were going to join him and some other church staff for lunch after worship, but the *Fergusons*," my voice rose as their name came to my mouth, "said it was for staff only. So Renee and I couldn't go."

Mom's brow came together in such a way that it looked like two narrow canyons had formed between her eyes. "The strain on time I get. The uninvited to lunch thing sits wrong with me, too." She shook her head. "There is something about those Fergusons that's not quite right. I've noticed people at church acting differently, too. I thought it was still the blow of hearing what happened with Ben Wescott—the affair and all that."

Now that Mom mentioned it, there did seem to be something off in the church. People were less friendly. Attendance was down. Some seemed happier than ever, like they'd won the lottery, but most of those were people I didn't know well. "That's true. I guess I've been so wrapped up in my own life I didn't really notice."

Mom patted my knee. "That's understandable, Baby Girl. You have a lot going on."

I think we all make choices about how to spend our free time. Matt's comment echoed in my head, making my skin cold. "Mom?"

"Yes?"

"Do you think I'm making a mistake by going back to school now? Renee is still pretty young, and I'm engaged. I have to work full time and pay the bills. Now I have another court battle with Derrick that could eat up all my savings." I felt my shoulders slump under the weight of the reality that was my life.

"Finishing college has been your dream for a long time. If you don't start now, when will you?"

I nodded. "That's true."

"Even if you don't *finish* now, getting in the classes you can moves you closer to your goal. Maybe you'll take a break after you and Matt marry. Or maybe . . ." Mom's eyes shone as her eyebrows lifted, erasing the lines of worry between them. "You'll want to take a break because you have another baby."

I couldn't help but smile at the thought. Having more children was my other dream. One too dear to me to even voice. "Maybe."

"I don't think we need to have every day and year of our lives planned out. I think there might even be something in the Bible about that. Proverbs, maybe."

Mom smiled, and at that moment she reminded me of Nannie so much that my heart both leaped with joy and ached with grief. "I think you're right. It's just . . . hard."

"Trust me, I know that for a fact!" Mom laughed.

My phone buzzed. A text from Matt popped up. He wanted to know if he could head my way.

"It looks like Matt wants to come over."

"Imagine that." Mom winked. "I think it's all going to work out."

As soon as Matt walked in the door, Renee ditched the movie she was watching and ran up to him. "Hi, Matt! Want to see what I did at school?" She bounced on her tiptoes.

"Of course. Can I have a hug first?"

Renee threw her arms up for a hug and Matt bent down to embrace her. "I think you've grown at least an inch since the last time I was here."

"That's because you haven't been here in for-ev-er!" Renee put a hand on her hip and tilted her head with enough attitude to put a teen girl to shame.

I stifled a laugh, both at her antics and words. Matt looked up at me, and I couldn't quite read the message in his eyes. I hope he didn't think Renee was echoing something she'd heard from me.

He turned his attention back to Renee. "I've missed you, too. Now, where's that project you're talking about?"

Renee ran into the kitchen, where her "All About Me" self-portrait hung on the refrigerator.

Matt stood and pulled me into an embrace before I could utter a word. "I've missed you, too." He whispered in my ear, his lips so close to my skin that a tingling warmth spread through my neck.

I closed my eyes, breathing him in, my frustration, the hurt and anger melting away. "Me too." Why had I let my emotions get to me earlier in the day?

Renee returned with her picture and proceeded to explain it in detail to Matt as we guided her back into the living room and sat on the couch. I leaned back and watched the two of them interact. Renee clearly loved Matt and looked up to him. In so many ways, he was already her father figure. The way Matt listened to my daughter and asked her questions. It was obvious that he cared deeply for her, too. I'd seen him with the youth at church and he always showed compassion, love, and a sense of humor. With Renee it was more, something deeper and closer. A fatherly love every girl needed. A selfless love I couldn't recall Derrick ever showing our daughter.

After about fifteen minutes of Renee catching Matt up on her life, my mom walked in. She nodded knowingly toward Matt and me, then spoke to Renee. "Hey, Sweet Pea. I have a package of cookie dough defrosted, how about you help me get some in the oven so your mom and Matt can talk?"

"Can't they talk while I'm here?" Renee looked at Matt and then me, her face set in a frown.

"Renee—" I began.

"Actually, I think your mom and I are going for a walk, and from what I remember, you're not a fan of walks unless it's in the forest." Matt gave Renee a dimpled grin.

Renee sighed dramatically. "Walks are boring."

I rolled my eyes, but Matt chuckled. "See, you're much better off making cookies. I can't wait to have some when we get back."

Renee acquiesced and went with my mom. Matt turned to me. "Does a walk sound good to you?"

I nodded and we headed out the door. The skies had cleared, leaving patchy clouds, a slightly muggy but pleasant temperature, and sweet-smelling air. Great weather for a walk, even if the scenery was "boring."

"Do you think Renee is overly indulged?" I asked Matt as we started down the sidewalk, hand-in-hand.

"Nah . . . she's just loved." He glanced over at me, dark circles around his eyes. "It has been a while since I spent time with her. I think it's okay to indulge her some, don't you?"

I nodded. "Yes." There was so much I wanted to say, to ask. I didn't know where to start.

"I'm sorry I've been so unavailable." Matt's voice was soft and strained.

"I understand. The church has kept you busy."

"Hmm. It's been more than busy. It's been downright confusing."

"What do you mean?"

Matt glanced away, and I noticed the tightness in his jaw. He was no longer smiling. I squeezed his hand. "Talk to me."

Matt exhaled loudly. "I'm not the only one they're

considering for the associate pastor position. Which is to be expected. There are a couple of other guys who have applied. Neither has more experience than me and aren't part of our He is Risen network of churches. I wasn't really worried about the competition. But now there's another hat in the ring, and I'm afraid he may have an advantage over me."

My heart dropped. I knew Matt really wanted this job. "Who could be more suitable than you?"

"It's another associate pastor at one of our affiliate churches. One who is apparently pretty good friends with the Fergusons."

The Fergusons. If I was a bird, my feathers would be standing straight up. "It seems like who he knows shouldn't matter."

Matt tilted his head toward me. "Maybe, but he also has more relevant experience."

"But you were the pastor of your own church for years!"

"True," Matt nodded. "But I wasn't an associate pastor of a large church. There's a difference."

My chest tightened. Was this why Matt had been so distracted lately? He was carrying this burden. I'd been so focused on my own needs I hadn't really seen it. "When did you find this out?"

"I first heard a hint of it about a week and a half ago. My suspicions were confirmed during lunch today."

"The staff of our church loves *you*. They don't even know this other guy. Will the Fergusons' opinion make that much of a difference?"

Matt was silent as we continued walking and turned a corner. The humidity was dampening my blouse. Or maybe it was the irritation caused by our conversation.

Finally, he spoke again. "Things have been tense since Ben left."

I nodded, thinking back to the conversation with my mom earlier in the afternoon. "What's going on with the staff?"

"People are on edge. Thomas Ferguson has been gentle but firm. He's raised questions about the strength of our staff as a whole. Asking how this could have happened right under our noses. I think James is really feeling the stress."

James Reynolds, our senior pastor, had always seemed like a wise man to me. I could only imagine how finding out his right-hand man was having an affair affected him. Then to have someone come in and question his abilities . . . that had to be a gut punch. "It seems really unfair for Thomas to do that." My anger came through in the hardness of my voice.

Matt looked at the sidewalk. "Yeah. I don't know. I think he's trying to make sure something like that doesn't happen here again."

I rolled my eyes. "Stuff like that happens everywhere all the time. Watch the news. It's just hard to have it happen to *our* church, with someone we know and care about." My mind drifted to Ben and his wife. I wondered how they were doing. How could either of them ever recover from such a fall? What did a pastor do with his life after that? How did a woman who had been cheated on and shamed recover her worth? I silently lifted them in prayer. I knew with God all things were possible. I'd experienced my own miracles to prove that.

Where was the balance between accountability and grace? I didn't know the answer. All I knew was my fiancé might be losing his dream, and my heart ached for him.

Matt remained quiet as we walked back home.

"When will they be making their final decision?" I asked.

"Final, in-person interviews with the other candidates are over the next two weeks. They could make a decision any time after that." Matt stopped and faced me, grabbing my other hand. "Whatever happens, I know God has a plan, so please don't worry."

I studied Matt's face, looking for words unspoken. "I want you to be happy."

A smile spread across Matt's face. "With my wedding to the most beautiful woman in the world on the horizon, how could I be anything but happy?"

I wrapped my arms around Matt and held him tight, hoping his words were true.

Chapter Sixteen

Sharon

FRANK SET A LARGE PIZZA BOX down on our dining table. "I should have asked first but assumed everyone would be good with pepperoni."

"I love pepp'roni," Renee piped in.

Frank smiled at her as he set one of those reusable canvas shopping bags on the table by the pizza. "I'm glad to hear that. This pepperoni pizza is really good, from what I've heard." He reached in the canvas bag and pulled out some other containers, including another small pizza box, a clear container of salad, and then another small cardboard box. "We have a little vegan pizza for the weird guy." He tapped the smaller pizza box and gave me a humored look, "And salad for all those wanting to add more vegetables to their diet."

"I don't like salad but thank you." Renee made a face.

I ruffled her hair. "A small serving of salad with ranch dressing will do you good, Sugar Bug. Grammy's having a salad."

Renee frowned. "What about Mommy?"

I looked toward the hallway. "She's doing her online class right now. We won't disturb her. She can eat when she's done."

I set plates, forks, and napkins on the table for the three of us. After Frank blessed our food, we dug in. The pizza looked and smelled amazing, but I forced myself to only take two pieces and fill my plate with salad. It was high time I started eating healthier, so I didn't end up having a heart attack like Frank. The last thing I wanted in life was to be condemned to rabbit food and fake cheese.

After dinner, I quickly cleared the table, set aside food for Cassie to eat later, and asked Renee to find a book to look at in the living room while Frank and I went over the class plans.

Frank set the curriculum notebook down on the dining table, along with some notes he'd typed up. I sat in the same seat I'd occupied for dinner, but Frank took the chair Renee had been in, which was right next to me. My pulse quickened.

"This is a schedule for the evening that I came up with and my idea of each of our parts, but I'm completely open to suggestions." Frank placed a typed page in front of me.

I read over the schedule. Talk about detailed. He had the entire evening broken down into five-to-fifteen-minute segments. There was a short part where I introduced myself, and another where I read a list of five questions. The rest was just housekeeping-type stuff. I was thankful he kept my speaking roles minimal, at least for now. Though I was no stranger to performing songs for an audience, this felt more personal. No guitar to hide behind. No lyrics to sing. "This looks good to me."

Frank nodded. "We'll see how things go and adjust for the next meeting as needed. But I think we can get into a rhythm that feels comfortable."

"How many people have signed up?" I asked.

Frank had agreed to take care of all the computer related items for the class, which included the online sign-up form.

He pursed his lips. "I only have three officially signed up, guys I've talked to at church about the group." He raised one shoulder. "But you know how it is. People may be hesitant to commit but decide on the night of to show up."

I nodded slowly. Samantha had made it sound like there was a significant need in our church for this group. Why had only three people signed up? "All men, huh?"

Frank gave me a half smile. "Well, that's mostly who I talk to at church about this kind of thing."

Made sense. "I'm sure there are women in the church that need this, too. We just have to find them."

"I'll leave that to you." Frank put the paper away.

I grunted. "I'm not much of an evangelist."

Frank gave a little laugh. "Oh, neither am I. I talk to people I feel a kinship with and about things I'm passionate about."

I chewed on his words. I supposed I was the same way, though I would need to start stepping out of my comfort zone more to be involved in this ministry.

He reached out and put his hand on mine. "I understand if you're nervous. I was, too, the first time I helped lead a group. It gets easier."

My hand warmed under this touch. Part of me wanted to pull it away, but another part enjoyed the intimacy. I shook my head, trying to clear it. "Yeah, I hope so," I cleared my throat. "We have some leftover cookies from Sunday night. Would that fall within your diet restrictions?"

"Did you make them yourself?"

Heat rose in my neck. The cookies were from prepackaged dough, and Renee helped me put them on the cookie sheet. I'd put them in the oven all on my own, though. "Yep."

He gave my hand a gentle squeeze before releasing it. "If you made them, then I'll make an exception. Just this once." He gave me a shy smile, his eyes shining.

Guilt mixed with my pounding heart, left me without words. I hoped the cookie didn't give him another heart attack. They were far from homemade and not worth it.

I had a feeling he didn't care.

Samantha met us at church the next evening to unlock the doors. We made our way to the small classroom that we would be using for our meetings, and Samantha flipped on the lights. The low hum of the overhead fluorescents seemed loud in the eerily quiet building. The emptiness of the space that was normally full of people was unsettling.

"You should have everything you need here." Samantha motioned to the room, which had two rows of four rectangular tables, all with chairs on one side of them facing the far side of the room. That side of the room held another, smaller rectangular table and a wall with both a whiteboard and a large television screen.

Frank walked toward the front of the room and opened a cabinet. He seemed to know what he was doing and was familiar with the space.

"I already showed Frank where the DVD player and other equipment are located, and I set a stack of pens and small notepads over there." Samantha pointed to a counter and cabinet area in the rear of the room, which also held a sink and water pitcher. "There are paper cups in the cupboard, if you want to provide water."

"Water's always good to have on hand."

"Always." Samantha smiled but her face wasn't as serene as usual.

Frank was still occupied with the technical details and didn't look like he needed my help yet. "Can I talk to you a minute?" I motioned toward the hallway.

"Sure."

I walked out of the classroom and Samantha followed.

"Is everything okay? You're not having second thoughts about the class?"

Second, third, and fourth, but I was here. "No, I'm good with the class. I was just curious about something else."

Samantha's forehead wrinkled. "What's up?"

Might as well get to the point. Frank was waiting. "Is everything okay with the church?"

"What do you mean?" Samantha's face went blank, the look of someone hiding their hand during a poker game.

"I don't know. Things seem kind of tense since the incident with the Wescotts, and then the Fergusons showing up."

"Yes, well, I think the Wescott thing shook us all up." Samantha's gaze flitted to the floor.

How could I be such a knucklehead? With Samantha's history, Ben's affair probably hit a little too close to home. "I'm . . . sorry." I inhaled, trying to find the right words. "I imagine it's been hard on the church staff. Some more than others."

Samantha looked away. "It's caused quite the upheaval, that's for sure." Her voice was soft, distant, and lacked its usual confidence. "God says we are to count our trials as joy. I'm trying to remember that, and to be okay with not understanding the why."

"I hope it all turns out all right."

"Me too, Sharon, me too."

When I got back into the classroom, Frank had the video ready to play at the push of a button and was writing some introductory information on the whiteboard.

"You look like you know what you're doing."

Frank peered at me over his shoulder, whiteboard marker still in hand. The bags under his eyes looked heavier today, and his cheeks more hollow in the unflattering lighting, but his smile brightened his face. "I have done this a time or two."

"What do you want me to do?" I looked around the classroom.

Frank stopped what he was doing. "There's a stack of handouts there." He motioned to the table behind him. "Go ahead and set one of those and a pen at about eight of the seats. Then if you don't mind filling the water pitcher, that would be great."

We finished setting up the classroom and put directional signs on the front door of the church and in the foyer. It was hard for me to stand still. Between wondering how many people would show up, and wondering if I'd botch my role, my nerves were in a bundle.

One younger man showed up just before 7:00 p.m., looking more nervous than I felt. Frank welcomed him and directed him to a seat. As the clock ticked past 7:00 p.m. two more men showed up, both older than the first. A young woman with dark, curly hair and tattoos hurried in at about fifteen after, just as we were getting ready to start. Thankful for the female company, I greeted her and invited her to sit.

I knew it was the first meeting and numbers didn't matter, but I couldn't help but feel disappointed by the lack of turnout. The benefit of the small group was the more casual feel, and my ball of nerves slowly unwound. When it was time to introduce myself, I felt at ease.

I told the group my story. How I'd been raised by loving Christian parents and married a good man who died too young. How I blamed myself for his death and the guilt of it led me to the bottle. How I eventually lost custody of my only daughter to my parents, who were able to take much better care of her. That I didn't get sober until my mom was at the end of her life, and then I fell off the wagon when my family needed me the most. I didn't tell them about the revealing of the family secret that had pushed me to the edge, but I did share how Cassie and I eventually made amends and now had a good relationship. As I told them about Cassie and Renee, a picture of Johnny came into my mind so clearly, it was like he was in the room with us. I could smell his cologne and even hear his tender but husky voice calling me Angel Eyes. I distracted myself by picking up one of the handouts, and telling the four participants in front of me that I couldn't credit the Higher Focus group, specifically, for my recovery, but I wished I'd had something like it in my life long ago.

The rest of the evening went well, and after the meeting was dismissed in prayer, the young woman, Hannah, came up to me. "Thank you for sharing your story. I'm so glad I found this group. It's just what I need in my life right now."

My chest warmed with the sense that I was actually making a difference. "Do you go to church here? I don't think I've seen you around, but it's a big church."

Hannah nodded. "I only started coming about two weeks ago."

"I'm glad you're here."

"Me too. I'm thankful I found out about this group. If it wasn't for overhearing Frank talking to Sam, I would have missed out. Is there a reason you don't advertise it?"

I cocked my head, confused by her question. "Well, it's in the church bulletin. I'm sure it's on the website, too, though to be honest, I haven't looked."

"Oh . . . odd. I never saw it in the bulletin."

That didn't make sense. I remembered seeing it when we first agreed to start, but I rarely read the bulletin. "I'll have to look into that. I'm glad you found us, despite the lack of information."

After everyone had left and we worked on cleaning up, I asked Frank about the bulletin and the announcement for the group.

"Yeah, I noticed that last Sunday and mentioned it to Samantha. She said she'd look into it." He set the leftover handouts into a briefcase. "I was wondering why there wasn't more in the form of announcements. Like something on the reader board or the screens before service." He shrugged a shoulder, but the deepened lines around his eyes told me the lack of advertising bothered him.

"Did Samantha say anything about it?"

Frank shook his head. "I haven't heard anything since I asked her about it."

I recalled the look on Samantha's face when I asked her about how the staff was doing. Something was definitely off. "I'll ask her, too."

As we walked out of the building, a question landed on me with the weight of a hammer. Did someone on staff not want Higher Focus to succeed?

If so, one person—or couple—came to mind.

Chapter Seventeen

Cassie

FOR WEEKS MISSY HAD HOUNDED ME to have lunch or dinner with her so we could catch up outside the confines of the office. When my boss, Cynthia, called in sick for the second time in less than two weeks, my workday was light enough to take an extended lunch break.

Instead of walking to a nearby restaurant, we drove Missy's truck to the Oakway Mall. I'd never been, but Missy claimed their sliders were the best in town. We found a seat on their patio. A true mid-Autumn summer day, the temperature was pleasantly warm. Missy already knew what she wanted, but I used my phone to bring up the menu. It was amazing how many places didn't have paper menus anymore. It made sense in the electronic age, but it felt like something was being lost. It made me miss my grandparents and their stories of the "good old days."

Looking over the menu prices on my cell phone, I regretted agreeing to lunch. I'd received the first attorney bill from Zane Morray, and my attorney fee retainer had already shrunk by a sizable amount. The thought almost made me lose my appetite, but I fought off the wave of worry, refusing to let it steal the precious time with my friend.

"I'll have the turkey dip," I told the waitress who appeared with a tablet in hand.

Missy ordered the sliders she'd been talking about, and then the waitress hurried off to the next table.

"So how are things with Pastor Man and the wedding plans?"

I took a sip of water. "It's been kind of stressful with both of our schedules, but we are good. I'm only at the beginning of wedding planning."

"But the date is set?"

I nodded. "We're dialing it in and thinking mid to late June." I smiled. Talking about the date brought a flutter to my chest, but not in a good way. "It's going to be here quick. I guess I need to really get busy."

"I talked to my mom," Missy raised an eyebrow, "and she's totally good with you having it at our place---if you'd rather have an outdoor wedding."

I laughed. "You're just trying to get out of setting foot inside a church."

Missy rolled her eyes. "I don't have a thing against churches. I wouldn't miss your wedding for anything." She sucked in her bottom lip. "Have you thought about your wedding party?"

"My wedding party?"

"You know, bridesmaids, groomsmen, all that jazz." Missy gave me a look that reminded me of an eager puppy.

"Oh, yeah." With everything going on, I hadn't given much thought to our wedding plans. How was I even going to pull the entire thing off? "Would you want to be my maid of honor?"

Missy slapped both her hands on the table. "I thought you'd never ask." She beamed.

"I'm sorry, things have been nuts."

"I know. I'm not offended, trust me. But I'd love to help with all the planning and stuff."

Help. That would be nice. And Missy had both a take charge attitude and a great sense of style. "I would love that."

Missy half-squealed and half-barked a laugh. "This is going to be fun!"

Several people on the patio turned toward us.

Hearing my friend's excitement rekindled my own happiness over the upcoming nuptials. It was a much more pleasant thing to think about than custody battles and church politics. "You know," I tapped my chin, "if you're going to help with all this wedding stuff, you're probably going to have to step inside the church before the big day."

Missy beamed. "That's all fine and well, girlie, but remember, you're the one who lost the bet."

"The bet?"

"Yep. As I recall it, if Matt *didn't* ask you to marry him during that mystery date you two had, then I was committed to going to church with you. "But if he *did,*" she raised her eyebrows, "then you agreed to go horseback riding with me."

"Oh yeah." I'd forgotten about our wager.

"I'm looking to collect on that debt before the weather turns bad. You don't want to ride a muddy trail in the rain, I'm thinking."

I laughed. "I don't want to ride a trail, period." I thought for a moment. "Are there any that go to waterfalls?"

Missy gave me a wink. "I'm working on that one, but we'll need to borrow my dad's horse trailer."

My heart lifted. If I was riding a horse to a waterfall, it might not be too bad.

"Speaking of bets," Missy waggled her eyebrows. "It's weird that Cynthia called in sick again. She's been looking a little exhausted lately."

"Yeah, I noticed. I'm kind of worried about her." I cocked my head, "What does that have to do with bets?"

"I'm betting she's pregnant."

"Really?" It did make sense. It'd been three years since she had her first child. Now would be the perfect time to have another. My chest ached. I wished I could've had another child when Renee was a three-year-old.

"Yep. What do you want to bet?" Missy's eyes twinkled mischievously.

"Oh, no." I shook my head but laughed. "No more bets for me."

"Chicken," Missy whispered, dabbing her last French fry into ketchup.

"Quack-quack."

Missy looked at me liked I'd sprouted a tail. "That's a duck, girlie. You need to spend some time on the farm."

We talked about wedding ideas as we ate, and my heart felt lighter than it had since I couldn't remember when. Toward the end of our meal, though, Missy's demeanor turned serious. "Any news on the custody front?"

The last bite of turkey sandwich scraped my esophagus as my throat tightened. "My attorney filed our response, saying that I should retain sole custody and all parenting time should be under supervision. Basically, the same as it is now. We have mediation next month to discuss things. Zane said I shouldn't expect to get everything I want. Unless there is some major issue we haven't found yet, I'm probably going to have to agree to let Derrick have Renee every other weekend, at the very least."

Missy nodded. "If he hasn't changed, mediation will show his true colors, don't you think?"

"I don't know." I pushed my plate away. "It's hard to imagine him changing. I'm pretty much just waiting for the other shoe to drop."

"He'll show his true colors." Missy held my gaze, her hazel eyes intense. "Don't let him push you around anymore. Those days are long gone, right?"

"Yes, of course."

Would time prove my words true?

Call me on your way home

The text from Matt arrived just as I got back to my desk. I wouldn't normally call him after work on a Wednesday because he had youth group to prepare for. What was so important that he could take time to talk?

My heart skipped a beat. The church leadership had finished all the interviews last week for the associate pastor position. Had they made their decision? The afternoon went by slower than old honey poured from a jar. I practically ran to my car at the end of the day, eager for the privacy and a call to Matt.

I tapped his contact in my phone as I backed out of my parking space and waited for my Bluetooth to connect. "Hey, there." I said, not hiding the excitement in my voice.

"Hey." Matt's voice was soft and not-at-all enthusiastic.

Oh no.

"Is everything okay?" But I knew the answer.

"Yes, everything is fine. I just wanted to talk to you really quick before youth group. Hear your voice."

"I miss you," I said. We hadn't seen each other since Sunday. It was only a couple of days but felt like eternity.

"I miss you, too." He was silent for a moment. "The leadership came back with their decision on the associate pastor position. I didn't get it."

"I'm sorry, Matt." My chest ached.

"It's okay. It obviously wasn't meant to be. God has different plans for me, and He knows what He's doing with the church."

I swallowed, hesitant to ask the next question. "So, who did they hire?"

"Mark Kirkpatrick." Matt paused. "He's the associate

pastor the Fergusons know."

I squinted at the road ahead of me, thankful no one but God could see my anger. "Of course."

"Cassie . . ."

"Doesn't something seem . . . I don't know . . . *manipulated*, to you?"

"He's very qualified."

"And he's friends with the Fergusons, who seem to be taking over the church. What does James think?" I knew James was fond of Matt. It seemed to me the lead pastor should have the most say in a decision like this.

Matt was silent for a moment before clearing his throat. "I don't know who voted which way. All I know is the final decision."

"Have you talked to him about what he thinks? Don't the two of you go golfing every other Thursday?"

Another moment of silence. "We haven't been golfing since the Fergusons arrived. Things have just been too . . . unsettled."

The strangeness of it all swirled around me. I felt like I was being sucked down a drain and I couldn't fight the current. "It just doesn't make sense! Why hire someone who has to move here from another state? You have all the qualifications they need. You already have relationships with all the staff, with the church members, everything."

Matt sighed. "I agree. We can talk more about it later. I have a drove of teenagers to get ready for." A hint of a smile lifted Matt's voice, making him sound more like himself.

"Will you have time to Facetime me after youth group tonight?"

"It'll be late. We are short on volunteers so I'm driving the church van to take kids home."

I wished I could help, but I had work, Renee, and school.

I hated not being able to do something, but I was doing all I could. "I love you, Matt."

"I love you too, Cassie. No matter what."

We hung up and I drove home with my hands gripping tight on the steering wheel. How had the church I loved so much turned into a political maze I didn't recognize? What did Matt's future look like at Cascade Christian Church now that he was turned down for the associate pastor position? I didn't know when another opportunity would come

Time was ticking for both of us. Would either of us end up where we wanted to be?

Chapter Eighteen

Sharon

CASSIE LOOKED LIKE A BOMB READY to explode when she got home. Creases in her forehead, narrowed eyes, tightened jaw. "Bad day at work?" I asked as she threw her purse onto the hook by the door.

I already had a simple dinner of fish sticks, tater tots, and carrots on the table, hoping to make her evening a little easier. Though she didn't complain much, I could tell school was starting to weigh on her.

"Work was fine."

"Hi, Mommy!" Renee ran up to her mom and hugged her.

Cassie's face softened. "Hi, sweetie. How was school?"

Renee presented a rundown of her day—one I'd already heard. I gave Cassie a little smile. "Dinner's ready, girls. Let's eat."

Cassie was unusually quiet as we ate. My every attempt at conversation was met with one-word replies. Finally, as we were finishing our meals, she spoke up. "Matt didn't get the promotion."

Oh, that explains it. "I'm sorry to hear that. How's he taking it?"

Cassie folded her paper napkin and set it on her plate. "He seems okay. Disappointed, of course, but not beaten down. I think I'm more upset than he is."

"Matt's a good guy. I'm sure he's going to be fine. There will be other opportunities."

"Maybe. Something feels off. I don't know." Cassie rubbed the bridge of her nose, looking lost in thought.

I silently agreed but didn't say anything. "How was your

lunch with Missy?" I hoped the change in subject would pull Cassie out of her funk.

The corners of Cassie's mouth lifted in a small smile. "It was good. She's going to be my maid of honor and help plan the wedding."

"And I'm the flower girl, right Mommy?" Renee interjected.

"Of course." Cassie reached over and brushed a stray curl from Renee's eyes. "Mommy needs to get homework done tonight, so let's get you ready for bed early. I want to read you a story this time, even if Grammy reads you one later when she tucks you in."

Renee's head bobbed up and down in agreement. I'd been the one to read to her and tuck her in the last two nights. Reading and studying had occupied Cassie's evenings. Her goal was to have enough free time this weekend to do something fun with Matt and Renee.

"Renee and I can clean up the kitchen. Why don't you go ahead and get a head start on studying?"

Cassie frowned. "I feel bad."

I dropped my chin and feigned a stern look. "Don't argue with your mother. You're setting a bad example for Renee."

Renee covered her mouth, stifling a giggle.

With an exaggerated and comic sigh, Cassie stood. "If you *insist.*" She bent down to Renee's level. "I'll see you in one hour for your bath and a story."

Cassie left for her room, while Renee and I made quick work of the kitchen. When we were done, I let her watch a Disney show in the living room while I grabbed my phone and stepped to the back porch. I found Samantha in my contacts but paused before touching her number. Should I even reach out and voice my thoughts and ask the questions I wanted to ask? She'd gone poker-face on me the last time I talked to her but hadn't completely withheld her thoughts. She knew firsthand the tension the Fergusons had stirred up. She most likely also knew who made what decision when it came to the hiring process, not to mention who was responsible for the Higher Focus meeting not being in the church bulletin. I could get all my questions answered. Was I over the line in asking her what she knew? After another moment of hesitation, I tapped on her name to make the call. If nothing else, Samantha was used to me not following most social protocols to a "T." Even if I was over the line, she wouldn't be surprised by my questions.

She'd also forgive my idiocy.

Probably.

"Sharon! What are you up to this beautiful evening?"

She sounded like she was in a good mood. Or she was faking it. Something told me it was the latter.

"Just being a grandma. You know, the usual." I gave a little laugh.

"We need to get our granddaughters together for a play date soon."

"Yes, we do." When was the last time they'd played together outside church? Seemed like it was the day Matt asked Cassie to marry him. "I was wondering if I could get your input on something." I rubbed the back of my neck and stared at the oak tree in the backyard. I wanted more than input, but that sounded better than "can I grill you for information?"

"I'll do my best." Samantha's voice dropped an octave. Her defenses were going up.

"I'm sure you've heard already that Matt didn't get the associate pastor position. Cassie came home and told me, and she is sure sad about that whole thing." I paused, trying to find the words for the question I wanted to ask. "I'm wondering---purely out of curiosity, 'cuz this church stuff is all new to me—who makes those decisions?"

"Oh . . . well . . . that's not top-secret information or anything." Samantha chuckled. "It's the church board."

"Okay. And who is on the board?"

"Well, there's James, Jeremiah—you know them---and Mark Schmidt and Mitch Jones---they are elders at our church. Then Ben was on the board but he's not anymore, of course, so the leaders gave Tom Ferguson temporary voting privileges."

My grip tightened on the phone. *Ferguson.* "So do they all have to agree, or is it whoever gets the most votes?"

Samantha laughed, this time at a higher octave. "It's a majority rule, but they discuss things and generally come to an agreement. It's not that exciting."

"So, they all agreed that Matt wasn't the right person for the job?"

"Yes, eventually they all agreed to hire Mark Kirkpatrick. He's an associate pastor of one of our affiliate churches in Oklahoma City, so I'm sure that gave him a foot up in the process."

"Oh, yeah, I guess that makes sense." I chewed on my bottom lip. "He probably has a lot more experience. How old is he?"

"I don't know exactly, but he looks fairly young. I'd say mid-thirties, perhaps?"

How much more experience could he have than Matt, if they were the same age and Matt had spent years being the senior pastor of a church? Granted, it was a small church and not the same denomination, but still. "Why do you think they chose him?"

Silence.

"Is there anything particularly special about him?".

"No, not that I know of." Samantha's voice was low. "He's a pastor's kid himself. Married. Two young sons."

"Is he a friend of the Fergusons?"

"Yes, but—"

"Did Thomas Ferguson talk the rest of the board into hiring him?"

"Sharon, I wasn't part of the conversation." Something in the tone of Samantha's voice told me she was holding back.

"But you know."

An audible sigh filled my ear. "Look, I don't know exactly. Like I said, I wasn't there, but . . ."

"Yes?"

"You know how I told you about things being on edge? How Thomas was questioning everyone's fitness for their position, trying to make sure that nothing like the thing that happened with Ben happens again."

"Yeah, I remember."

"Well, I wouldn't doubt he put pressure on everyone else to make sure the person who was hired checked all the boxes, and, well . . . from what I heard him saying, he didn't think Matt fit the bill."

"How so?"

"Sharon . . ."

"I'm not going to go blab to anyone. I won't even tell Cassie, if that helps. But this is bugging me because in my eyes, Matt *is* the perfect fit."

Another sigh from Samantha. "I don't know everything involved in their decision. I do know I heard Thomas question . . . well . . . have doubts, I guess, about Matt getting married at this point."

"What's wrong with Matt getting married? He's not sworn to celibacy as a pastor, is he?" My voice rose, and I glanced over my shoulder to make sure Cassie or Renee weren't on the other side of the sliding glass door.

"No, of course not. But there are some people who believe that a divorced person should never remarry unless the divorce was based on the biblical grounds of infidelity."

"Matt's not divorced, he's widowed."

"But Cassie . . ." A hint of sadness tinged Samantha's voice.

What? They were worried about him marrying my daughter? My blood turned to lava, making my skin hot. "What's wrong with Cassie remarrying? Her husband was abusive!" I hissed the words through my teeth, spit spraying my phone screen.

"Yes, but he wasn't unfaithful, was he? Myrtle asked lots of questions about Cassie's divorce, wanting to know what caused it and all. She brought up scriptural references about it and—"

"That is the most ridiculous, heartless, and downright belittling assumption to make of a woman." I shook my head. I wanted to wring Myrtle's neck. "My daughter was supposed to stay in an abusive marriage?"

"No, of course not. Leaving an abusive situation is understandable for safety purposes. But according to some, remarriage is not an option. Not biblically."

"Anyone who thinks that can take a long walk off a short pier, in my oh-so-humble opinion."

"I hear you. I certainly don't agree with that theology."

Silence filled the air between Samantha and me. All I could hear was the runaway thumping of my angry heart. "You don't even know how much I'm biting my tongue right now." It was true. I could taste blood in my mouth as the part of my mind who knew better fought off the furious mother bear of my heart.

"Look, Sharon, one reason I'm telling you this is because I'm afraid Cassie is going to find out, one way or the other. I'd highly prefer if you didn't tell her you heard it from me. But when the time comes, I can only imagine how upset she's going to be. She's going to need you."

I closed my eyes. Cassie was going through enough right

now. She already doubted whether she had what it took to be a pastor's wife. Hearing that Matt didn't get the pastor position he wanted because he was engaged to her would be the blow that knocked her flat. The protectiveness I felt toward her in that moment made me miss my own mom with a fierceness I was sure could open up the barrier between heaven and earth. I lifted my chin toward the darkening sky and opened my eyes. All I saw were a few faint stars. "No kidding. Does Matt know about this?"

"I believe so." Samantha's voice was barely a whisper.

Would Matt keep that secret from Cassie? I couldn't imagine being him and put in that spot. I also couldn't fathom continuing to work for a church where the leaders didn't accept my fiancée.

My curiosity about the church bulletin information faded away, the issue as insignificant as a fruit fly in the summer compared to what Samantha had told me about the board. Which left me with one question. What part of his life was Matt going to change?

The question clung to me as I got ready for bed that night. I couldn't imagine Matt choosing church over Cassie. I saw the way he looked at her. He was gentle and kind and patient. Having suffered his own great loss when he lost his wife to cancer, he seemed, in some ways, wise beyond his years. Still, even the possibility of my daughter's heart being broken wrenched my stomach, making it hurt. Not too long ago I'd have found solace in a Jack and Coke. Now, though, I knew alcohol wasn't the answer.

Lying on my bed, I prayed. I asked God to be in charge of the entire situation, to stand guard over Cassie and Renee in both the issue at church and the custody battle with Derrick. I implored the Lord to bless their future. I prayed for wisdom for Matt.

As I lay in the dark, I heard a ping from my phone. When I was done praying, I picked up the phone from my nightstand and saw a notification from Facebook. Curious, I tapped on the icon.

Black words on a blue background, next to a picture of the California coastline. "Johnny Beckett has accepted your friend request."

I stared at the screen, my brain trying to wrap itself around the words. How long ago had I sent that request? One month? No, it was more like six weeks. Maybe even eight. He was just now accepting it? Irritation bit at my already taught nerves. The gall of him! What made him decide to accept it *now*? Did he have a girlfriend run off and leave him lonely? I dropped the phone back on my nightstand.

Johnny Beckett. Just moseying on into my life, at his leisure. I grunted. Men! And God had made them *first*! Some things I would never understand.

I lay there staring at the dark ceiling, telling myself to sleep, but my eyes stayed wide open. Too much adrenaline—and questions. Why now, Johnny? I'd quit checking his Facebook page weeks ago, getting the hint from his lack of response. He wasn't interested in me. He'd moved on to better things. La-de-dah. Fine.

I was fine.

But I wasn't.

I grabbed my phone again and opened the Facebook app and clicked on the notification, which took me directly to Johnny's page.

"It's hard seeing my dad like this. He was always so strong. Up at dawn every day. Never needed help from anyone. Now he can't even get out of bed without help."

Alarm bells went off in my head. I scrolled down the page.

"Home for a while now. Things were so hectic I lost my

phone when I got here. Just now getting back on the good ole' Facebook. Hope everyone is doing good. If you're one of those praying people, send up one for my dad. He needs it."

What had happened to Johnny's dad? Was losing his phone the reason why Johnny hadn't accepted my friend request sooner? I internally kicked myself for even thinking the question. If his dad was that bad off, responding to friend requests was probably the last thing on his mind.

My chest swirled with emotion. All this time I'd thought Johnny had written me off. But perhaps he'd simply had his hands full. I knew what it was like to have an ill parent, to be facing the possibility of losing them. A band wrapped itself around my heart. Whatever was going on with Johnny's dad, it was bad enough for him to make a public request for prayer. That told me all I needed to know about how well his dad was doing.

I put in another request to God. My words were scattered and jumbled, but I trusted He understood. When I was done, I searched for the right words to say to Johnny. Somewhere in the wee hours of the morning, I succumbed to sleep before I found them.

Chapter Nineteen

Cassie

I WONDERED IF MATT AND I were trying to pack too much into one Saturday. Our plan sounded simple enough: He'd come over for lunch, then we would take Renee to a movie and do a quick stop at the park afterward, if weather cooperated. The cloudy sky could go either way, and the forecast called for a fifty percent chance of rain. We'd then bring Renee back home for an evening with my mom, and Matt and I would go out to dinner. Afterward we'd head back to his place, where we would talk about wedding plans and maybe watch a romantic comedy. That was two movies in one day, but as the mom of a seven-year-old girl, I longed to watch something other than animated movies and princesses.

It would be fun. Too much sitting after spending the week in front of a computer screen, but fun.

Listening to Renee talk to Matt gave me enough smiles to make up for the busy week.

"Matt, my teacher said I read as good as a third grader. Grammy said I'm a smarty pants. Do you think I'm smart?"

"Matt, when I'm a teenager will I be in your youth group? Can we go to Taco Bell on those nights?"

"Matt, Mommy said I'm too young to play Minecraft, but lots of kids in my class play Minecraft. What do you think?"

Matt did a great job of referring that request back to me. Then her last question, as we said good-bye and left for our date. "Matt, Mommy says I gotta wait until the wedding to call you Daddy, but can I call you that sooner? For practice?"

The emotion on Matt's face had mimicked the swelling, hopeful, this-is-my-dream-come-true feeling in my heart. He knelt to Renee's level. "I can't wait until you can call me Daddy. Just like I can't wait until your Mommy can call me her husband. But waiting until it's the special day in front of your family and friends and God makes it mean even more. Waiting is hard, but we can do it." He lifted his hand to do a fist bump, something that was a ritual with his youth kids, but Renee wrapped him in a tight hug.

"She has me wrapped around her little finger already, you know that, right?" Matt took my hand as we walked to his car.

"Yes. It reminds me of how my grandpa was with me." I smiled at him. "But you're a little younger than he was."

Matt laughed. "Just a little, huh?"

We drove to our favorite restaurant, in downtown Springfield. It tended to be noisy due to the acoustics, but we were able to get a booth toward the back of the building. I tried to order something off the small plates section of the menu, but Matt wouldn't let me. "We haven't been out in a while. Let's do this right. I'm having the sirloin."

He had a point.

"Okay. Then I guess I'll have the snapper."

The waitress took our orders and left.

We sat for a moment, taking each other in. We hadn't been on a real date in weeks. Matt reached across the table and took my hand. "I'm looking forward to wedding planning."

"Me too." I squeezed his hand. "I told you I have my maid of honor picked out. Have you given any thought to your best man?"

"I have. I asked my old friend, Chad, and he said he would be honored."

"Chad?" I tried to place the name. "He was one of the original members of my old church. He lives up in Silverton."

"Oh. Yes. I remember you talking about him, but I've never met him."

"Now you will." Matt's eyes glimmered, but his smile seemed forced.

"I thought you would've asked someone from the church."

"I considered it. But I thought it'd be nice to bring things full circle, as well as give my church friends the opportunity to simply attend the wedding."

I nodded. "I guess that makes sense." Did it have anything to do with him not being hired for the associate pastor position?

"Do you—"

"How are you holding up?" Matt interrupted before I could finish my sentence. "With juggling work, school, and the ridiculous legal stuff with Derrick?"

"Oh . . .uhm . . .fine. I mean, I'm tired. But work is good. Things are pretty smooth there. Did I tell you that Missy thinks Cynthia might be pregnant?"

Matt's eyes widened. "Good for her."

"Yeah, it is. If it's true." I didn't tell him how much it reminded me of my own longing to have more children. "School is fine, too. It's not that hard, just a lot of reading. The whole Derrick thing has me worried, honestly, but you know that."

Matt nodded, the smile leaving his face. "Yeah, me too. We need to keep praying. Have you said anything yet to Renee?"

"No." My stomach twisted into a knot. "I'm going to wait and see how mediation goes. That's coming up soon."

"Too soon."

Our food arrived, perfectly plated and smelling delicious.

"Thank you for this food, Lord." Matt said, then dug into his sirloin.

I laughed. "You must be starving."

Matt shrugged one shoulder. "This smells amazing." He

took a bite and nodded. "Yep, definitely amazing."

I smiled and took a bite of my snapper. "It's weird. I haven't heard a word from Derrick since that letter to Renee—other than being served the custody papers. My attorney said he calls *him* all the time with the stupidest questions. I swear he's trying to rack up the attorney fees for me." I shook my head, my mouth full of snapper. "If he's changed, I'm not seeing it yet."

"I suppose the mediation will show you his true colors."

"Yeah, that's what I'm thinking." I looked down at the plate of food, my appetite waning.

"I wish I could be there with you."

"Me too, but it's not allowed." What I wouldn't give to have Matt at my side when I faced Derrick for the first time in over two years.

"God *will* be with you and in control." Matt quit eating and gave me a solemn look. "He hasn't failed you yet, has He?"

"No."

Matt was right. Except for the whole promotion thing for Matt, it seemed God had been abundantly faithful in answering my prayers and taking care of me and Renee.

"How are *you* doing?" I asked. "And how are things with the church stuff?"

Matt squared his shoulders. "I'm doing fine. Like I said, I know God has a plan. For now, he's blessed me with a youth group and I'm embracing that." His words were right but sounded rehearsed.

I stabbed at the salad that came with the snapper. "How's the atmosphere with leadership? Still tense?"

Matt waved his hand. "It's calmed down, somewhat. Chris Kirkpatrick will be here in a month to start work as the associate pastor, but the Fergusons love Eugene so much they're talking about staying here."

"What?" Dread ran through me. Between the hiring

drama and then hearing about Myrtle's little trick with the group my mom was co-leading, I didn't like that couple. Mom said Frank looked into why the Higher Focus group was left out of the events portion of the bulletins. Turned out, it was Myrle, the new *promotions director* who was responsible for that content, or lack thereof. "What would they do?"

Matt shrugged. "Tom is near retirement age. He could retire a little early and volunteer at the church."

"Hmm. I guess the church could always use more volunteers. Good ones, anyway." I took a sip of my water.

Matt raised his eyebrows at me inquisitively. "I assume you're referring to the oversight by the new promotions director."

I rolled my eyes. "Oversight? Two weeks in a row?"

"It *could* happen."

"Uh-huh."

Matt shook his head. "She got it fixed. The Higher Focus meetings have been in the bulletin."

"But no other mention of it has been made."

My mind ran back to the conversation with my mom. She'd been upset, though not nearly as much as I would've expected her to be. Myrtle had somehow managed to leave the group off the list of meetings in the bulletin for two weeks. The meeting also had not made it onto the website. According to Mom, Frank had asked that an announcement about the group be put on the television screens before and after service, but it had yet to happen.

Matt headed off the rest of my questions. "There's a lot of hands that go into getting information out. We don't have a full-time tech person for the website, and reader boards are all volunteer based."

"I get that. But someone is telling them what to put where, right?"

Matt sighed. "Correct. There is a communication

breakdown somewhere."

I tapped my fingers on the table, my meal forgotten. I didn't want to spend our entire evening talking about church stuff. "You're right. And the communication seems to be getting better."

"Yes, it's getting better." Matt's tone didn't sound as certain as his words.

After a late night with Matt, it was hard to get up early for church. Maybe during Thanksgiving break I'd get to finally sleep in. We made it to church a little late. Worship had already started. Mom had to work, so I rushed Renee through the donut line. "Eat what you can in five minutes. We'll save the rest in my purse for after service." I cringed at the thought of putting a napkin-wrapped, half-eaten donut in my purse, but I didn't want to miss all the songs. The sermons had fallen flat with me lately, and I never had time to read my Bible anymore, so I found the musical part of the service to be the closest I felt to God. It wasn't the same as going to a waterfall, but almost.

I scanned the rapidly emptying foyer for Matt while Renee ate. I didn't see him. He was probably already in the youth room, beginning their service. Renee somehow managed to finish the entire donut. I rushed her to the check-in for kid's church and then made my way into the sanctuary, which was the fullest I'd seen it in quite some time. I found a seat toward the back and made my way down the row, apologizing to people as I went.

After worship, our outreach pastor, Jeremiah Hanson, came on stage and did the announcements. I listened for news of Mom's group, or the announcement of the new associate pastor, but Jeremiah didn't mention either. After that he introduced Tom Ferguson as the speaker for the day. The hope that filled me during worship dissipated faster than the air from a popped balloon. Great. I internally chastised myself. Just because I didn't like Tom didn't mean God couldn't use him.

"Thank you, Pastor Hanson." Tom turned to the congregation, a wide smile spread across his face, making his wrinkles more pronounced. "I have a couple of announcements, also."

The room was quiet, and my curiosity was piqued. Was this when we'd hear about the new associate pastor? Wouldn't it make more sense for our lead pastor to do that?

"As most of you know, the church has been searching for a new associate pastor."

There were several nods from the congregation, and a few murmurs. Was Tom going to talk about why there was a search? I doubted it.

"I have the privilege of letting you know that the church's board has reached a decision, and our new associate pastor will be here next month! I know Chris Kirkpatrick personally, and I'm confident he will be a perfect fit here at Cascade Christian." Tom looked up at the screen at the side of the stage, where a picture of a man now showed, with his name and title. Chris Kirkpatrick was a slightly overweight but not bad-looking man about my age. The congregation broke into applause. I joined them, out of courtesy.

Tom went on to talk about Chris's experience and some of his personal history. He was married, had two children, both in grade school. He was the son of a pastor, went to seminary in Maine, and his favorite football team was the Oklahoma Sooners. "But," Tom joked, "I'm sure he'll be an Oregon Duck fan soon enough." Laughter rippled through the congregation.

Jealousy gnawed at me, despite trying to fight it off. He didn't sound any more qualified than Matt, who was already an Oregon Duck fan, because this is where he grew up.

"Now, technically, my job here is coming to an end." Tom walked across the stage, scanning the faces of the audience. "But my wife, Myrtle, and I have fallen in love with this town. With this church." He paused as he paced the opposite direction. "We don't want to leave." Tom came to the center of the stage and stopped. "We've decided to make this our home."

Applause erupted from the seats, though not from all of them. Some people looked at those sitting beside them, their faces full of questions. I was one of them, but I kept my eyes on the stage, afraid that someone else might see how much Tom's announcement rankled me.

"I'm close enough to retiring that I won't need to be on staff at church and collect a salary but still young enough to be involved in the ministries that Cascade Christian is known for."

What ministries were our church known for? Higher Focus was not one of them, and I had a feeling if Myrtle stayed on as Promotions Director, it never would be.

"In fact, we've done such a good job of talking up this town and this church, that our youngest daughter, Emily, has decided to join us here all the way from Santa Barbara, California, and make this her home, too." Tom's face glowed with joy and he focused on a seat near the front of the sanctuary. "Emily, go ahead and stand up."

A young woman with blonde hair cut in a short bob stood in the front row. She looked around her, a big smile plastered on her face. I wondered if she was Myrtle's daughter or her younger clone.

More applause. After it died down, Tom continued. "Emily is a talented interior designer and has landed a great job with a remodeling company in town. She also loves the Lord and is excited to serve here. Her experience in youth ministry will be a blessing, I'm sure."

Chills went down my spine. Her experience in youth ministry? Was he trying to replace Matt now? No, that couldn't be it. He said Emily had a full-time career. The most she could do was volunteer in the evenings and weekends. Matt had said he was short of volunteers. The extra help would be welcomed, I was certain, but Tom's comment seemed pointed.

After Tom was done highlighting himself and his family and all their amazing virtues, he went on with his sermon, but I didn't hear a word of it.

Chapter Twenty

Sharon

HAVING WORDS IN YOUR HEART IS completely different than putting them into writing.

The morning after Johnny's Facebook friend acceptance, I spent way too long trying to make the words in my head sound as good as what my fingers tapped out on my phone. When I had to get up and ready for work, I finally hit send on my best effort:

Sorry to hear about your dad. Can't tell from your post what all is going on, but I know an ill parent is a tough road to walk down. If there's any way I can help, or if you just need someone to talk to, let me know. You're in my prayers (yeah I'm one of those, LOL)

Sharon

Johnny had responded to my message by my lunch break. He told me his dad had fallen off a ladder while climbing into the loft of his barn. Johnny's mom had found him later. No one knew how long he'd been lying there, but he'd suffered a concussion, broken wrist, and ruptured vertebrae. He'd had surgery, but he would never walk again without assistance. He could no longer take care of their property—the orchard, a few head of cattle, and horses. Johnny had come up to help during his recovery and support his mom. It remained uncertain what would become of "the farm," as Johnny called it. The news saddened me, but the last two lines of his message sent my heart on a runaway train. "I've sure missed you Angel Eyes, and if you have time to talk, I'd love to catch up sometime. Give me a call."

I knew I should call him to offer emotional support, but I

couldn't bring myself to dial his number. Plus, he'd called me Angel Eyes—his term of endearment for me. It said he had more in mind than a casual conversation. I messaged him back, saying again how sorry I was and that I would keep praying, I told him I'd call him soon.

It'd been a week.

In that week, Frank and I had managed to pull off another meeting of Higher Focus. We still had only four students, but I figured if everyone continued coming, it was a win. Frank and I had been talking regularly throughout the week but hadn't spent any time together outside of the meetings. I kept getting the feeling he was interested in me, but he hadn't made any moves Which was fine by me. He wasn't really my type anyway.

That's what I told myself every time his face popped up inside my head.

Sunday, after a long and weary shift at work, I decided it was time. I told myself it was my Christian duty.

I drove down to Island Park and found a shady parking spot by the river. The sight of the water rolling by soothed the anxiety that wanted to lay claim on my heart. I rolled down the windows for the fresh breeze. The sound of children playing in the park mixed with the slow murmur of the river and the hum of traffic from the bridge overhead. The perfect white noise.

"I was starting to think you wouldn't call." Johnny's voice was smooth, perfect, and yet sincere.

"You know me, always hedging my bets." That probably wouldn't make sense to most people, but I knew Johnny understood.

"Driving to Watsonville a year ago was the longest drive of my life."

My heart pitter-pattered, but I couldn't let him know. "How are you holding up at the farm?"

"I'm doing okay. It was a hard seeing my dad after his fall. We never got along great, you know. He's about as stubborn as they come. Seeing him depend on my mom, sister, and me is . . . humbling."

"I can imagine. Your poor mom. From what I remember, your dad could get a little ornery and short-tempered, but she seemed to have a way of settling him down."

Johnny chuckled softly. "She'd put him in his place if the situation called for it, but sweet-talking was her specialty."

I smiled. I'd only been around the family a handful of times all those years ago, but that was exactly the picture I remembered.

"I'm sure she's glad to have you home." If I were in her shoes, Cassie would be the only one I could call for help. The thought scared me. But I'd never be in her shoes. To have a husband fall ill required, well, a husband.

"Yes. She is." Johnny sighed. "I took a leave of absence from my job in California, and I've been managing to keep up on the payments at my place with savings. Believe it or not, I took the plunge and bought that house I was leasing. My leave is running out here pretty soon, though, and my piggy bank is getting a little hollow." Johnny's chuckle was a dry laugh.

A little tug at my heart. He was heading back home soon. "When are you leaving?"

I could hear a television show playing in the background. After a long silence, Johnny spoke. "I can't leave my mom in this situation. Dad's not going to be able to manage this place but absolutely refuses to sell it. I'm staying. I'll pick up work somewhere now that Dad doesn't need heavy-duty care. I'll live with them and keep things going around here."

"What about your sister? Your brother-in-law?"

"They've got their hands full with teenagers and a grandbaby on the way from their oldest. Plus, they both have full time jobs they love.”

Johnny was staying? It seemed impossible. Yet it made perfect sense. Somehow our lives had ended up mirroring each other. I lived with Cassie and helped with Renee. He now lived with his parents and helped with his dad and the farm.

“Do you think your dad will agree to sell, eventually?”

“Nope. I don’t think so. The land’s been in the family too long. He wants either my sister or me to get a loan on it to buy the other out and set up a little manufactured home for him and mom on the property. The buyer gets to live in the house and run the land.”

“Sounds like a good retirement plan.” I mused. Would Johnny be up for it? It was hard to imagine him that settled.

Johnny laughed. “Yeah, I’m thinking maybe the old fella should’ve had a few more contingencies in his plan.”

Did that mean Johnny was up for the buyout? “I guess we all do the best we can.” I didn’t like the yo-yo bounce my heart was doing. I’d called to offer my support and here I was, dying to know if Johnny was staying for real and for how long. Good grief.

“I guess you’re right.”

“I should go. I stopped on my way home from work to talk to you. Cassie and Renee are home from church by now.”

“How are they doing?”

I wasn’t up to going into the details of Cassie’s life. Not now. “They’re doing well.” Johnny’s last words to me, by text, before he left for California played through my mind. *Have a nice life, Sharon.* I did have a nice life, and I wanted to keep it that way.

“I’m glad to hear that.” He cleared his throat, sounding uncomfortable. So unlike him.

“I’ll talk to you later, Johnny. Let me know if there’s anything I can do.”

“I appreciate it. I really do.”

The call ended and I drove home, wiping my eyes.

Cassie's car was in the driveway when I got home, but once inside, I saw no sign of her or Renee. Their bedroom doors were open, rooms empty. I poked my head out the sliding glass door and scanned the small backyard. The leaves of the oak tree had started to change color, and the grass was turning green again. Signs of cooler temperatures and more rain. Fall was in the air, and I breathed it in, looking forward to the cooler season, but there was no sign of my family.

This wasn't right. I pulled my phone out of my purse and sent Cassie a quick text. She responded almost immediately.

On a walk. Right around the corner on B Street if you want to join us.

I wasn't really in a mood for a walk and itched to get out of my work uniform. But something told me meeting Cassie and Renee needed me.

I found them still on B Street. They must've been walking slow to wait for me. Renee ran up to me with her signature grin and a large maple leaf in her hand. "Look, Grammy!" She breathed heavily when she reached me, full of excitement. "This leaf has so many colors. Red, purple, yellow, green!" She said each color slowly, as if she was the teacher and I was the student.

"That's pretty neat." I gave her a quick hug then grabbed her hand to lead her back toward Cassie. The shadow in Cassie's eyes told me something was off.

"I'm surprised you got this one to go for a walk on city streets," I teased, fluffing Renee's hair. We weren't actually in the city. Our neighborhood was a few blocks away from downtown and full of older, modest homes and mature trees, but Renee, like her mother, preferred the forest trails.

"We're on a search for leaves that are changing color."

Cassie spoke in the voice mothers use when they are faking happiness for the sake of their kids.

"I see." Nodding toward the leaf in Renee's hand. "Looks like you're off to a good start."

"I needed the fresh air. The air at church left me queasy." Cassie tilted her head. "Know what I mean?"

I was catching her drift. Had Matt told her today about the underlying reason he hadn't been chosen as the new associate pastor? "Fresh air is good." We continued along the sidewalk, and Renee returned her focus to finding leaves. "Anything you want to talk about?"

Cassie looked away for a moment before turning her focus back to me. "Oh, well since you weren't at church, you probably haven't heard the news." She took a deep breath. "The Fergusons have decided they love it here so much they are going to stay permanently. In fact, they even talked their daughter into moving here."

That wasn't what I was expecting to hear, but the mention of the Fergusons put my guard up. "Oh? That's . . . great."

"Yeah, great. You know what else is great? Their daughter has all kinds of experience helping with youth ministry. Which will be *great* because Matt needs the help, you know."

"I see." A tendril of dread wrapped itself around my stomach. What were the Fergusons doing? Taking over? And Cassie still hadn't said anything about Matt telling her the reason he didn't get the position. He would tell her, I was certain. Or would he?

If he didn't, what did that mean?

"Anything else?" I asked.

Cassie's face scrunched. "Does there need to be anything else?"

I sighed. Great. Maybe it was good she didn't know the whole story. Yet. "I can understand why you are upset about the Fergusons. They rub me the wrong way, too." I wished with all I had that I could tell her how much and why they rubbed me the wrong way. How the thought of them made me want to punch a wall. How anyone anywhere thinking my daughter wasn't good enough had *me* to reckon with. But I held my tongue. For now.

"There's something about the way they look at me, especially Myrtle, that is so, so . . ." Cassie shook her head. ". . . demeaning, I guess. Like they are looking at a stray dog that showed up at the back door and is begging for dinner." Cassie turned to me, her eyes on fire. "Like, you call yourself a good person, so you can't turn the dog away, but you just throw it some scraps and send it on its way. Don't bother looking for a collar. Don't bother seeing if it's hurt. Just throw it some scraps, and if it still stays around, call the humane society."

Goosebumps covered my arms. Cassie didn't know the whole story, yet a part of her *knew* the heart of the story. "I get that impression about them, too." Guilt nipped at my heart. A voice in my head screamed to tell her what I knew, but reason held me back. I had to give Matt a chance.

"I don't want to say anything to Matt. He already knows how I feel about them. Even though he acts like he's fine, I can tell he's disappointed about not getting the associate pastor position."

I nodded. "That's understandable. But you should still talk to him about it."

Matt had to tell her. Because if he didn't, soon, I would have no choice. I couldn't let my daughter walk around wolves unaware. Even though she already sensed what kind of people the Fergusons were, how could I keep the secret from her? What could be worse than being the last to know, and then finding out those closest to you kept it hidden?

"I guess I should talk to him. Maybe later this week."

"No, you should soon. Maybe even tonight." I tried to keep my voice even and encouraging.

Cassie's shoulders sagged. "I guess you're right. If we're going to be married, we need to be open about our feelings and fears."

"I hear that's key." I didn't feel like I could offer marriage advice. My marriage to Steven was long past and relatively short lived. But I knew beyond the shadow of a doubt she needed to talk to Matt, and he needed to talk to her. Openly. Honestly.

"He said he was going to stay at church a little later today and work on planning stuff for the youth group and making some phone calls. Maybe now that you are home, I'll leave Renee with you and run back over there to see if he needs help." She sighed. "And to talk."

"I think that's a great idea." I was bone tired. My heart twisted in a knot over Johnny. My back ached and my stomach demanded food. It all faded in the light of knowing Cassie needed me right now. I would watch Renee, and I would be here with open arms when my daughter came home with news that would undoubtedly break her heart.

Lord, please work this all out. I know you must have the answers because I sure don't.

I squeezed Renee's hand as we walked home, an amen to my silent prayer.

Chapter Twenty-One

Cassie

WHEN I ARRIVED AT THE CHURCH, Matt's car wasn't the only one in the lot. A few others were parked near the front entry. A red Nissan Maxima had a California license plate. Alarm bells flashed in the back of my mind, but I ignored them. I needed to talk to my fiancé.

The front door was unlocked so I didn't have to call or text Matt to let me in. A murmur of conversation punctuated by a light, high-pitched laugh emerged from the youth room as I approached. The door to the room was ajar, so I walked in, like I'd done many times before when I'd shown up to help Matt. A small group was gathered in the middle of the room, some sitting in chairs, and a couple, including Matt, standing. I recognized them all. Alice and Doug were a young college-aged couple that helped when their schedules allowed. Larry leaned back in one of the chairs, with his always-at-ease smile showing above his gray beard. He was retired and one of Matt's favorite co-leaders. Kathy sat across from him, her genuine smile and full cheeks belying the lines around her eyes that revealed her true age.

Standing next to Matt was a new face, one I'd seen for the first time that morning. Emily Ferguson. With her cute blond bobbed hair, big blue eyes, and petite figure accentuated by white pants and pale pink sleeveless blouse. Everyone stopped in the middle of their conversation and turned toward me.

My face turned hot as the blood rushed up my neck and to my cheeks. "I . . . uhm . . . thought I'd stop by and see if you needed any help." I spoke toward the group but made eye contact directly with Matt. His slightly opened mouth and widened eyes told me he was genuinely surprised to see me.

"We always need more help!" Kathy bellowed as she stood. "It's good to see you." She ambled to me and wrapped me in a hug. "We've missed you around here."

I hugged her back, thankful beyond words for the friendly welcome. "I've missed you, too. School keeps me busy."

Kathy patted me on the back as she released her embrace. "It's great you're going back to school. Sets a good example for the kids." She pulled me back toward the group, one arm around my shoulders.

Matt cleared his throat. "Cassie, I'm glad you could make it. Have you met Emily?" He motioned to the woman beside him.

I shook my head. "No, not officially, but I saw her during the service this morning." I swallowed hard, trying to stuff down my emotions.

Matt's head bobbed up and down, a sign, I had learned, that he was either excited or nervous. "Emily, this is Cassie Peterson, my fi-an-cée." Matt accentuated my title with a flourish. He smiled and rolled his hand toward Emily. "Emily Ferguson has moved here all the way from southern California and is already jumping in to help with the youth ministry."

I inhaled, hoping my voice didn't betray my feelings. "Nice to meet you, officially. And how great that you're already getting involved." And weird. And suspicious. *And why are you standing so close to my fiancé?*

Emily laughed the light, high-pitched titter I'd heard from the foyer. "Oh, I'm really looking forward to getting involved." She turned to Matt and then the rest of the group with a big, white-toothed smile. "I've heard such amazing things about this congregation from my parents. I can't wait to see what the Lord does here!"

Matt put his hands behind his back and smiled but stared at the floor. "You know, all we have left to do for the evening is divide up the phone calls to students and parents for the week." He pulled a white paper with a list of names from the chair next to him and handed it to Larry. "Hey, buddy, would you mind delegating? I need to put away some paperwork in my office and then head home for the night." Matt looked up and made eye contact with me. "I owe Cassie some ice cream."

I tilted my head. "You do?"

He winked. "I do now."

I followed Matt to his office. Emily started to follow us, but Matt turned and spoke to her. "Larry can give you a couple of parents to call. You can introduce yourself. I'm sure they'd love to have you reach out." He grabbed my elbow and we walked briskly to his office.

"She's a bit much." I breathed, once we were in his office.

Matt nodded. "Let me just grab this folder and then we'll head out. Don't need rumors starting." He picked up a folder from his desk, and then led me out the door, which he locked behind him.

"Rumors?"

He waved his hand, but his eyes looked pained. "I'll explain later. Let's go."

Questions raced through my mind. Why was Matt in such a hurry to leave? What made him decide we should get ice cream? Why did he seem nervous? When we got to the parking lot, though, one question was at the top of my mind. "Whose car are we taking?"

Matt paused. "Good question." He looked back and forth between his Toyota Camry and my Ford Explorer. "How about if I follow you home, and then you jump in my car, and we head to Prince Pucklers?"

"Okay, I guess that makes sense."

I drove home and Matt followed. I tried to be quiet pulling into the driveway, not wanting to rouse any questions from Mom or Renee. My daughter would be sad she was missing out on ice cream if she knew. Once I was in Matt's car, I breathed a sigh of relief. Something about the evening made me feel like I was on a mission. Or on the run. "I really did show up with the intention of helping you tonight, but it looks like you had plenty of help."

"Yeah, I was thankful. We have a youth event coming up next weekend and you know that always takes extra volunteers, plus doing all the phone calls to make sure the kids and parents know and have all the forms filled out."

I studied his profile. Lines had deepened in the corners of his eyes. His jaw was tight. His hair appeared thinner at the temples. He clenched the steering wheel like his life depended on it. I wanted to ask him what he thought of Emily being there. I wanted to tell him what I thought of the Fergusons. More than anything, though, I wanted to know he was okay. "Matt, is everything all right?"

He breathed through his teeth as he weaved through the mostly empty downtown streets that would take us to the ice cream shop. "Not really."

"Is it because of the associate pastor thing?"

"Yes, but it's more than that."

He maneuvered his car into a street side parking space and turned off the engine. "Cassie, there's something I need to talk to you about."

Was Matt having the same misgivings about the Fergusons as I was? "I need to talk to you, too."

Matt chewed on his bottom lip, as if contemplating his words. "This entire thing with Ben and the affair, the Fergusons' arrival, the search for a new associate pastor . . .

it's brought out an ugliness in our church." Matt dropped his chin and stared at the steering wheel his hands still gripped. "I hate to admit. It's thrown me for a loop."

"Me too." I exhaled, a weight releasing from my chest. "Something is not right. I can't quite say what it is. I just know that the Fergusons aren't"—I shook my head, trying to put in a few words everything I'd told my mom—"what they seem, I guess."

Matt shifted in his seat and looked at me. Trouble brewed in his stormy blue eyes. He reached for my left hand and took it in his, tracing the curve of my engagement ring with his thumb. "I didn't tell you this before because I didn't know how to tell you, and honestly I was still trying to process it myself, praying and figuring out what to do."

Was it more bad news about the church? My stomach sank. "What is it?"

"They gave me a few reasons why I wasn't hired for the associate pastor position. The first one was that Chris had the most relevant experience. It's basically a lateral move for him." He squeezed my hand and looked away for a moment, then took a deep breath. "The second reason, though, was complete bull, to put it bluntly." He leaned closer to me, his voice deep, loving. "I want you to know, I don't agree with what they said, and I know a lot of other people don't either."

My pulse skyrocketed, throbbing in my neck as my mind raced, trying to figure out what Matt was going to say next, while a small, quiet part of me already drew the picture of his words in my mind. "What?"

"The Fergusons have been all about getting to the root of any sin in our leadership that might be unseen." His eyes narrowed. "In their quest, I guess you could say they felt I might bring in unbiblical standards unfitting of an associate pastor." His jaw worked as if he was chewing on his words.

"They took the standards for a church leader laid out in first Timothy and Titus to a religious extreme." He slowly shook his head. "It's not worth going into all the technicalities, because my defense, which was also biblical, fell on deaf ears."

"What standards? I'm confused." I tried to remember what Titus and first Timothy said, but I couldn't think with the beating pulse in my ears.

Matt ran his free hand over his head, seeming pained. "They said a pastor can't be divorced, which, in their opinion, means he also can't be married to a divorced woman. 'Anyone who divorces a woman causes her to commit adultery.' They reason that I'm committing adultery when I marry you."

Silence fell between us. The only sound I heard was the rushing of blood through my veins. "You didn't get the job because of *me*?"

Matt leaned in closer. "They were *wrong*, Cassie."

"But it was me. All because you're marrying me." I pulled my hand out of his and leaned back against the car door. My breath came quick and I tried to slow it, fighting the urge to open the door and run.

Run where?

My fear had become reality, and there was no place to hide from it. I wasn't qualified to be a pastor's wife. The church leadership said so. What's worse, my lack of qualification had kept Matt—a good, kind, Godly, loving man—from getting the position in the church he longed for. I was holding him back. Was he better off without me? The weight on my chest was more than I could bear.

Matt reached for my face, but I turned away from his hand. "What did you say to them, when they told you?"

His brow furrowed. "I told them I respected their opinion, and then offered my own." He reached for my hand, the one I had pulled away from him. I let him take it, but every part of me felt closed off. A wall was being built, brick by brick, at rapid speed, around my heart. "Cassie," Matt's voice held a gentle pleading to it, breaking through my rising defenses, "you have to know they are wrong, and I don't agree with them. I countered their arguments using the same Bible passages. I brought up grace and the heart of the scriptures. They already had their minds made up. When it comes down to it, they are more concerned about the image of holiness than holiness itself."

Tears welled in my eyes as I imagined the scenario in my mind. "All the leadership?" I asked, my voice barely above a whisper, "They all agreed you aren't qualified because of me being divorced?"

"No, not all." Matt sighed. "But they felt the pressure, the scrutiny, we've all been under. They all eventually gave in to the argument."

The face of each leader flashed before my eyes. I had considered them to be friends. How could a friend judge another the way they had me? Had their friendship been fake?

A realization dawned on me, another stab in my chest. "If they don't think you're qualified to be an associate pastor, then how are you qualified to be a youth pastor?"

Matt swallowed. "Another point I brought up. Long story short, I'm already in that position. It's also not as visible of a position as the associate pastor, though if I was on their side of the argument, I'd say it's more important to set a good example for the youth than the adults."

Was it coincidence that the Fergusons' daughter who had just moved here had experience with youth? Or was it part of their plan to make the church more "above reproach"? Looking at Matt's face, I knew what he thought. "What are you going to do?"

Matt looked out the front window of his car at the darkening sky. "I'm looking for another job."

I knew it wouldn't be easy to find another pastoral job in town. Was Matt going to lose his calling in life because he had chosen to marry me? What did that mean for our future?

I remembered the moment years ago, when I'd held onto a tree limb for dear life, the water of the river nearly pulling me away and over the fall. I'd seen God then. Felt His love, His protection. I saw He'd been with me during my divorce and the fight for my daughter. No matter how big my shame was, He was bigger.

Where was God now?

Chapter Twenty-Two

Sharon

SOME THINGS A MOTHER NEVER FORGETS. The first tooth. First steps. The sight of their little one walking into kindergarten. Regrettably, I'd been gone for other milestones. Cassie's first day of high school. Her driver's license test. I was there, though, the night she came home and ran to the bathroom to throw up because her self-worth was shattered by people who called themselves followers of Christ.

I stood on the other side of that bathroom door, begging her to let me in, but she refused. She didn't have to tell me what was wrong. I knew. I'd held the secret and bided my time. When she came out of the bathroom, there was no comforting her. She didn't want to talk. Her eyes were red and swollen but completely dry. All she wanted was to go to bed.

She didn't tell me the reason for her distress until the next morning, when she called in sick to work. I'd heard her in the bathroom throughout the night, dry heaving. She looked horrible. Dark blue rings encircled her eyes. She was pale, hollow looking. That's when things turned from bad to worse. Because when she told me, I had to nod. I had to say, "Yeah, I know."

"You knew?" Cassie's voice was hoarse, crackly.

"Yes, Samantha told me, but asked me not to say anything." I'd ran my fingers through my hair, pulling a strand around my finger the way Cassie did when she was nervous. "If Matt hadn't told you soon, I was going to. That's why I wanted you to talk to him last night. I couldn't keep it from you any longer."

I hoped my voice, my eyes, my every movement conveyed

how hard it was for me, as her mom, to see her in pain. I hoped she knew I was between a rock and a hard place and only trying to make the right decision. Like a flame under the force of a flood, my hope was extinguished when Cassie turned and walked away, slamming her bedroom door.

Since then, our home held a cold silence that was only broken by Renee's chatter and laughter. Whenever I approached Cassie and tried to bring up the situation, she changed the subject or simply walked away. I understood her anger, but it was also getting under my skin. One more day. That's what I told myself as I drove to the Higher Focus meeting. I'd give her one more day to sort it out, then I was going to make her talk. That's what my mom would've done, and she usually got things right. Usually.

Walking into the church felt like walking into a morgue. It was the people in this building who had hurt my daughter. Part of me didn't even want to be there, but I'd made a commitment to the attendees and to Frank. Plus, I guess God had told me co-leading the group was what He wanted me to do, though I wasn't happy with Him right now, either.

"Is everything okay?" Frank asked after I walked into the room and threw my purse on a table.

I grunted in response and picked up the handouts to put on each table. The group now had nine students out of a church with six hundred attendees between two services. I didn't have to be a math genius to know Higher Focus was not what you would call a success, at least not when it came to attendance. So far, no one from outside of the church had signed up. As far as I knew, our outreach to community was nonexistent.

Frank paused writing on the whiteboard. "Want to talk about it?"

"It's probably best for me to keep my mouth shut right now." I responded, setting the last of the handouts on the table and walking toward the sink to fill the water pitcher.

"Have I done something to upset you?" Frank's voice echoed slightly in the empty room.

I stopped and turned toward him, hand on my hip. "Why in the world would you think that?" Men. Always assuming a woman's world revolved around their actions.

Frank's lips pursed in a suppressed smile. "Well, you walked in angry. Maybe you don't want to be here? I don't think any of the attendees would make you feel that way. It's a matter of elimination." He held up his hands, the left one still holding a dry erase marker.

I waved my arm at him and returned my attention to the water pitcher. "It's not you, Frank. It's stuff at home. With my daughter."

"I see."

I heard the dim, squeaky sound of the dry erase marker continuing its work before I turned the water on. As the pitcher filled, I thought, why not? Of all the people to talk to about this whole mess, Frank seemed like a reasonable choice. He was a member of the church but not part of the inner circle. A mature Christian with a broken past. Plus, he was older and wiser, presumably.

Once I set the water pitcher on the table, I blurted out everything. Matt being turned down for the associate pastor position and the reason why. How I'd known but held my tongue. Cassie not talking to me since Sunday night. Her obvious heartbreak. My uncertainty of what to do next.

Frank listened attentively, his face showing acknowledgment, surprise, concern. When I was done, he said. "That's a lot. I can understand why you're upset."

"You think?" I threw my hands up in the air. "This is the first church I've been to since I was young and went with my parents to a little church with pews and one pastor who preached pretty much every Sunday until the day he died. I don't even know what to do with this mess. Is it a church or political campaign or a gossip factory?"

"Probably all three." Frank deadpanned, not missing a beat.

That wasn't the response I was expecting. "Seriously?"

Frank shrugged. "Church is full of people. From the lead pastor down to the person who walks in the door for the first time, they're all human. Imperfect. Flawed. Everyone has their own struggle they are dealing with, but they try to hide it, most of the time."

I knew he was right, but I didn't like it. I'd been afraid to come back to church because of all I'd done in my past. I knew how hard it was to walk in those doors and to keep coming back when regret haunted you. When your own shame stood in the way, keeping an invisible shield between you and God. The last thing a hurting person needed was those who were supposed to be representatives of God getting in the way, too.

"I get it. I really do." I glanced over my shoulder, checking the door, making sure we were still alone. "But sometimes people go too far. What they do is evil. Pure and simple."

Frank nodded. "That's true. They need to be held accountable. Often, when you look closer, those same people are already paying the price for what they've done. If not now, they will be." Frank studied my face, his eyes holding a gentleness beyond what I'd seen before. "Few of us escape this life without facing the consequence for our choices in one way or the other."

His words hit home. I knew the truth of them all too well, but it wasn't me we were talking about. "Yeah, well, sometimes it's hard to see where that's the case. As for me, personally, I need to know this situation is being dealt with." I sank onto a chair, the realization of what I was about to say weighing me down. "I can't stay here if it isn't."

Frank looked away. "I understand. Been there." His voice

was distant as his eyes seemed to gaze into a memory I couldn't see.

Had he been through something similar? I wanted to pry, but it was almost time for people to arrive. "If you have any advice, I'd love to hear it." I said instead.

He laughed, but it was a small, tight sound. A polite chuckle. "Are you up to having coffee after the meeting tonight?"

Coffee. With Frank. Another not-a-date get-together with the man who kept looking at me like he was interested but acted like he wasn't. Why not? I needed all the advice I could get. Shoot, while I was at it, maybe I could ask him what he thought about Johnny. I agreed to coffee and held back my laughter as the first attendee walked in the door.

After group was finished, Frank suggested Shari's restaurant for coffee.

"Uh, how about someplace else? Denny's maybe?" I couldn't go to Shari's with Frank. Their coffee and pie reminded me of Johnny.

Frank lifted an eyebrow. "It's a little farther drive, but sure, if that's what you want. I'll meet you there."

I followed Frank to the 24-hour restaurant. It was probably unreasonable of me to refuse to go to Shari's, but the idea caused a pain in my chest I couldn't deal with right now. When we arrived, we were seated at a booth and given menus. "I just want coffee. Decaf, with a touch of cream." I told the waitress.

"Regular for me. No cream."

We handed our menus back to the waitress, then sat in silence for a solid minute. I shifted nervously in my seat, unsure of where to start. "Group went great tonight, I think."

Frank nodded. "Yes, it did. Everyone who's coming seems

fully invested. That's a good thing."

He had a point. We didn't have any dropouts yet, though it was still early. Each person did seem genuinely interested in growing and getting better. "The small number of people showing up doesn't bother you?"

Frank shook his head. "Nope."

The waitress returned with our coffee. Frank added a packet of sugar-free sweetener to his and took a sip. "Not bad," he said.

"Why doesn't the lack of attendance bother you?"

Frank set his cup down. "Well, I suppose I could say I'm glad there are only nine people in our church that struggle with addiction." He smiled. "But I know that's not true. Statistics confirm that."

I nodded, urging him to continue.

He laid his hands on the table and took a deep breath. "It really gets to the heart of what I wanted to share with you. About the church. The leadership, the people."

"The leadership is to blame for the lack of attendance." I spit out the words, confident of my assumption.

Frank tilted his head. "Perhaps, but that's not the point."

I looked at the ceiling, took a deep breath. "Okay, I'm listening."

"The church I attended before this one, when I lived in San Diego, was quite different from Cascade Christian Church."

"How so?"

"A little smaller. Much more charismatic. Far less structured."

"Is that where you first led a Higher Focus group?"

Frank nodded. "Yes. I started with twenty people, at the end I had seven that regularly came to the meetings. I can't tell you how many are still sober today, because I've lost touch with many of them."

A cool wave flowed over my body, making my heart slow. "Oh . . . that had to be hard."

"Yes, but I knew it was coming. I knew that there was a fervency in some that would not be sustainable." He took a deep breath. "I also knew I was doing what God wanted me to do, and I was where He wanted me to be. So, I didn't focus on the numbers, or lose too much sleep over the people who didn't come back, because I trusted God had His hand in everything."

"I bet you had more support from the church there."

Frank shrugged a shoulder. "In a word, yes. But in deed, not so much. It was a very unstructured church. Not enough oversight. Not enough accountability."

I chewed on his words. "The opposite of where you are now?"

"I don't know about the opposite. But I do know this—" Frank held my gaze, his yellow-brown eyes serious, "There is no perfect place or circumstance. I'm doing what God has called me to do. Whether nine people or ninety show up. Whether the group is advertised in the bulletin or not. God brought me through my own struggles for a purpose. He longs for the broken to be healed. He fights to set the prisoners free. I can trust that anyone who doesn't, who isn't working in His will, ultimately, they are *not* going to succeed." Though Frank's words could have been part of a passionate sermon, he spoke them evenly, almost devoid of emotion, yet I knew by the seriousness in his expression that he meant every word.

"So even though the church you're in now might not be the most supportive, you're sticking with it?"

Frank took another sip of his coffee. "Yes, until I hear otherwise from the Lord."

I stared at the dessert menu standing up at the end of the table. If only making big decisions was as easy as choosing a piece of pie. "I get what you're saying, but this thing with Matt and Cassie, it's different. I know my daughter feels judged. I imagine Matt feels that he can't succeed in any ministry. That's a big obstacle to overcome."

"You're right. It is. But in all of it, you can't lose sight of what God has called you to do, Sharon."

Goosebumps erupted on the back of my arms. "I don't know what He's called me to. I mean, yeah, He wants me to help with this group, but I don't know for how long." I forced a laugh. "The course is only twelve weeks."

Frank gave me a small smile. "It might be the group. It might be something else. My point is, you can't let what other people do—even other Christians, other leaders—deter you from the path God has for you." He sighed. "I'm not saying don't seek counsel. I'm not saying ignore words of wisdom or encouragement from others. What I'm saying is, don't be afraid of the giant. God equips you with what you need."

I appreciated Frank's wisdom, but it also scared me. What if God's path for me took me away from my daughter? My granddaughter? I couldn't see why God would do that. Then again, Cassie was getting married. She needed a new start with Matt. I was beginning to wonder how new and unfamiliar that start would be for all of us.

As if on cue, my phone buzzed.

Will you be home soon? Need to talk.

Cassie. Ready to talk. Finally. Why now? My heart quickened.

"I need to go." I reached for my purse to get some change out of my wallet.

Frank waved his hand. "Please, it's on me. Is everything okay?"

I nodded. "Yeah, I think so. It was Cassie. She wants to talk." I gave him a half smile. "I've been waiting for her to be ready."

"The way you were hurrying out of here, I thought it must be your boyfriend wondering why you're having coffee with some other guy."

I froze. Johnny's face flashed in my mind. Frank didn't know about Johnny. Did he? "I don't have a boyfriend." A nervous titter followed my declaration as I scooted out of the booth.

"I was making a joke." Frank replied. His hesitant smile didn't reach his eyes. "But I was wondering."

He was wondering? Why was he wondering? I stood. No time to think about *that* right now. "Nope, single and fancy free. That's me." Even as the words left my mouth, I knew the last part of my sentence wasn't quite true.

"Good to know." Frank said as I turned to leave. "Good to know."

Chapter Twenty-Three

Cassie

AFTER TEXTING MY MOM, I MADE myself a cup of chamomile tea, popped a couple of Tylenol to ward off my growing headache, and sat in the living room with the television off. I'd briefly Facetimed Matt because it was our routine, but the events of the evening had me longing to talk to my mom.

The evening replayed in my mind like an echo in the silence of the night. Derrick had called, requesting to talk to Renee.

I hesitated, yearning to say no, but remembered the words of my attorney. "If this goes to court, you don't want to come off as the parent who kept Renee away from her father."

I told Derrick to hold on a moment and then muted my phone so I could speak to my daughter in private. "Renee, your daddy is on the phone and wants to talk to you. You don't have to talk to him very long. You don't even have to say anything if you don't want to, but I'm going to give you the phone so he can say hello."

She shook her head. Her emerald eyes widened. I took her in my arms and gave her a hug. "I know this is hard, honey, just try. That's all you have to do."

Her body relaxed in my arms, familiar and warm and trusting. I unmuted the phone and handed it to her. She took it from me, her mouth set in a frown and her eyes still big, waves of uncertainty turning them a dark blue. She didn't speak. I was close enough to hear Derrick's voice. "Hi, sweetie. It's daddy. How are you?"

Renee's bottom lip trembled ever so slightly, but she croaked out a timid, "Okay."

"I sure miss you." He said, his voice smooth and sweet. My stomach turned, remembering how his voice could turn from sweet to threatening in the blink of an eye.

Renee didn't respond. She looked at the ground.

"I'm hoping I can see you soon." He continued, but now there was a strain in his voice. Whether it was from frustration or sadness, I couldn't tell through the muffle of the phone.

Renee looked up at me, her brow furrowed. "Mommy?"

I nodded. "I'm here, honey, it's okay."

"Is your mom listening to this phone call, Renee?" Derrick's voice was elevated now, a hint of hardness in it.

"Uh-huh." Renee responded.

"I see." Derrick snickered. "That's okay. Pretty soon I'll have you all to myself. You can come over and meet your little brother."

Renee swallowed but didn't say a word.

"I have a nice house. My new wife, Brooke, she is nice. She set up a bedroom for you with a pretty pink bed and white dresser. I think you'll like it a lot."

My stomach turned. What was he thinking? This was too much, too soon.

Renee's bottom lip quivered. "Okay." She handed the phone to me. "Mommy, can I be done now?"

I nodded. "Yes." I reached out for her as I took the phone from her hand, but she ran to her room and slammed the door.

"She handed the phone back to me, Derrick. I think she's done talking." I couldn't hide the anger in my voice.

Derrick laughed. My skin crawled as memories flashed through my mind of all the times he'd laughed at my heartache and distress. How had I put up with him for so long?

"That's fine, Cassie. I'll be seeing you in mediation next

week. I'm sure we can work something out that's best for our daughter." He said the right words, almost, but the concern wasn't there. It was like each word was made to taunt me instead of showing real love for our daughter.

I ended the call. I took several deep breaths, steadying my shaking hands.

Renee.

I rushed to her room and opened the door. She sat on her bed with tear-streaked cheeks, her last school photo on her lap, the frame it had been in discarded on the floor. In her right hand was a pencil, and she was stabbing hard at the picture. I sat beside her and gently pulled the photo out of her hands. She allowed me to take the picture but looked away and dropped the pencil at her side. I held the picture in my hands, staring at it, tears welling in my own eyes. She'd poked the picture of herself with the pencil so much that nothing was left of it. She'd obliterated herself from the photograph.

"Renee." I reached for her, but she scooted away from me, backing herself in the corner of the bed.

What had I done? What could I do now? I withdrew my hands, and she stopped her recoil, staying perfecting still.

"I'm so sorry, honey. I know that was hard." My voice cracked.

Renee didn't respond. She buried her head in her knees, refusing to look at me.

I sighed. "Sometimes, if we talk about things, it makes the sad things less heavy."

We sat in silence for a few minutes. Me waiting, Renee ever so slowly relaxing, and finally raising her head to look at me. "Am I a bad girl, Mommy?"

"What? No." I shook my head. "You're just upset." I picked up the picture and bit my lip. I could always order another class photo.

Renee shook her head. "No, I'm bad." New tears streamed down her face.

I pulled her into my arms. "You're not bad. You're hurting. Mommy's heart hurts, too." I held her until the tears dried. We skipped the bath and story time, but it was still past her bedtime before I tucked her in.

Now it was me and chamomile tea, waiting for my mom to get home. I longed to talk to her. Because of my bitterness and past hurts, I'd cut my mom out for days. I'd been angry with Mom for not telling me what she knew about Matt not getting the job. My mom loved Renee as much as I did. Of that I was certain. Derrick's call, and the pain it caused Renee, made me realize what had been eating at me. I realized that the main thing that bothered me about her not telling me was it reminded me of her drinking days and the secrets and lies she told then. Once I understood my feelings were from events of the past, not the present, my anger subsided.

The front door quietly creeped open, and my mom slipped in, worry lines across her brow. She threw her purse up on a hook and then joined me in the living room. "What's going on?" She asked before even sitting down.

I told her everything about the phone call from Derrick and Renee's reaction.

"Well, that does it. Don't let him talk to her again. He's bad for her!" Mom huffed, still not sitting down.

"I wish it were that simple." I slumped against the back of the couch, the throbbing in my head increasing in tempo.

Mom shifted, her eyes boring into my soul, then sat beside me gently. "I'm sorry you and Renee have to go through this, Cassie. How can I help?"

"I don't know what you can do." I looked at the ceiling. "I'll write down what happened. Tell my attorney. Which will cost me about fifty dollars just to make that phone call." I sighed and turned to my mom. "I honestly don't understand how mediation can go well. I can't see Renee having parenting time with him alone. She can't even talk to him on the phone. And the *way* he talks to her. Either he doesn't have a clue, or he wants to hurt her. Or me." I rubbed my temples. The more I thought about the entire thing, the more my head throbbed.

"Your attorney can't go with you to meditation?"

I shook my head.

"What about Matt or me?"

"No, it's not like that. It's supposed to be a chance for Derrick and me to talk things out with an unbiased third party." I sighed. "It's dumb, really. A hoop to jump through before court." It was the same thing I'd told Matt when he'd asked.

"He still doesn't have an attorney?"

"No. I'm guessing he's waiting to see how mediation goes before putting the money into one." I shrugged. "But who knows, it's Derrick."

"What does Matt think about the whole thing?"

"He's concerned and sad for the whole situation." I shrugged. "I'm trying not to burden him too much about the entire thing. Right now, his job has him stressed."

"What are his plans, job-wise?" Mom's tone turned hard.

"He's putting out feelers for other pastor positions in town. It's not an easy thing to do under the circumstances. He needs his job."

"I understand that." Mom patted my knee, but her eyes were on the wall, seemingly lost in thought.

"Everything seemed so perfect a few months ago. Now, it feels like my whole world is on the verge of falling apart." I blinked away tears. "Why is God letting so much happen all at once?"

"I don't know, Baby Girl." Mom put her arm around me

and pulled my head down onto her shoulder. "What I do know is that we've had other storms and got through them. We'll make it to the other side of this one, too."

I clung to my mom's words, hoping and praying she was right.

"You better be free the Saturday after next, because I've got our horseback ride all planned out." Missy sat on the edge of my desk like she owned it, eating a mozzarella stick.

"Uhm . . ." my mind raced, hoping I had some not cancellable plan I could blame for having to back out of the horse ride. Nothing came to mind. Homework, as always, but that could be done around other things. "I think I'm free?"

"Good! It's going to be a blast."

"What if it's raining?"

"Wear rain gear." Missy winked. "But let's hope it doesn't. I don't want to hear you whine." She playfully hit my shoulder.

I wouldn't even dare to whine about rain to Missy. She'd call me a tourist or a Californian or something. "Where are we going for our ride?"

Missy shoved the last bit of cheese in her mouth and stood. "I thought about fibbing and telling you we were going to some waterfall. Less incentive for you to call in sick."

I rolled my eyes. "I wouldn't call in sick on you." What I didn't tell Missy was that any excitement I may have had about the horse ride was extinguished by finding out there were no waterfalls on the trail. My heart longed to return to the falls, but time had not been on my side.

"Uh-huh. Well, that's good, because I've arranged to get my dad's horse trailer for the day, and we're taking the horses up to Quinn Meadows and riding the trails there."

"Meadows sound nice." They did. Sort of.

Missy nodded with enthusiasm. "Those are good trails for

newbies. Pretty easy to ride."

That was a relief to hear. I'd tried horseback riding once when I was eight. It hadn't ended well. I wondered, though, if Missy's idea of easy and my idea of easy were even in the same ballpark.

"There are a few spots that are a little tricky, but you'll be fine. I'm taking our older horse, Scout. He's gentle and experienced. He's the babysitter."

"Babysitter?"

Missy rolled her eyes. "That's what my mom calls him. He's the one she has little kids ride."

I raised an eyebrow. "I'm comparable to a little kid?"

Missy guffawed. "Nah, just when it comes to horses. And farm animals." A mischievous twinkle lit her hazel eyes. "What is that sound chickens make, again? Quack-quack?"

I laughed, my first real laugh in days. It both hurt and felt good. "Good one. You got me."

Missy gave my arm a soft punch. "Mark your calendar and find a real babysitter for Renee. This is going to be the ride of your life."

"I'm sure it will be." I looked at the clock on my computer. "I'm surprised Cynthia isn't back from lunch yet."

"I heard she had a doctor's appointment."

"Oh? That's odd that she didn't say anything to me."

"I'm telling you." Missy waggled her finger at me and then leaned in and whispered. "That woman is P-R-E-G-N-A-N-T."

I pursed my lips. "I wonder when she's going to share the news?""

Missy gave an exaggerated shrug and sauntered off. I turned back to my work. How far along in the pregnancy could Cynthia be?

And what did that mean for my future employment?

Chapter Twenty-Four

Sharon

SOMETIMES, PLUCKING AWAY AT MY GUITAR was the only way to soothe my soul. Today was one of those days. I had the day off, Cassie was at work, and Renee at school. The peace from making amends with my daughter was tainted by the story of Derrick's phone call. My purpose in the Higher Focus group was uncertain because I didn't see myself staying at Cascade Christian Church much longer. Then there was Johnny. He kept popping up in my mind like a jack-in-the-box, surprising me at the most unlikely times. Folding laundry. Driving to the grocery store. Flipping pancakes for Renee's breakfast. No rhyme nor reason, just Johnny's face in my mind, and I couldn't shake it.

Focus on the good. Mom's voice. How I wished I could talk to her now, but all I had were memories. Sweet and golden like honey, they soothed my aching heart but didn't take away the pain. I focused on the chords I played, working on the song I'd found for Cassie and Matt's wedding. I still hadn't talked to Cassie about it, thinking it may be best to get the song down right so I could play it for her myself, rather than have her listen to it on her phone. I'd tweak it a little, make the tune more wedding-like.

I had the upcoming Sunday off and dreaded going to church. Cassie had confided in me that she wasn't looking forward to it either. What a crummy situation to be in. That girl had loved church up until now. I'd go this Sunday to be by her side, just like she'd been by mine when I couldn't face the unpleasant parts of my life. That's what family was for. I quit strumming and hit the heel of my hand on my guitar. Family. Wasn't that what church was supposed to be?

I put down my guitar and picked up my phone. It'd been a while since I'd texted my new-found half-brother, Andy. It wasn't an easy thing to build a relationship with someone you didn't even know existed until the middle of your life. Having that person be a somewhat famous country musician added an extra layer of awkwardness, at least for me. Ignoring my nerves, I sent him a text that could qualify as a mini novel. He usually responded in kind, so we had that in common. I told him the latest with Cassie and the custody battle with Renee. Let him know how the Higher Focus group was going. He already knew about Cassie and Matt's engagement, so I asked if he had figured out if his schedule would allow him to make it to the wedding. I didn't want to start in about the things at church. Not yet.

After sending the text, I picked up my guitar again to practice the song, but my mind kept drifting and soon I found myself playing "She's My Kind of Rain" by Tim McGraw, a song that Johnny had sung terribly off key to me on more than one occasion. I stopped on the lyric, "like love from a drunken sky." We'd both been heavy drinkers back then. I'd given up that lifestyle. Last time I saw Johnny, he'd changed a lot, but it didn't appear he'd given up drinking entirely. I put down the guitar, my shoulders and chest aching. Why did I keep thinking about someone who wasn't good for me?

Pray. I could do that. It was simple enough. Sometimes so simple it seemed like it couldn't work, but it so often did. If nothing else, it helped me hand over to God what I couldn't control. I prayed for Johnny. That everything would work out with his dad and the family land. I asked that he find happiness. Most importantly, I prayed that Johnny would know God—a prayer I'd repeated more times than I could count over the last year.

After my "Amen," I picked up my phone. Andy had responded. My heart leapt. He said he would be at the wedding. Cassie hadn't yet sent out the invites, so now I could tell her to add him to the list. He'd be finishing up a small tour just before the wedding but would have time to recoup for a couple of days at home and then head this way. His grown children, who I hadn't yet met, might even be able to come with him. Like me, Cassie had been an only child. Now she had cousins, and she'd finally be able to meet them. He told me he'd keep praying for Cassie and Renee and the custody battle. Hearing him say he was praying brought a comfort to my soul that I didn't expect.

Thank you, God, for family, near and far and everywhere in between.

I was about ready to walk out the door to pick Renee up from school when Johnny called. My heart skipped a beat in excitement, and yet I wasn't surprised. He'd been on my mind all day. The song. The prayer. Maybe he'd been thinking about me, too.

"Hey, Angel Eyes." His voice was smooth and husky and yet light. So Johnny.

"Hey." I closed the door behind me and walked to my car. I didn't have Bluetooth in my ancient vehicle, but I'd figured out a way of mounting my phone to the dashboard and using the speakerphone. It worked in a pinch, but I'd sit in the driveway and talk to Johnny as long as I could.

"I hope this isn't a bad time to call. I'm not sure what your schedule is these days."

"I'm getting ready to pick up my granddaughter, but I can talk for a bit. How are you?" I opened the door to my car and slid in.

"Good. My dad is improving, and being a little less stubborn, so that's a plus." Johnny laughed. "I listed my house in Watsonville for sale. Looks like I could make a pretty penny with the market being what it is right now."

He was selling his house in California? Did that mean . . . "You decided to buy out your sister?"

"That's the plan."

I could hear the smile in his voice.

"Look at you, Johnny Farmer now, huh?" I chuckled. It was hard to believe. I thought he'd changed a lot by taking the trucking job in California that had him home each evening. Now he was signing up for the family farm. Talk about commitments and putting down roots.

"Never say never, right?" His voice held a gentle tease. There was a pause before he continued. "I've got to admit, this entire thing with my dad has opened my eyes. It's given me a real change in perspective these last few months."

I knew how those times could be. "I bet. I'm sorry it's been rough." Should I invite him to coffee so we could talk more? I opened my mouth, ready to ask.

"I've got something else to tell you that's probably gonna shock you. Are you sitting down?"

"I'm sitting in my car, so yeah." What more could there be? Had he won the lottery?

"My mom has this neighbor, she's a real sweet gal."

"That's shocking?"

"Well, hopefully not." Johnny chuckled. "But I'm not done. Anyway, she's been an angel . . ."

A vine of jealousy knotted in my stomach. Did he call her an angel? That was his name for me, Angel Eyes. "I see."

"Yeah, it's been a real help. Bringing meals over and such. She goes to a church in Junction City, and I guess she got my parents signed up for one of those meal train things. There's been quite a few folks dropping off food, but she's brought over more than her fair share of meals."

"I'm glad you've had the help." I meant it, but my throat was tight, speaking the words.

"It's been nice. Anyway, her name is Christy, and she invited my parents and me to her church this Sunday. Would you believe I said yes?"

No, but yes. Hadn't I just been praying for him? How many times had I prayed for Johnny to find God? More than I could count. I just didn't think it would be through another woman. My chest tightened. "I'm pleasantly surprised to hear that, Johnny."

"Like I say, never say never."

"You've got a point." Maybe now wasn't a good time to invite Johnny for coffee. It sounded like he had other interests, and I couldn't say it was a bad thing. Why, then, did my heart ache so much? "You'll have to let me know what you think of the church and all." By 'the church' I meant if he was ready to commit his life to the Lord, and by 'and all' I meant how things went with Christy. Hopefully he understood.

"I sure will." Another pause. "How are things with you?"

I gave him an abbreviated version of my life. The Higher Focus group. Cassie engaged to Matt and back in court for another custody battle.

"Wow, other than the custody mess that all sounds like life is going good for you and your family. I'm happy to hear that." He sighed. "I've always wanted you to be happy, Sharon."

I wanted him to be happy, too. The problem was, there was a stubborn part of me that still hoped that somehow, someway, we'd be happy *together*. "Thanks. I am. For the most part." He didn't need to know about all the things that were weighing me down, though a tiny voice inside my head screamed to tell him it all. Another, quiet and gentle voice said, "Not yet." Maybe never. "I should probably get going so I can pick up my granddaughter. It's been good talking to you."

"Okay, I'll let you get to it." He sounded slightly disappointed by me ending the conversation. "Take care, talk to you later."

I hung up the phone and started the engine. It was only after I backed out the driveway that I realized Johnny hadn't called me Angel Eyes when he said goodbye.

Chapter Twenty-Five

MOM RODE WITH RENEE AND ME to church.

Something about the drive reminded me of our trip to California the previous year. The two things had nothing in common on the surface. The road trip to California had been about me supporting my mom in the search for her father. Initially unsuccessful, we ended up with enough clues to get Mom on the path that led to her finding my grandpa, Michael Smith. It'd been a fun trip, a mini vacation.

Mom accompanying me to church was no vacation. It was something we did regularly. This time, though, didn't have the happy Sunday vibe to it. Instead, it felt like we were going into battle. The irony wasn't lost on me. Wasn't church supposed to be a safe place? A haven in the storm?

Now it seemed like the storm would be found walking through those double glass doors.

After I pulled into a parking spot and killed the engine, Mom spoke. "I've been sitting here trying to think what your Nannie would say, if she was here now."

I stared out the front window, watching people get out of their cars and walk into the church. Families, mostly. Dad, mom, kids. Some modestly and casually dressed. Many more, though, wearing their Sunday best. I'd first come to Cascade Christian Church because I heard they had a group for single moms. People like me. I'd felt welcomed, but the participants of that group cycled through so quickly I hadn't stayed in the circle. Most of them ended up in other churches. A few, like me, ended up joining a family home group.

Then I had found the group for adult children of

alcoholics. I was still a part of that group, though I went far less frequently than I had in the past. I had connections there, but most of them were older than me.

I hadn't gone to my home group this week. Rick and Trish were a part of that group, and they were also leaders in the church. Though they may not have been part of the hiring decision, they were undoubtedly in the know on who was chosen and why. I was too embarrassed to face them—and hurt. They knew. Did they think the same thing the Fergusons did of me? Was I not qualified to be a pastor's wife in their eyes, too? Their friendship suddenly seemed shallow, uncertain.

"Cassie?" Mom again.

"Yes, sorry." I swallowed and looked at my mom. Her eyes were the deepest shade of brown I'd ever seen them. I saw pain and righteous anger there, but also a small sliver of peace. I imagined Nannie with us. A peacefulness would come from her that would calm us all. I refused to cry. "What do you think Nannie would say?"

Mom inhaled. "I think she would say, 'hold your chin up and remember, God loves you and already knew what was going to happen. He has a purpose for you, and sometimes people can't see it, but that doesn't mean it's not going to happen.'" Mom nodded once, seeming satisfied with her words. "She also probably would have told you that anyone who can't see your worth deserves a good, swift, kick in the pants." Her chin jutted out with a little laugh.

I smiled in reminiscence. I could see Nannie saying both things. The spunky part of her had been handed down to Mom, in spades. "I think you're right." I turned to Renee. "Ready for church, Sugar Bug?"

Renee nodded enthusiastically. "Grammy said I could have whatever donut I want today."

I squinted at Mom, who gave me a sideways grin and held

her hands up. "That's what grandmas are for, right?"

At least Renee would be happy and distracted. Hopefully so much so she wouldn't notice if I struggled.

We exited the car and walked into the building, three generations, side by side. Mom and Renee headed for the pastries. I almost joined them as a distraction, but this was the time I usually used to chat with people. I saw someone from my Adult Children of Alcoholics group and exchanged a few pleasantries with him. I scanned the foyer for Matt. He was standing by the entry to the youth room. It took me only a second to notice that Emily Ferguson was standing on the other side, as if she was part of a welcoming team to youth group.

Was she already on the youth ministry team and Matt hadn't told me?

I walked that way but was stopped by Trish. "Cassie! We missed you at small group on Tuesday." She smiled, her face bright and sunny.

"Oh, I was sorry to miss it. I've been so busy with schoolwork and all." It was a partial truth. I had missed a few home groups since starting school because of my schedule.

Trish tilted her head, a hint of emotion flitting across her green eyes. "That's what I thought. I hope everything is going well for you."

Was that code for 'I know what happened and I hope you're okay?' I didn't ask. Instead, I nodded. "Everything is good. Busy but good."

"Glad to hear that." Her gaze flitted to something behind me. "Talk to you later."

I continued my way to the youth room. Now Emily, Matt, and the college couple who liked to volunteer were talking to a small group of teens. Whatever they said made the teenagers laugh, and the group of young people enthusiastically went inside the room. I waved in Matt's direction, hoping to get his attention, but he didn't notice. Small, sticky fingers clasped my other hand. I looked down to see Renee's chocolate rimmed mouth beaming.

"Mommy, this donut has chocolate on the outside and pudding on the inside." She held half of it up in the air toward me, as if inviting me to take a bite.

"That looks yummy." I glanced over my shoulder, searching for my mom. I spotted her talking to Samantha. Renee took another bite of her éclair and the filling dripped out, falling on the front part of her dress.

"Uh-oh." Renee swiped at the pudding filling with her chocolate fingers, creating a bigger mess.

Great. Mom was still involved in conversation with Samantha. I clasped Renee's less sticky hand. "Let's go to the bathroom and get you cleaned up before church starts."

"I'm not done with my donut."

I glanced toward the youth room. Emily was standing next to Matt now, laughing at something he was saying. Heat and irritation ran through me like a drop of water hitting a hot skillet. I couldn't very well go waltzing over there with a child covered in a sticky mess. "You can finish it on our way to the restroom. But hurry."

The first beats of worship music poured down the hallway as I entered the restroom with Renee. She stuffed the rest of the donut into her mouth and now looked like a chipmunk. A couple of ladies gave me knowing smiles on their way out of the room. I tried to stay calm and not rush through cleaning her up. I didn't *have* to see Matt before service. I could always see him afterward. The image of Emily standing close to him and enthralled by whatever he was saying felt like bugs crawling on my skin. By the time we exited the bathroom, I was practically dragging Renee behind me as I rushed to the youth room. The foyer was nearly empty, worship in full swing. Mom stood near the entry of the sanctuary, shifting from one foot to the other and looking at her phone. I turned toward the youth room door, but it was already closed. Matt was gone.

"There you are." Mom approached me, concern written all over her face.

"Renee needed to get cleaned up." I explained.

"Shouldn't we take her to kids church now?"

"Oh . . . yeah." I'd been so concerned with getting to see Matt, I hadn't done the logical thing—the responsible, parental duty of taking my child where she needed to be. I pinched the bridge of my nose. "I'm sorry. I don't know where my brain is."

Mom patted me on the side of my arm. "It's okay. I get it. I'll take her. You go find us a seat."

I nodded and watched Renee happily take Mom's hand and leave for kids' church.

I glanced at the closed door, hoping someone would arrive late so I could peek in. I could, of course, walk over, open the door and just go inside myself. It would be awkward since I wasn't signed up to help and they were probably in the middle of a warmup game or something. It was tempting, but I knew it was an irrational thing to do. Best to go to service and find Matt afterward.

Entering the sanctuary, the worship music tapped at my chest with its beat, the melodic voice of the lead singer pulling at the strings of my heart. I found two seats in the back, near the aisle, and stood to wait for Mom. I tried to focus on the lyrics of the song, but it was all a jumble in my head. The row was full of people I didn't really know since I didn't usually sit in the back row. I stepped into the aisle, walking slowly toward the front and scanning the seats for empty ones. I spotted the Fergusons up near the front, standing next to Rick and Trish and another couple I didn't recognize, though the man seemed familiar. Realization dawned on me. It was Chris Kirkpatrick, the new associate pastor. I thought he wouldn't be here until next month, but maybe he had come to visit before making the move. I saw a couple of empty seats on the side near Trish. I continued that way. Trish looked toward me and made eye contact. I smiled at her, hope lighting my heart. She was my friend. I waited for her to wave at me, to motion toward the seats next to her. Instead, she looked back toward the stage, not acknowledging me standing in the aisle. My heart clenched in my chest. I turned and headed to the back row just as Mom entered the sanctuary. I motioned to the two seats still there.

I sat during worship. Mom stood at first, singing in her beautiful voice. When she noticed I was sitting, she stopped singing and sat, too. Putting her arm around me, she still sang, but with the soft, tender voice of a mother soothing her child's broken heart.

Mom offered to get Renee after church, so I was able to head right toward the youth room to see Matt. Teens poured out of the room. I waited until the group slowed to a trickle and then made my way in. Matt stood at the front of the room, talking to a boy who looked about fourteen. The college couple worked on cleaning up, and Emily was talking to a parent, a serious and concerned expression on her doll-like face. I hung out in the back of the room, waiting for Matt's conversation with the boy to end.

The parent Emily was talking to turned to leave, looking upset. I didn't know the mother, but if I had to guess, she was angry. Emily spotted me and waved, then headed my way. I shot a glance at Matt, hoping he was done talking to the boy, but no such luck.

"Cassie, right?" Emily sashayed up to me, sticking out her hand in greeting.

I offered my hand in return. "Yes, Cassie."

"Oh my goodness. It's so nice to have a chance to talk to you."

"Thanks. It's umm . . . nice to get to chat with you also." I looked over her shoulder at Matt. Still talking.

"I heard you love to go hiking. You'll have to let me know where the best spots are."

That was odd. Most people who heard about me knew that I didn't like hiking for itself, but to go to waterfalls. I shoved the thought away. Small details weren't something to be concerned about. "Yes. I'm particularly fond of waterfall hikes. If you want to know the best ones to go to nearby, I can definitely send you in the right direction."

"Oh, that's so cute." She wrinkled her nose in an exaggerated smile.

Cute? What was that supposed to mean?

"You like hiking?" I asked.

"Oh, yes. I've hiked most of the California section of the Pacific Crest Trail. Now that I'm in Oregon, I'm planning on doing the Oregon and Washington sections." She tilted her head. "There are a few waterfalls to be seen along the way, I hear."

I looked her up and down. She was tiny, but looking closer, I noticed she was lean, muscular and fit. I spent most of my days sitting. My waterfall hikes were the extent of my outdoor adventures. The Pacific Crest Trail was serious business. "That's impressive."

She giggled. "Oh, thank you. Being single I have plenty of time for that. But you have a young child, right? I'm sure she keeps you busy."

I nodded, a smile spreading across my face at the thought of Renee. "Yes, I have a daughter. She's seven."

Emily lifted her shoulders and exhaled, her head once again tilted. "That is so sweet. And Matt, marrying a single mom. He's such a good guy. You are so blessed."

If skin could wrinkle and squirm and knot up all at the same time, that's what mine would've been doing at that moment. Instead, all the blood rushed to my head, having nowhere else to go, and turned my face red. "Yep. He's a keeper." I looked over her shoulder again and saw Matt was finally done with his conversation. I shot him a look that I hope said, "Help!" or better yet, "Get over here, NOW."

Emily lowered her head, and spoke out of the side of her mouth, a smile still on her face as her eyes twinkled. "Talk about an eligible bachelor. Let me tell you, men like him are hard to find. I've looked." She tittered and waved her hand, apparently amused.

"Hi, Cassie."

"Oh hey, we were just talking about you." Emily turned and put her hand on Matt's arm. My hands clenched into fists. How much more would Matt be disqualified from pastoral jobs here if I punched a woman in the face? Especially the daughter of another pastor?

"Really? And what were you all saying?" He asked, a hint of playfulness in his voice.

Was he really that oblivious to Emily's ploys? I shot him another look, but it apparently went right over his head because he didn't flinch.

"We were just talking about what a great guy you are." I spoke up, my voice sounding strangely mechanical.

Emily giggled. "Yes, we sure were." She brushed her hair back with her hand. "Oh, I better catch up with my dad and mom. They are wanting to go to lunch." Emily turned to me with a fake smile. "It was so nice to talk to you, Cassie."

Turning back to Matt, she said. "I had such a good time with you at youth group today. You really minister to these young people." She put her hand on her heart. "It is so refreshing."

She sauntered out of the room.

Matt looked at me, a half grin on his face. "She can be quite . . . expressive."

I rolled my eyes. "I think she likes you."

Matt shook his head and laughed. "Cassie, you're funny."

"I'm serious."

He stopped laughing and lifted his eyebrows, stepping closer, he leaned in. "You're not really serious, are you?"

I glanced around the room. The helpers were still cleaning up. This wasn't the place or time for a long or intimate conversation. "I'll talk to you about it later." To me my voice sounded barely audible over the pounding in my chest.

Matt's eyes widened. "You don't have to raise your voice." He cleared his throat and stood back. "I'll call you tonight."

What? Tonight? "You're not coming over later?" Weekends were about the only time we saw each other anymore.

He shook his head. "I can't. The leadership is meeting later this afternoon. Chris decided to come for a visit, so we are having a last-minute meet and greet."

I studied Matt's face. Though he remained stoic, I couldn't help but wonder how hard that meeting would be for him. "I'm sorry. That's a lot for a Sunday."

"I know. Higher ups think it's what is needed right now." Matt's voice was flat, devoid of emotion.

Higher ups. Probably led by the Fergusons.

"Could you come over afterward?"

"It'll be a long day." He lowered his head, touching his forehead to mine. "Spend time with Renee. She needs you right now. We'll talk later."

I turned to leave. He was right. Renee needed me now.

What Matt didn't seem to realize was, I needed *him*.

Chapter Twenty-Six

Sharon

Cassie's obvious distress during worship, along with her mood after talking to Matt, kept me from telling her about what I heard in the restroom after service. She didn't need another thorn in her side.

The entire situation was almost laughable. Like something you'd see in a movie. Samantha talked to me before service about the Higher Focus group, and how she planned on mentioning to Myrtle, again, the importance of getting the word out to the community. I'd agreed that was a good idea, though it made me anxious. Not because I didn't want more people to come, but because I wasn't sure how long my role with the group would last.

After we were dismissed from the church service, and before picking up Rence, I needed to use the restroom. The main restroom was full, but because I was involved in church behind the scenes, I knew there was another restroom down the hall from the kids' church entrance. It was in its own alcove of the building with small signage, and primarily used by staff and others who knew it existed. It was also not brightly lit.

The restroom was empty when I entered and I went to the last stall, a habit of mine. As I sat on the commode, I heard women enter. I recognized Samantha's voice. "There's a need in the community for Higher Focus, but no one outside the church knows about it. Maybe we could put a small ad in the newspaper or on social media. I could even reach out to some Christian counselors I know. If we have some fliers about the group made, we could give them out."

Samantha must be talking to Myrtle now about the group. Someone entered the stall one down from mine. Wherever they were, they didn't see my feet. I should've coughed or flushed or done something to make my presence known, but I found myself breathing quietly instead.

"From what I understand, there are plenty of AA meetings out there for addicts, and a couple of other churches in town do a different recovery program. I don't think we need to put time, energy, or finances into reaching out beyond the church." Myrtle's voice was decisive and cold.

Guilt, anger, and shame mixed in my chest, making me freeze. I should've made my presence known. Now it felt too late.

"We don't know about that. There could be people in AA who long for something more. Ones that don't have a church home. This group is a great way to reach them." A flush came from one of the stalls, followed shortly afterward by the sound of the water from the sink.

Another flush. Footsteps. "Perhaps, but I'm not sure we have the right leadership in our group to reach those people in an effective, Godly way."

I bit my bottom lip as the water faucet was turned off.

"What do you mean by that?"

Myrtle gave a little, dry laugh, followed by a sigh. "Frank seems like a good guy. Solid. Walked with the Lord for some time now. But Sharon . . . I don't know about her."

"What do you mean, you don't know about Sharon?" Though I couldn't see Samantha's face, by the tone of her voice I could imagine her expression. Probably frowning, jaw tight.

"Oh, you know, I just see that her walk with the Lord is still in its infancy. She has a lot of growing to do. She doesn't seem to have much in the form of a higher education, judging by the way she speaks and dresses." I heard a paper towel being pulled from the holder.

"I've known Sharon for a while. I don't know if you've heard about our history, but I assure you, God has changed her mightily. Her growth is inspiring."

"Perhaps, but I haven't seen that, personally. Regardless, there are other churches out there better equipped to serve addicts and their issues."

The way Myrtle said the way 'issues' sounded like she was choking on the s's, or she was trying not to sneeze.

"What about those with addiction issues that are already a part of our church? What message does not reaching out send to them?" Samantha didn't back down.

"Well," Myrtle cleared her throat, obviously uncomfortable under the scrutiny, "I honestly don't think there's a real need in our congregation. The ones who do have that need may find this isn't the church for them."

"Hmm. Sounds to me like you need to reread The Great Commission."

Footsteps echoed in the small room, on the way to the door.

"I'm perfectly aware of what the Bible says!" Myrtle hissed. The door opened and their voices faded as it shut behind them.

My hands were shaking when I left the restroom. Whether it was nerves or anger, or both, I wasn't sure. I imagined I felt much like Cassie as I walked out of that restroom. Judged. Deemed unworthy, inadequate, lacking. The difference between my daughter and I was I had a good twenty plus years of dealing with all kinds of people. Some were the ugliest, meanest ones you could come across. I knew a lie spun as a truth when I heard one. My insides were a simmering volcano ready to erupt at the audacity of Myrtle Ferguson. Luckily, seeing Renee lifted my spirits, and by the time I saw Cassie I was able to pretend everything was okay.

Which was good because I could tell Cassie was anything but okay.

After we were home, fed, and had Renee down for a Sunday nap, Cassie told me everything she'd witnessed and experienced at church that morning. The blood in my veins turned to lava, seeing my daughter's pain. The restroom incident was bad enough, and after hearing what Cassie had endured, I decided to wait to share my tidbit with her. I needed to talk to someone who could give me advice.

I thought about calling Samantha, but that would require me admitting I eavesdropped, though mostly unintentionally. It was a confession I should make, but not yet. I had a whole new level of respect for Samantha after listening to her defend Higher Focus—and me—in the restroom. It took courage to stand up to Myrtle and call her out. It took another level of integrity and mission-minded purpose to defend a woman who had an affair with your previous husband.

The only other person that came to mind was Frank. He had a stake in the success of our group, plus he had experience with other churches.

Wanting to make sure I had privacy, I went for a drive and called while parked in the lot of the supermarket down the road. He picked up on the second ring.

"Hi, Sharon. Good to hear from you."

"Do you have a minute to talk? It's about the Higher Focus group."

"You're always all business." There was a smile in the tone of his voice, but his comment made me feel a little guilty.

"Sorry. How are you? Having a good Sunday?" I wanted to hit myself on the head for doing last minute pleasantries and not being more friendly to begin with.

Frank chuckled. "I'm fine. It's a nice day. Relaxing. What

do you want to talk about? You sound stressed."

"Yeah, well, I guess I am stressed." I took a deep breath and then told him about the overheard bathroom conversation. "I'm not sure what to do. And when I see Myrtle again, I'm not sure I can hold my tongue."

"Can't say that I blame you for feeling that way."

At least he was understanding, but did he have any solutions? "What should we do? We have to do something, right?" I rubbed my temple with my spare hand. Tiny rain drops fell on the windshield of my car as a black cloud darkened the sky.

A sound somewhere between a sigh and grunt came from Frank's side of the line. "I've been praying about this a lot since we had coffee at Denny's." I'd been praying too, but not just about the group. There was the custody issue with Renee filling my prayer time. Second to that were my confused feelings for Johnny. Praying about the group hadn't been at the top of my list. "Yeah, me too, but not enough."

"I don't think God keeps a score card of performance." Again, there was the hint of a smile in his voice. "But praying has given me some thoughts. Some convictions even."

"I'm listening."

"What is happening in the leadership isn't healthy. It probably is having a direct impact on our group, among other things. I think it's time I talked to Pastor Reynolds directly about my concerns. Based on what you've told me, I'm going to ask Samantha to accompany me for that conversation."

Satisfaction and thankfulness flowed over me. What a relief to have someone other than myself stand up and take notice. I was certain Samantha would be willing to go to Pastor Reynolds and discuss the situation. Hopefully once that happened, something could be done about the Fergusons and their effect on the church. "That's great to hear, Frank. I don't like the direction this church is going. You should hear what Cassie experienced today." The rain was coming down harder, creating a soothing but almost-too-loud hum in the background.

"I'm sorry she's going through that. Did it involve the Fergusons?"

"The youngest of them. Their daughter."

Frank clicked his tongue. "I guess the apple doesn't fall far from the tree. Hopefully once the tree realizes the effect they are having, all attitudes and outlooks can be adjusted." He didn't ask for details. I supposed that was wise. It didn't have to do with him and could be considered gossip.

"You're going to contact Samantha?"

"Yes, I'll probably text her tomorrow."

I scratched behind my ear, uncertainty nibbling at my insides. "I guess you'll have to tell her about the bathroom incident."

"I don't have to say anything about that, but you probably should."

"Yeah, I know." I sighed. "Talk to you later, Frank. Good night."

After hanging up, I tapped my hands on the steering wheel. Might as well get it over with. I shot Samantha a short text, getting right to the point. I was in the restroom stall during her conversation with Myrtle that morning. Sorry I didn't make myself known. I told her I shared what I heard with Frank because I felt he needed to know. Lastly, I thanked her for sticking up for the group. Samantha responded almost immediately.

Oh, my friend, I knew you were.

She ended her text with a wink-face emoticon.

My heart skipped a beat.

You knew? You didn't say anything.

In my 55 years on this earth, I've learned two things as a

woman. 1. Only talk in public places about things you are comfortable with the public hearing and 2. Always look for other pairs of feet when in a public restroom.

I laughed out loud at Samantha's second line of wisdom. But Myrtle didn't know?

I'm assuming not. But I didn't ask her. By the time she said things she shouldn't have said, it was too late to point it out. I was going to reach out to you to make sure you were ok, but thought it best for you to contact me first. I know you are strong.

The tension in my shoulders eased. Samantha wouldn't be surprised by Frank's reaching out to her tomorrow. Myrtle apparently was unaware of me being in the restroom. Part of me felt guilty about that, like it was still eavesdropping.

I pecked out another text to Samantha.

I still feel deceptive. Myrtle didn't know I was there.

Out of the abundance of the heart the mouth speaks. Myrtle made her heart known. God always reveals the heart, one way or the other. Maybe you should have made your presence obvious, but the bigger issue is Myrtle needs to be held accountable for her words and actions.

Accountability. It was a big part of recovery. So was grace. I didn't know how the Ferguson situation would end up. Who was accountable for what, and where grace should be given. The one thing I did know was I would have to trust God had the answers.

Chapter Twenty-Seven

THE CLOUDS WERE FULL AND DARKENING, blocking any chance of the sun breaking through. I knew I needed to pray before getting out of my car and walking into the Family Justice Center to attend my mediation appointment. Would God hear my prayers? It'd been a long time since I doubted His love for me, but between Matt being turned down for the associate pastor position, and then what happened Sunday at church, doubt had crept into my faith, chipping away at everything I thought was solid and impenetrable. Mom had waited until Monday to tell me about what she overhead in the restroom, giving me time to recover from the blows. Sadly, her story didn't surprise me. It was yet another chip in the crumbling dream I held for my life and future.

I lowered my head against the steering wheel. I'd already prayed about this day more times than I could count. What else was there to say? I searched my heart, remembering all the times God had answered my prayers, all the ways He had taken care of me and Renee. "Lord, you know what's best for Renee. That's my prayer. That your will, your perfect will for her life, would be done today. Or, at least, the seed would be planted for it to be accomplished. I'm leaving this all in your hands." I wiped a tear from my eye.

When I opened my car door, the cool air had a bite to it, making me shiver. I looked up at the sky. It might rain any moment. I hoped the weather wasn't a sign of how today would go.

The front of the two story, white building containing the mediation center was all windows with white columns, creating a look that was almost inviting, and yet imposing at the same time. I fingered the cross necklace I'd worn, one that had belonged to Nannie, as I walked in the front doors. As I had in the beginning of this custody battle, I felt comforted by knowing she had prayed, and by her faith that everything would work out. She was no longer here to pray for me or Renee. Someone had once told me that prayers, like God, were timeless. I was counting on that being true.

After checking in with the receptionist, I was shown to a waiting area outside the room where I'd be meeting with the mediator and Derrick. I breathed easier seeing Derrick had not yet arrived. Maybe he wouldn't show at all. Not keeping the appointment wouldn't be out of character for him and would simplify things immensely.

"Ms. Peterson?" A short, bearded man approached me, his hand held out in greeting.

I stood and reached for his hand. "Yes."

"I'm Presley Johnson, I'll be facilitating your mediation today." He scanned the room with pale brown eyes. "It doesn't look like Mr. Peterson is here yet."

"Nope, not yet." I couldn't hide the happiness in my voice.

"Well," Presley studied his watch. "We will give him a few moments."

Great. I sat back down and took out my phone as a distraction. Matt had texted me. I touched on the notification. **Praying**, he wrote. **Let me know as soon as you can how things go.** The simple text brought a smile to my face. He had called me just before I drove here, and then sent this text, knowing I'd probably be checking my phone before going in the mediation room. His devotion was clear. Why had I let Emily's flirtation get to me? When I'd talked to Matt about her extra friendliness with him, he had a good laugh. "You have nothing to worry about. I'm not an eligible bachelor. I'm yours."

I heard a cough and looked up from my phone. Derrick

stood in the waiting area, hands in the pockets of jeans. Jeans, not trousers. He also wore a half-zipped Oregon Duck hoodie instead of a dress shirt or sweater. He was certainly dressed casually, and a different style than I knew him to wear.

What else about him had changed?

Presley introduced himself to Derrick, and then called us both into the mediation room. I walked into the room first, avoiding eye contact with Derrick. My heart was running at jack-rabbit speed. I breathed slowly through my nose, willing it to slow down. Would my fear of my ex-husband ever subside?

Derrick and I sat opposite each other. No table between us. The mediator sat to the side, a small table with a laptop next to him. He introduced himself again, elaborating on his experience, and then explained the process of mediation. Today's appointment would last up to ninety minutes. If we didn't reach an agreement today, we could have up to two more meetings, but only if we both agreed it would be helpful.

Derrick and I both affirmed our understanding of the rules. As we sat there, I garnered the courage to look directly at Derrick, but his gaze was averted, seemingly focused on Presley's laptop, though the screen was turned in such a way that neither of us could see it. Derrick had aged since I last saw him. New lines accentuated his eyes and mouth. His hair was a darker blonde and cut closer to the scalp. He looked healthier, something about him had more perkiness, and he seemed more relaxed. Maybe he truly had quit drinking.

"Looking over both of your court documents, there is obviously a great discrepancy how you each believe parenting time should be divided for Renee." Presley looked back and forth between us. "Our goal is to come to a compromise between the two. That means each of you will give up something you want."

"Ms. Peterson, let's start with you. What parts of your proposal are most important to keep?"

I couldn't imagine giving up anything, yet I knew that wasn't realistic. The prayer I'd spoken in my car came back to me, guiding my words. "The most important thing to me is what is best for Renee. I've seen how she reacts when she reads a letter from her dad or talks to him. I heard from my mom how she reacted when she saw him at the park." I could feel Derrick's eyes on me, but I focused on Presley. "My concern is that because of the amount of time that has passed since she last was alone with her father, and because of things that happened when he was around, she needs some kind of slow re-introduction process. Something that takes her needs and wishes into account."

Presley nodded to me, then turned to Derrick. "What about you Mr. Peterson. What is the most important element in your proposed parenting time?"

Derrick shifted in his seat and cleared his throat. Instead of looking at Presley, his moss green eyes fell directly on me. My pulse, which had finally slowed to something less than heart attack speed, quickened. There was no apparent hate or malice in Derrick's eyes. They didn't even look calculating, though there was something about them that reminded me of how he behaved whenever he was up against a problem he couldn't quite figure out. "I just want to see my daughter. It's hard to reconnect over the phone, or with someone else standing there watching your every interaction."

Presley typed something into his laptop. "Okay, so you both can agree there should be some kind of reunification, but you don't agree with what that should look like."

Wasn't that obvious from our court documents? I leaned back in my seat, wondering how long this ordeal would take. There was no way Derrick and I would reach a resolution.

"You're asking for a gradual reintroduction." Presley

scanned something on his laptop, and then turned his focus to me, mouth set in a frown. "It looks like you are asking for supervised time once per week for six months, and then unsupervised daytime only visits for six months after that, before moving into any kind of overnight visit."

I could tell by the tone in his voice Presley thought my request was unreasonable. My attorney had said I was unlikely to be granted the plan we'd proposed, but he said we might as well shoot for the stars and see where we landed. I touched the cross necklace around my neck, thinking of Nannie, remembering my prayer in the car. "I want what's best for Renee. Whatever happens needs to be very gradual, so she has time to adjust."

I expected a snarky remark from Derrick, or a derisive laugh. Instead, his voice came softly across the six feet between us. "I understand and I'm willing to start out slow."

He was willing to compromise. I felt my chin drop when I looked at Derrick. Something that might have been concern showed on his face, but I couldn't believe it.

Presley nodded, looking pleased. He turned to Derrick. "What kind of gradual plan seems doable to you?"

Derrick shrugged one shoulder. "I'm not an expert in child psychology, so I don't know. But Renee is still really young, and I think she can adjust quickly." He tilted his head, his eyes falling on me. "I'd like her to meet her little brother while he's still . . . little. It doesn't seem fair to keep them apart."

Guilt poked at my chest. I hadn't really considered that I was keeping Renee from having a relationship with her younger brother. But I had to know she was safe, and that the reunification wasn't mentally harmful for her.

"I'm concerned for Renee's mental health in all of this. I don't want any more trauma for her." I looked at the floor. "I'm no expert either, I just know what I see in my daughter."

Presley spoke softly, "You both agree you're not experts and seem open to suggestions. Where could we go from there?"

An idea popped into my mind. I remembered when Brian had spoken to an expert divorce attorney on my behalf during the initial court case. That attorney had suggested Renee see a child psychologist. With Derrick getting arrested, the initial court case had been a slam dunk, and there was no need for an expert witness. Which was good, because I couldn't afford one. I had good health insurance now, and money in the bank. Also, if Derrick wanted this to work, he should be willing to financially invest in it. "What if we have a counselor oversee the reunification?" I asked.

Presley lifted an eyebrow, but gave a short nod, then turned to Derrick. "What do you think about that?"

Derrick studied me, his gaze unrelenting. My heart pounded in my throat. I couldn't read his expression, but it seemed he was thinking hard. Calculating. "I'm willing to do that, but it has to be a counselor we both agree to."

He was willing to relent from his stated plan? I blinked several times, shocked.

"What do you think about that?" Presley asked me.

"I . . . umm . . ." I searched for words. There had to be a catch to Derrick's proposal. He was never this accommodating. "How would we come to an agreement for a counselor? And how the parenting time starts out?"

Presley stroked his chin. "Good question. I would say you both would evaluate counselors and then present each other with your top three picks. As far as how the time starts out, that is something you two need to come to an agreement on, and perhaps be willing to let the counselor re-evaluate."

I stared at the floor, but in my head, I was praying. *Lord, what do I do? What do I do?*

An image flashed in my mind, the remembrance of a

dream I had during the scariest time of my divorce from Derrick. Grandpa ahead of me on the trail, calling my name against the wind. I had to keep my eyes on him and keep moving forward. Don't look down. Don't doubt.

"I'm good with that." I inhaled slowly, drawing out the courage I needed. "I'm willing to work on coming up with three counselors I'm okay with. What if we don't both agree on one?" Presley smiled. "You have two more mediation sessions."

That's right. "All right." I forced myself to look at Derrick. "I'm willing to offer my suggestions for a counselor. I can email those to you over the next few days. As far as time goes, I think it would be ideal if the first meetings with Renee were with the counselor, assuming he or she is willing to do that." I turned to the mediator, looking for guidance.

Presley nodded. "I've heard of that happening in similar situations."

Derrick shifted in his seat again, stared out the window. He didn't look at me or Presley when he spoke. "Fine, Cassie. We'll meet with the counselor the first time or two. Then we do what he or she says."

Presley typed on his keyboard. "Let's state the number of times for the mediation agreement. Does two sound good to both of you?"

My stomach turned. It didn't sound good to me at all, but Derrick had given in, agreeing to something I would have never thought he'd agree to. It was only reasonable that I agree to the two supervised-by-the-counselor visits. "Yes." I replied, my voice sounding like a dying frog.

Derrick gave me a sideways grin, a familiar glimmer in his eyes. "Works for me."

My chest tightened. What was that look for? Did he have something up his sleeve? "I need my attorney to look over the mediation agreement before I sign it."

Presley nodded. "Of course." He turned to Derrick. "And

what about you Mr. Peterson. I don't see that you have an attorney of record."

Derrick smiled. "I'm representing myself. For now." He looked at me, the glimmer animating his green eyes. "Hopefully, mediation keeps us out of court, and I won't need one. They are expensive, aren't they, Cassie?"

My shoulders tightened. He knew how much this was costing me, and it gave him pleasure. Some things would never change. I didn't respond to his remark, and instead asked Presley. "How long until the agreement is ready for review?"

"A couple of business days." He closed his laptop.

It was time for me to get to work finding the best counselor in Eugene.

Chapter Twenty-Eight

Sharon

I WRINKLED MY NOSE AT THE smell of over-bleached laundry. I'd never get used to that aroma.

"My daughter sees a counselor. I can ask her for the phone number." Janice lifted the set of sheets off the laundry cart and waddled to the bed with the heavy load in her arms.

I walked to the other side of the bed to help. The housekeeper who was supposed to work with Janice today had called in sick and I hadn't been able to find anyone else to fill the spot.

"Her attorney gave her some suggestions, from what I understand." I grabbed the end of the bottom sheet and tucked it under the bed. "I still can't believe they agreed to something on the *first* mediation appointment, and it looks like they are staying out of court."

Janice walked up to the head of the bed, sheet in hand. "That must be a relief. Is she happy?"

I couldn't say Cassie was happy. She was still unsure how the entire thing would roll out and how Renee would react. Even Matt seemed somber about the entire situation. It was obvious the atmosphere at church was still weighing on them both, snatching the happy out of their lives. "She's cautiously optimistic, I think."

"Makes sense."

We finished cleaning, then headed for the breakroom. "How's that recovery group at your church going? You haven't talked about that much lately."

Sometimes Janice felt more like my counselor than a coworker or friend. Then again, maybe that's what I needed in a confidant. I hadn't told her yet about what I'd overhead in the restroom at church. Frank and Samantha were meeting with Pastor Reynolds today. I'd prayed about it and knew my future participation in the group would depend on the outcome of the meeting. "It's going. I'm not sure I'll do it again, once we are done with this round."

"Really? Why?"

We reached the breakroom. Janice made a beeline for the vending machine. I took my home packed lunch out of the fridge. Something about hearing Janice hit the buttons on the machine made me crave a Diet Coke. I'd cut down, way down, on the beverage, finding that something about my addiction seemed to be mentally tied to the bubbly concoction.

"Long story." Our lunch break wasn't enough time to go into the details, and I could share more once I knew what I was going to do. I pulled a piece of string cheese out of my lunch sack and peeled off the plastic wrapper, then took a bite. "Let's just say it's not what I thought it would be, so I'm debating whether I will continue with it."

Janice returned from the vending machine with a bag of chips, a Snickers, and a Mountain Dew. She plopped down in a chair. "I was almost certain something would spark between you and Frank, but it didn't take me long to change my mind." She still had tiny droplets of perspiration on her forehead, and she dabbed at them with the back of her other hand.

I put my string cheese down. "Do tell. What made you change your mind?"

Janice's dark eyebrows arched as she tilted her head. "You are obviously still in love with Johnny."

I felt heat run up my neck. "What makes you say that? I hardly even mention him."

"It's more than what you say, it's what you *don't* say." Janice pursed her lips.

I picked the cheese back up. "I have no idea what you're

talking about."

"I've heard you talk about Frank, but never in a romantic way, even though you've gotten together with him a couple of times, and spend a lot of time with him at the church."

"So? That doesn't mean I'm still in love with Johnny."

Janice opened her bag of chips. "Yeah, except every time I ask you about Johnny, you either seem irritated or look like a sad puppy dog. I can't even count how many times I've seen you checking his Facebook page on your phone."

The heat in my neck reached my ears. I'd been looking at Johnny's Facebook page the day before, in the breakroom, because I hadn't heard from him since he said he was going to church with his neighbor. His angelic, sweet, home-cooking female neighbor. The only new thing on his page was a picture of an apple in a tree, with the line, "Exciting things to come." I could only guess what that meant.

"Yeah, well, call me curious. That doesn't mean I'm in love with him." I took a ham sandwich out of my lunchbox, though my appetite was waning.

Janice giggled. "You don't have anything to hide with me, girlfriend. I'm not judging the torch you're carrying." She wiped her hands together, cleaning them of chip crumbs. "I'm just wondering why you don't do something about it."

"There's nothing to do." I forced myself to take a bite of the sandwich, which stuck to the roof of my dry mouth. I reached for my water and took a long swig. "It looks like he's interested in someone else."

Janice's brow wrinkled. "Really?"

"Yep, some neighbor lady's been cooking for him."

"So you're saying the guy who wanted you to run away with him last year, *and* who stayed in love with you for well over a decade even though he didn't see you, has been won over by a casserole?"

When put that way, it did sound ridiculous. "People

change." I shrugged a shoulder, hoping to appear nonchalant. "Seems he's looking at taking over the family land and settling here for good. He wouldn't have done that before. And whoever this lady is, she got him to go to church. That's another surprise."

"Interesting." Janice ripped open the wrapper of the Snickers bar. "If it wasn't for this other woman, I'd say God was setting everything up for you and Johnny to live happily ever after."

Though I knew Janice didn't mean any harm, her words stung. There was no happily-ever-after for me, but I was doing my best to be happy for Johnny. She was right about Frank, though. Spending time with him was enjoyable, mostly, and he was a good friend, but I didn't have any truly romantic feelings toward him. The realization settled on me like a thorned weight. Yep, no romantic tales of love for this middle-aged woman. I checked the time on my phone. "We need to hurry up and eat and get back at it."

Janice nodded. Her mouth was full, but she managed to say. "Yes, boss." She swallowed. "You know, maybe this whole thing with Johnny and the mystery woman had to happen to clear the way for you to fall in love with Frank." She shrugged. "It's a possibility."

I rolled my eyes. "I think you need a new hobby. My love life—or lack of—is taking up way too much real estate in your head."

Janice belly laughed, covering her mouth. "Maybe you're right. But I'm also eager to see my friend ride off into the sunset with her prince charming." She grinned. "Call me a romantic."

"*Hopeless* romantic." I replied, closing my lunch bag.

My break room conversation with Janice was still bouncing

around in my head when Frank called later that night, making me feel guarded when I answered the phone.

"How has your day been?" Frank said. He sounded tired.

"You know, another day, another dollar." I was in the living room, watching a show with Cassie and Renee. "Just a minute, Frank," I gave Cassie a look to let her know I was excusing myself, and then headed to my room so we could talk in private. "How are you? How'd the meeting go?" I closed my door and sat on my bed.

"Not as well as I hoped." Frank sighed. "It was a little discouraging."

My heart dropped to my stomach. I felt bad for Frank. Higher Focus was his passion. Yet, sadly, hearing the meeting hadn't gone well didn't surprise me. Still, I had hoped. "What happened?"

"Samantha and I both talked about the lack of advertising for the group, and Samantha brought up her conversation with Myrtle in the restroom. Pastor Reynolds listened, and empathized, but then he basically excused everything she had done."

"What excuse could he possibly give for her behavior?"

"Well, for the promotion stuff, he said she was still getting used to the systems we have and learning the ropes and such. He pointed out that she's doing that in a volunteer capacity."

"But other people were doing those things before: did they just disappear, or did she run them off?" I tried to think if I knew who oversaw or volunteered for those things before Myrtle stepped in, but with the size of the church, I didn't know everyone and what they did. There were many who were still strangers to me. People I'd barely recognize if I passed them on the street.

"From what he said, there was a big decline in volunteers after the incident with the Wescott's. Attendance in general went down. Giving is still down." Frank's voice lowered a notch when he talked about giving.

Cassie and I had both noticed the decline in attendance, though things seemed to be picking up in the last couple of weeks. Matt had obviously been overworked and short on volunteers, according to Cassie. I thought of my daughter and how torn she was, wanting to help but not having time. Seeing Emily, the Ferguson's daughter, working side-by-side with Matt and seeming to flirt with him didn't sit well, either. I wondered if Ben Wescott realized the fallout that would happen to people beyond his own family when he had an affair? The domino effect one person's actions could cause to others. If having an affair was anything like being an alcoholic, I'd bet he didn't how far-reaching his actions could be.

I grunted, frustrated by the entire scenario. "Okay, so I guess we can kind of understand why Myrtle wouldn't have been able to get things in the bulletin in time and all of that, and I did see the meeting listed the last time I checked the bulletin, so I guess we can lay that to rest." I sighed. Even though the Higher Focus meeting was now advertised, attendance was still low. No doubt it didn't help that the course was well underway. "What about what Myrtle said to Samantha?"

"He was a little more unsure when that was brought up." Frank gave a short laugh. "The look on his face said he was unhappy, but not surprised."

"What did he say? Is he going to speak with her?"

"Well, yes. But he also said that she probably meant well. She understands the church's resources are being stretched and is only trying to be a good steward."

I looked at the ceiling, counting to three in my head to keep my anger from reaching a boiling point. "And what she said about me? Does he have an excuse for that, too?"

Frank sighed but didn't speak for a moment. "He said she

shouldn't have shared those thoughts with Samantha in the way she did. He's going to meet with Samantha and Myrtle to discuss it."

What did that mean? She shouldn't share those thoughts *in that way*? Did he think her ideas about me were valid? I chewed on my lip, trying to calm my own thoughts into words that didn't contain expletives.

"I don't think I can continue co-leading this group, if that's the kind of support we are going to get from leadership."

Silence came from the other end of the line. I began to wonder if Frank had heard me, or if the line was dead. Or if maybe I should've held my tongue, for now, and given the situation more thought.

"I'm not sure I can, either, Sharon." Frank replied, a heavy sadness accentuating each word.

Poor Frank. But no one had brought his abilities into question. Though support wasn't great at the church right now, the group still had a fighting chance. "I don't think you should give it up. You said you were called to do it. That hasn't changed, has it?"

"I know I'm called to lead a Higher Focus group, yes. I'm just starting to doubt whether I'm called to do so at Cascade Christian Church."

"Then what are you going to do?"

"That remains to be seen." Frank's voice was deep, thoughtful. "It's going to take some prayer."

I hung up the phone. My room felt smaller, darker. This whole situation put a damper on any hopeful thought that formed in my mind. Picking up my guitar, I fingered the strings, trying to find the chords to a song that had not yet been written.

Chapter Twenty-Nine

Cassie

AFTER REVIEWING THE MEDIATION AGREEMENT BETWEEN Derrick and me, my attorney said he was cautiously optimistic we would stay out of court. He gave me the names of a couple of counselors he knew and after I researched them and checked my health insurance, I had him forward those to Derrick.

Derrick presented his own list of counselors, none of which matched the ones I had picked. "Do we have to go back to mediation?" I asked my attorney, Zane, dreading the idea of facing Derrick again.

"Perhaps not. I'll draft him a letter and ask if he's willing to go with any of the counselors on our list. I'm not familiar with any of the ones he suggested, and quite frankly, two of the three don't even have the kind of experience I'd want for this case. You never know—he might say yes to one of ours."

I didn't hold on to hope for that. Derrick had never been cooperative. He always insisted on his way, no matter the cost to anyone else. Which was why I was shocked to the point of laughter when Zane called a few days later to tell me Derrick had agreed to one of the counselors on our list.

"What do I do now?" I asked Zane.

"Call her and ask if she's willing to take this on. If she's not, we'll go to the next one on the list."

And so the process had begun. I was almost in a daze by how quickly and easily everything fell into place. Because time was of the essence in our case, the counselor, a sweet, older woman with a lifetime of experience, made the initial appointment for only two weeks out. She said she'd begin by meeting with me and Derrick individually to discuss our concerns, and then schedule the first supervised meeting with Derrick and Renee. From there she would assess if she should see either of them individually before continuing.

Once everything was set to go, it was time to tell Renee. After praying about it, I decided it would be best to have Matt with me when I told her. He was the one she saw as her father figure, even if he wasn't yet, at least officially. "If you assure her everything is okay, and that you're still there for her, I think it'll be easier for her to accept."

He'd agreed to come over after I got home from work that Tuesday night. "We all have a lot at stake in this," he said.

That night, while we ate dinner, Matt talked about the youth group event scheduled for the following evening. "We rented a trampoline park. It's a great back-to-school event to generate excitement about youth group and to get kids to invite their friends."

Mom was quiet during dinner. I figured she was worried about Renee and how she'd react to the news about Derrick. "Reel them in." She responded when Matt talked about the youth event, her mouth half full of fried chicken.

I raised an eyebrow at her, unable to tell if her remark was genuine or sarcastic. I decided to let the comment slip into oblivion. "I wish I could help," I told Matt, "but my workload for the term is really amping up."

Matt wiped his mouth with a napkin. "I wish you could, too. Are you sure you can't get away?"

I stared at my half-empty plate, feeling guilty. Taking the extra time tonight with Renee would already put me behind, so I had a valid excuse for not going tomorrow. What I didn't want to admit to Matt was that the idea of crossing paths with Emily was an extra deterrent. "Sorry, maybe I can be available for the next event."

Matt frowned, obviously disappointed. "I understand." He studied me with his blue eyes as if he was looking for more than what he could see on the surface. "Hopefully next time works out."

After dinner, Mom went to the store, and Matt and I took Renee to the living room. Renee was happy to have Matt over, and too excited to notice we were both on edge about the conversation ahead.

We sat on the well-worn couch, the blank screen of the television across from us. Renee sat between me and Matt but was barely able to sit still. "Are we going to watch a show?" she asked.

"Not yet, maybe in a minute." I looked at Matt, seeking courage and strength. In the dim light of the living room, he looked older. Bags had started forming under his eyes, which looked red and strained, probably from lack of sleep. He nodded at me, his mouth in a straight line.

"Renee, we need to talk to you about something." I tried to add enthusiasm to my voice.

Renee's head bobbled between me and Matt. "Is it about my flower girl dress?"

I smiled, the mention of her dress bringing a bittersweetness to my heart that I couldn't quite put words to. "No, remember, we are waiting until closer to the wedding date for that to make sure we get the right size. You're growing fast."

Renee formed her mouth into a large "O". "Oh, yeah."

I returned my gaze to Matt, hoping he would jump in, even though I knew him doing so wasn't fair or even his place, at least not yet. His gaze was averted to the blank television. A cold wave shot down my spine, bringing with it a sense of foreboding. I cleared my throat, willing the sense of doom away. "It's about your daddy, Renee."

"Oh." She scooted her bottom to the edge of the couch and focused on the area rug at her feet, digging her toes into its thick fabric.

I put my hand on her shoulder. "Your dad wants to see you again"—Renee's shoulder tightened under my hand—"and I know that sounds kind of scary, maybe, but the good thing is there's going to be a nice lady named Elizabeth who will be there with you when you see him. You won't be alone with him."

Renee turned to me. 'Why can't you be there?" Her eyes narrowed.

"I wish I could be, Sugar Bug, but that's not the way this works." I frantically tried to think of a comparison, something I should have thought of sooner. "It's kind of like when you go to school. Your teacher is there, but I'm not."

Renee's head jerked to Matt. "Can you be there?"

Poor Renee. I wondered if my example had made her think that since Matt was a youth pastor, he'd be allowed?

Matt's focus turned from the blank television screen to Renee. "Sorry, kiddo. This is something I can't go to, either." He tapped her on the nose with his finger. "But I'll be praying for you, and I'll be here for you to talk to afterward, if you like."

Renee kept looking at Matt. I couldn't see her face, but I could tell by the sadness in Matt's eyes that she wasn't looking happy.

She turned back to me. "Do I have to talk to him?"

That was a tough question to answer. Mine and Derrick's meeting with the counselor was the following week, just two days before Derrick and Renee's appointment. I didn't know exactly how the visit would go. "I don't know, but I do know that the nice lady, Elizabeth, wants you to be comfortable. If you don't want to talk, you can let her know."

Renee turned to me, her fearful emerald eyes filling with tears. "When do I have to go?"

My heart felt like it was being clawed by an angry cat. I knew I had to trust God with Renee but seeing the fear in her eyes was almost more than I could bear. I tried to find comfort in knowing she would have another adult there, someone trained to notice her distress and to intercede. It was still so hard. *Why do we have to keep going down these difficult paths, God? When do things get easy?* The image of Grandpa leading the horse on the trail popped up in my head again, easing the anxiety in my soul. I didn't understand. Not yet. Perhaps, someday, I would.

"It will be next Thursday. A little over a week from now."

Matt put his hand on Renee's other shoulder. "Maybe, if it's okay with your mom." He made eye contact with me, the slightest of grins lighting his face. "We can celebrate how brave you are by going out for ice cream that evening."

I nodded in agreement. "Yes, I think we could definitely do that."

Renee wiped a tear from her face, shaking her head. "Not even mint chocolate chip will make me happy after that."

Though my heart hurt, I had to bite the inside of my cheek to keep from laughing at her response. From the glimmer in Matt's eyes, I gathered he felt the same. I leaned forward and kissed the top of Renee's head. "Chocolate chip mint ice cream might not make everything better, but it won't hurt. Plus, it means we all three get to be together. That's always something to look forward to."

Matt nodded in agreement, but again turned his focus to the television with nothing on it. "Yes, we can look forward to that." His voice was too soft, hesitant.

My heart clenched in my chest and this time it had nothing to do with Renee.

Guilt and unease plagued me Wednesday as I tried to study. Matt needed extra help and I wasn't there. Then the look on his face when I talked about all three of us being together next

Thursday as a good thing. All of that coming on the heels of his yet unsuccessful search for a job at another church. The only ones Matt had found so far were out of town, most out of the state. With it looking like Derrick and I would soon be having shared custody of Renee, moving wasn't an option. It would take Derrick agreeing to it, and I knew he wouldn't. A court would likely agree, especially since he was trying to rebuild his relationship with Renee, which would take consistency and time.

I tried to focus on my studies but kept finding myself checking the time. At ten p.m. Matt should be home and available for a call. With all the doubts and fears niggling at me, I needed to talk to him and longed for reassurance. Plus, I missed him. Having him over the night before had been nice, but it had been family time. Tense family time. Our time together as a couple was getting slimmer by the week.

Finally, it was 10:00 p.m. I closed my laptop and textbook, eyes blurry with fatigue. After brushing my teeth, I settled on my bed and tried Facetiming Matt. He didn't answer. I shot him a text, asking him to call me when he had a minute. I let him know I'd wait up because I wasn't feeling sleepy—which was true because I didn't feel like I could sleep until I talked to him.

I waited for a half an hour, but still no return text or call from Matt. Feeling bored and trying to stay awake, I opened the Instagram app on my phone and scrolled through friend's pictures. I came upon a post by the Cascade Christian Youth Group page, one that Matt struggled to keep up on and delegated to various volunteers. There was a picture of the outside of the trampoline park, with the tag line, "Time to jump into the new school year!" I scrolled the pictures on the post and my breath caught in my throat when I came upon a photo of the volunteers helping with the event. It was all the usual people, with Matt and Emily in the center of the group, standing close together. Too close. Matt had a huge smile on his face. Emily looked cute and stylish, younger than her age, like she could almost be part of the youth group instead of a helper.

I set my phone down and took a deep breath. *You're being irrational.* Picking my phone back up, I sent Matt another text. **Hey, are you home yet?** I typed, hoping I didn't sound desperate.

My mind running through a dozen possible scenarios for Matt not responding, I came up with an idea. I typed 'Emily Ferguson' into the search bar on Instagram. There were only a few results, making finding Emily's page easy. I clicked on it. Her account wasn't private, so there were several pictures for all to see. The latest one appeared to be from this last Sunday and was a photo of her standing next to Matt in front of the Cascade Christian Youth Logo inside the room where the teens met at church. Alice and Doug stood beside them, their arms around each other. The caption on the picture said, "This is where the cool people at church hang out."

I swallowed against the growing nausea in my stomach. The way Emily and Matt stood next to the married couple made it look like they were a couple, too. They were part of something I wasn't. I was on the outside, they were in. I studied the picture closer. Matt was smiling, his eyes bright. Just like in the photo from the event this evening—in the other picture where he stood next to Emily.

Memories from the last few weeks gathered, creating a tumbleweed of fear inside me. Matt's sadness when he told me about losing the associate pastor position because of me. The irritation on his face when I'd shown jealousy of Emily. Him staring at the blank television while we talked with Renee about her future. Emily's proclamation of Matt being an "eligible bachelor." Matt telling me the only job opportunities for him were out of town, and out of his reach because moving wasn't an option. Because of me.

The chilling, foreboding sensation that had wormed its way into me the night before grew, taking over every inch of my mind, filling every crevice that had dreamed of a future with Matt. A new understanding took the place of my dreams. A cold realization that made me feel as small and insignificant as I had the day the police showed up at Derrick's and my home three years ago and threatened to take me to jail.

Matt was better off without me.

I was holding Matt back from a better life. Whether or not he had feelings for Emily, she was a more suitable match for him. She was much more like his deceased wife, the one he would still be happily married to if she hadn't died too young. With someone like Emily, there were no complications from an ex-spouse or shared custody to cloud their future. Her father was a pastor, not a deceased race car driver. Her mother was the devoted wife of a pastor, not a recovering alcoholic. Just like Emily could backpack rugged paths such as the Pacific Crest Trail while I could only master the shorter day hikes to waterfalls, she was more solidly made for the challenges of being a pastor's wife.

My phone dinged with a notification, but I didn't look at it. *Couldn't* look at it. I needed the night to confirm what my heart was telling me, the truth that I had refused to see out of my own selfishness, my desire to build a life that wasn't meant for me.

I had to find the courage to break up with Matt.

Chapter Thirty

Sharon

I'D COME A LONG WAY IN the last couple of years. Gave up drinking for good. The itching, uneasy, restless feeling that haunted me when I'd quit no longer plagued me. I owed it all to God. I felt Him free me the night I stood on that karaoke stage and sang *Father I'm Coming Home*. The memory still brought a smile to my face because never would I have dreamed of singing a church hymn in a bar, but I guess when God leads you to something, you do it, no matter how crazy it sounds.

I'd also quit smoking. Started eating healthier. Faithfully went to church and now even served in a ministry. It was a mountain of change in a short time, but one thing remained the same—sometimes the only thing that soothed my soul was a long car drive with the stereo blasting.

So I drove, the radio dialed in on an oldies but goodies station, turned up loud so I couldn't hear any of the road noise of my old Buick chugging its way along, even when I rolled down my windows to let in the cool autumn air.

When Cassie told me she was thinking of calling off her engagement with Matt, it took all the self-control I had not to ask her if she'd lost her mind. What was she thinking?

Then I saw the pain in her eyes, a pain I realized she was trying to hide behind the wall she'd been slowly building around her heart. How had I not seen it coming?

I couldn't blame her, not really. Look at everything that had been thrown her way in the last few months. Derrick showing up, and no doubt bringing a whole host of painful memories that poked at old fears and insecurities she'd worked hard to overcome. Then watching her beloved find out his mentor had a dark secret and seeing the fallout at the church she called home.

Before she could catch her breath, along came the Fergusons and their pious, judgmental attitude, which led to their influence on other leaders. Ones Cassie thought of as friends. Matt getting denied the associate pastor position, apparently because he was engaged to her. After hearing Myrtle's summation of me in the restroom, I knew firsthand how that had to sting. For Cassie, the rejection was bigger, more personal.

Then the proverbial cherry on the cake—Emily. My fingers gripped the steering wheel so tight my knuckles turned white when I thought of that woman. She'd been the one to deal the final blow to my daughter. Emily and her smug, fake ways, flirting with Matt like he was some celebrity, and she was a star-struck teenage girl.

And Cassie thought that woman was somehow more qualified to be a pastor's wife. Talk about the lies of the enemy.

I tried to persuade Cassie to think rationally. I empathized with her predicament. Reminded her of the good. Racked my brain for scripture to quote like my mom would have, but my heart was racing so fast nothing came to me.

In the end, she agreed to wait and give her relationship with Matt more thought, more prayer, before breaking it off. It wasn't a win, but it was close enough to the finish line I could breathe, at least a little.

Now I was driving. Praying. Singing. And finding myself on the road that led to Johnny's parents' place.

How had I ended up all the way out in the Junction City area? I initially drove toward Fern Ridge Reservoir, but it took only one right turn on that road, for the most part, to head north and into farm country.

Johnny called the day before my drive. I didn't answer.

Couldn't take the time or emotional energy to talk. Too much turmoil filled my heart to hear more news that might bring me down. While I still hoped and prayed Johnny had found church to his liking, and that he would find the Lord, I didn't want to hear about what probably came with that conviction. About the sweet angel of a neighbor who led him there. The woman who gave him the hope I couldn't offer the last time we were together, because I was lost and trying to find my own way, hands held out in the darkness, grasping for light.

I drove slowly past the gravel road to the Beckett land. Stopped. Pulled into another gravel drive, turned my radio down. Backed up and headed the way I came, easing my old car past the entrance again. I couldn't see anything from the road. Trees lined the drive and the space between the main road and their house. Lots of vegetation and space blocked me from seeing whatever was happening at the house. I came to another gravel drive, pulled in. As I did so, I wondered if it was the one that led to what's-her-name's place, the one who had baked a casserole and invited Johnny to church.

So you're saying the guy who wanted you to run away with him last year, and who stayed in love with you for well over a decade even though he didn't see you, has been won over by a casserole? Janice and her sense of humor. Now the thought flicked like flames at my insides. How could he be swayed by some other lady showing up with dinner? My mind drifted to last year, when he'd driven me up the very road I'd slunk past two times in the last five minutes. The romantic evening that would be forever etched on my heart. The night he'd set up the picnic date of my dreams on his parent's property and presented me with a ring. A ring, but no proposal. A ring I still owned, hidden in the music box that represented the secret my mom almost took to the grave. How long had it been since I opened that box, relived those memories?

It'd been a year. Because my heart couldn't handle it. Could I endure it now?

There was only one way to find out. I reversed out of the gravel drive and headed back to the Beckett road. Ready or not Johnny, here I come. I gritted my teeth and found the accelerator.

Even as I drove down the country road, I berated myself. What would I do if his new love was by his side? Talk about awkward. What would his parents think of an old flame showing up at their home? Yet here I was, creeping down their driveway like a stalker.

I guess love mixed with anger and grief makes one do outrageous things. Then again, what did I have to lose?

I drove past the field where Johnny had taken me on our last date—the night he'd offered me a ring, but not marriage. There was no evidence left of the makeshift gazebo he'd built for our romantic dinner that night. Only the bricks of the fire pit remained. I sped past it, unable to bear the memory. I came to the orchards of pear and apple trees and wondered which one had been the focus of Johnny's Facebook post. "Exciting things to come." He couldn't possibly already be engaged to his casserole-toting neighbor, could he? I saw a backhoe on the side of the road, and an area of land that had been cleared and leveled. What was Johnny up to? I supposed I'd find out.

The Beckett house looked pretty much the same as the last time I'd seen it over a decade ago. Not the typical farmhouse, it was a one level ranch design, modest but wide, with faded green paint. The grass surrounding the home appeared freshly mowed. Smoke came from the chimney. The thought of a fire was cozy, another reminder of the night Johnny gave me the ring. Three vehicles were in the driveway.

One was a Ford truck I recognized. Johnny's.

I thought of turning around, heading back the way I came. Maybe I would have done just that, but the front door to the house opened. Johnny stepped out on the small concrete entry, his hand shielding his eyes from the sun. My pulse pounded in my ears, and I reflexively slammed on my brakes. Though I wasn't going fast, a cloud of dust rose from the rear of my car, covering the sad creature in even more dirt. Johnny stepped down off the porch, his eyes still shielded. His shoulders shot back and his hand raised to a wide wave as he continued down the front walkway.

I took a deep breath. Unless I wanted to look like a crazy stalker, I had no choice but to pull forward and park. My hands trembled annoyingly as I steered my car to the side of the drive, put it in park, and killed the engine. Johnny stopped at the end of the walkway and put his thumbs in front pockets of his faded blue Levi's. A huge smile spread across his face. He tilted his head ever so slightly. Even from where I sat, I could see his eyes twinkling. My heart picked up its staccato rhythm, making me dizzy. I sucked in on my cheeks and counted to three, all the while unbuckling myself and opening the door.

When I got out of the car, I shot Johnny a short wave and headed toward the walkway where he still stood. I couldn't help but look in his eyes and smile as I walked up to him. Part of me wanted to run to him, but I knew that was foolish. I forced my hands to be still and took my time.

"Well, this is a pleasant surprise!" Johnny's familiar voice, husky and smooth, warmed me from a few feet away.

"You know me . . . unpredictable."

Johnny lifted his chin, a smile still on his face. "I always liked that about you."

I wanted to throw my arms around Johnny and give him a hug but stopped myself. Who knew where casserole-toting lady was? She may be in the house. I offered my hand instead. "It's good to see you, Johnny."

His smile faltered, but he took my hand in his and shook it gently. "I got to say, you're a sight for sore eyes." Johnny's voice deepened, and he held onto my hand for a moment before letting it go.

I put my hands in my back pockets and looked toward the orchard, unsure of what to say.

"I called you yesterday." Johnny offered.

I nodded and turned back to him. 'Yeah. I know. I had a lot going on and today I went for a drive." I looked back toward the road I'd driven down to get to his house. "Next thing I knew I was driving by your place, so I thought, why not?" I shrugged one shoulder.

The twinkle returned to Johnny's eyes, along with a sideways grin. "Imagine that." He ran his hand over his goatee and gazed at the trees across the drive. "Want to see what I've been working on out here?"

I looked back to my car and then to Johnny. There was nowhere I needed to be. Cassie was getting off early to pick Renee up from school so she could spend some quality time with her, as well as get homework done before she spent her Saturday with Missy. They were going on a horse-riding adventure, which surprised me. Cassie was afraid of horses, or at least of falling off them. Kind of like I was a little afraid to have Johnny show me around his parents' place.

Or was it *his* place now?

And soon to also be the casserole-toting lady's place.

My stomach knotted. Before I could say yes or no, Johnny tilted his head toward the trees and began walking. "Let's start over here."

I followed Johnny's lead and stepped up beside him. "How's your dad?"

Johnny kept looking forward. "Getting better every day.

Still ready to lay down the land though."

"What are you going to do?" Gravel crunched under our feet as we walked down the road, back toward where the backhoe sat.

"I already have an offer on my place in California. The money from that will be my down payment, enough to give my sister a generous sum and get my parents into smaller, ADA friendly living quarters."

I stopped. "Your parents are moving out?"

Johnny gave me another sideways grin. "Yes, but not far." He nodded toward the leveled land in front of us. "We're getting a manufactured home put right there. It'll be set up with all the things Dad needs. A walk-in tub, wider doorways, handrails. Plus, it'll be much smaller than the house and easier for Mom to keep up without having to ask for help." He gave me a conspiring wink. "She's kind of stubborn like that. Guess I take after my dad in falling for the stubborn ones."

Was casserole-toting lady stubborn? Or was he talking about me? My heart pitter-pattered, unsure of whether to break or swell.

We came to the expanse of freshly turned dirt and stopped. "So . . . you'll be living in the house?"

Johnny chuckled. "That's the plan. I offered to move a single wide onto the property and stay in that, but Mom wouldn't have it. She said this made more sense."

I nodded. "I can see your point. It's a big place for a single guy."

"It sure is."

He continued down the road toward the orchard. I stayed put, wanting to ask more questions but unsure of how to pose them. Johnny stopped and looked back at me. "You coming?"

I exhaled. Nodded. Caught up with him.

"So you went to church last Sunday?"

Johnny smiled, his focus still on the orchard. "I did. I

called to tell you all about it."

I took the bait. "I'm listening."

Johnny stepped into the trees and I followed him. We were in the shade now and the chill made me shiver. My t-shirt was inadequate for the autumn weather. I should've brought a coat.

He pivoted toward me, an almost dreamy smile still plastered on his face. His eyes held something they never had before. He'd always been a gentle guy, even if he was rough around the edges, but there was more than tenderness now. "Let's just say the entire morning was more than I expected. Better than I could have ever imagined."

I nodded, but a noose tightened around my ribs. He sounded like a man in love.

"Christy inviting me and my folks. It was definitely . . . providential."

So that was the casserole-toting woman's name. Christy. It made sense for her name to have something holy about it. I forced a smile. "Did . . . did your parents go too?" I stumbled over my words, unsure of how to ask him what I wanted to know. Two questions begged to be answered, but one was more important than the other.

Johnny chuckled softly, his gaze shifting to one of the apple trees. "Mom did. Dad chose to stay home, claiming he liked the idea of having the house to himself after having all of us around constantly. Maybe someday Dad will come to church, too. Christy said it's something she'll be praying for."

Did Johnny believe in prayer now? I shifted from one foot to the other. "I will pray, too. I have been praying. For all of you." I swallowed the rising lump in my throat.

Johnny turned back to me, tilting his head. "Thank you. I think it's made a difference." He put his hand to the back of his neck and looked at me with earnestness. "I've started praying, too."

Goosebumps ran up my arms, making me quiver. The sadness I'd felt at losing Johnny to Christy was wiped away, at least momentarily. "You have?"

Johnny gave one quick nod, then looked at the trees again, but the dreamy smile had returned to his face. "The preacher on Sunday. Great guy. He preached this message on the prodigal son. It hit me. Hard." His smile faded, but the peacefulness in his eyes remained. "Something about the father and son in that story reminded me of the relationship between my dad and me." When Johnny looked at me, his brow was crinkled. "Him having the accident, me being here. It was all a second chance to get things set right between us. When the preacher talked about the father running toward the lost son, all dignity thrown aside, I knew that no matter what, that'd never be my dad." Johnny paused, took a deep breath. Then I understood there was a father who would run to me." Emotion added an edge to Johnny's voice. "He'd already been running to me with open arms, and it was on Sunday I finally saw Him, so to speak."

I chewed on my bottom lip, trying not to cry, but tears gathered in my eyes anyway. I knew that feeling, in all its will-crushing and overflowing of love and glory. "I'm so glad to hear that, Johnny."

Johnny smiled, the familiar twinkle back in his eyes. "I thought you would be."

I took a deep breath. "I'm sure Christy is happy to hear it, too."

He shrugged. "Well, sure, I mean, she took me there." He laughed, a deep, melodic sound that may have made the tree leaves shake. "I suppose she was on a mission. Like Peter or Paul or one of those other disciples."

I grinned, wiping tears away with the back of my hand. "You're reading the Bible now, I'm thinking."

Johnny pursed his lips and gave a quick nod. "Yes,

ma'am."

We stood in silence for a moment, a whisper of wind shivering the leaves around us.

"I'd like to meet Christy." The words hurt to say, yet they were true.

"She's at my folks right now, unless she took off while we've been shooting the breeze." He lifted an eyebrow. "I could introduce you, and you can say hello to my mom. Dad's probably in his room, resting."

Might as well get it over with. It would be a good way to say farewell to Johnny and then head down the road and get on with my life. I nodded my agreement, and we walked back toward the house. As we ambled along, Johnny told me his plans for the farm. He was going to turn most of the orchard into a you-pick, as well as plant more strawberries in a nearby field for the same purpose. On another patch he planned to have a field of pumpkins and hoped to put on a fall festival each year. He'd sold the few farm animals his parent's had and was making improvements to the barn with plans to host holiday craft fairs there as well as weddings and other events in the spring and summer.

I thought of Cassie's upcoming wedding. Would it still happen? If so, would it still be at the church? I pushed the anxiety away that the ponderings brought me. I'd have plenty of time to fret over those things when I drove away from the Beckett farm.

"Do you think you'll make a real profit doing those things?" It seemed like a lot of work, and the potential for income was questionable.

Johnny shrugged one shoulder. "I'd like to give it a whirl. With a partner, I think I could make it a success."

A partner. Must be talking about Christy. "I'm sure you can."

We arrived back to the house and Johnny opened the

front door, motioning for me to go in first. I stepped into the entry way and was greeted by the smell of cinnamon and apples. Casserole-toting woman . . . er. . . Christy, must've been making an apple crisp. *She made herself at home fast, didn't she?*

"Mom! Christy. We have a visitor."

A rosy cheeked woman with gray hair pulled back in a braided bun approached from around the corner where the kitchen was, if my memory was correct. "Well, hello!" She said in a welcoming voice, holding out her hand.

I took the woman's hand. I couldn't remember exactly what Johnny's mom looked like, but I'd say she'd aged well. Her tanned but wrinkled skin glowed. Though she was wide around the midsection, she had a healthy vigor to her appearance. She was definitely a woman who could spend the evening in the kitchen after having toiled all day in the garden.

I took her hand. "It's been a long time." I smiled, hoping Mrs. Beckett didn't mind my intrusion into her home.

She shook my hand vigorously, but her brow wrinkled. "We've met before?"

Johnny lifted an eyebrow at me.

I flustered. "Oh. Well, yes. It's been a long time." I looked to Johnny, pleading with my eyes for help. Maybe she wasn't keen to see Johnny's old girlfriends coming around. Or maybe she wasn't as young in mind as she seemed, and her memory was failing.

Maybe I was completely forgettable. My shoulders sank.

"Oh, well. I'm sure I would remember meeting you." She smiled broadly. "My name is Christy."

"Yes, I'm Shar—"

What did she say? Her name was—Christy?

This was Christy? She looked nearly old enough to be mine or Johnny's mother. I shot a glance to Johnny, who had a confused, but also amused, expression on his face.

Christy squinted her eyes. "Your name is Shar?"

Johnny's chuckle echoed in the narrow entryway. He stepped closer. "Christy, this is Sharon. The one I was telling you about."

"Ohhh!" Christy's eyes widened, and she gave me a big-toothed smile. "I've heard so much about you. It's nice to meet you. I wished I'd known you were coming by. I'd have had this crisp done sooner."

"Who do we have here?" An older woman, shorter and with slightly hunched shoulders, entered from the hallway.

Now that she was standing in front of me, I recognized her. *This* was Johnny's mother. "Hi, Mrs. Beckett."

Johnny spoke to his mother. "Mom, do you remember Sharon?"

His mother laughed and shook her head, while playfully slapping Johnny on the arm. "How could I forget her? You talk about her enough to kill a parrot."

I shifted my gaze from Mrs. Beckett to Johnny. His face had turned a deep red, but he was smiling. "Well, I guess it's a good thing we don't own any birds."

Chapter Thirty-One

Cassie

MY ALARM WENT OFF AT FIVE a.m., entirely too early for a Saturday. I grabbed my phone from the nightstand to turn the beeping off, nearly knocking over the glass of water I kept there in the process. It'd been another nearly sleepless night.

My mom convinced me to give my relationship with Matt more thought before breaking it off but doing so had only increased my torment. It was like walking around with a large splinter in your hand. It ached and throbbed, and the longer I waited to pull it out, the deeper it went, causing more pain.

Looking at my phone screen, I noticed three missed text messages from Matt and one phone call. So far, I'd done a good job of pushing him off. I'd made excuses for not answering his calls and sending only short, to the point, text messages. Things couldn't continue this way. It wasn't fair to him, and my heart was breaking piece by piece. Better to crush it with a hammer and be done.

Before I could change my mind, I dialed his number. He didn't answer, which I expected. It was early on a Saturday. Working with teenagers, Matt had become accustomed to going to bed later and waking after the sun came up, not before. I listened to his voicemail greeting, tears slipping down my cheeks. I remembered the first time I ever laid eyes on him. Nannie had been with me then, patting my knee and winking at me as we watched Matt preach at her church. What would Nannie say now? I couldn't bear to think about it.

Dread washing over me, I left a message. "I just wanted to call you before I headed out for the day with Missy." I was surprised by how robotic my voice sounded. "I'm sorry I haven't been very . . . available these last few days." The hammer was ready to strike my heart. I knew what I was going to say would hurt Matt, too, but in the long run, it would be what was best for him. I took a deep breath and blurted out my decision. "I've been thinking about us a lot lately, and our upcoming marriage and it's made me realize a few things. Well, actually, the events of the last couple months have opened up my eyes." I gulped and inwardly begged God to give me the right words, but as I continued, I didn't feel Him with me. "I'm holding you back, Matt." I took a deep breath and continued. "I love you. I'll always love you."

The tears came like a waterfall now, dripping on my nightgown. I scrunched my eyes closed. "I love you too much to let you throw your dreams away on me. You are called to be a pastor. It's a God-given gift and I can't take that away from you. I know leaving a voicemail is a horrible way to do this, but I had to get it out. I couldn't keep dodging your phone calls and texts and I just . . ." I stammered. "I'm so sorry. I want to talk to you in person, but I'll be home really late tonight. Maybe tomorrow after church we can talk more?"

I ended the call. The hammer had struck its blow. My heart was crushed. I prayed Matt's heart would not be broken, too. But if it was, I knew he would bounce back. He had a lot going for him. A future of possibilities. Maybe it even included Emily.

Missy arrived promptly at a quarter to seven, pulling a horse trailer behind her big truck and blocking the road, waiting for me. I ran out the door, having kissed Renee goodbye while she was still sleeping. Mom was set to take care of her the entire day and told me to have fun. I didn't tell her about the voicemail I'd left for Matt. That could wait until later. Mom seemed in an especially good mood, considering the circumstances, and I was thankful. No reason we should all be miserable, and Renee needed the positivity to make up for my sulkiness the last few days.

Missy sat behind the steering wheel wearing a cowboy hat, and the local country radio station blasted the air around me as I opened the truck door.

"Hey, cowgirl, ready for the time of your life?" Missy added a southern drawl to her greeting.

I jumped into Missy's truck and pulled the door shut. Despite my broken heart, I smiled at her words, which could've qualified as a bad pickup line in a bar. "If it makes me forget all my problems, I'm game." I threw my bag with a change of clothes and a packed lunch in the back seat.

Missy put the truck into gear and pulled forward. I could feel the weight of the trailer behind us, hear the engine work harder.

"How long of a drive is this?"

Missy glanced in the passenger mirror and turned on her blinker. "Almost three hours."

"Oh, wow." No wonder she wanted an early start.

"We'll still have plenty of time to explore the trails before heading home."

"A good, long day away from life is what I need right now." I looked out the window so I could wipe away the tears that refused to stop.

"Anything you'd like to share with the group?"

I wasn't going to make it through the day without more tears, and though I'd come accustomed to covering up my emotions when needed, doing that for nine or more hours with Missy would be impossible. It made sense to tell her the truth, plus I needed someone to talk to about the whole thing. "I broke up with Matt."

"You what? Why? What happened?"

I told Missy a modified version of the story, doing my best

to make church people not look bad. I explained that Matt had a possibility for a better pastoral job, but because of new leadership and their interpretation of the rules, he didn't get it because he was engaged to me. I told her he thought they were wrong, as did others, but it made me realize that I was holding him back from his dreams. He needed a wife who could be his helper, not one who made his life more difficult.

"Besides," I said, doing my best to sound determined and confident. "I have my own dreams. I want to finish school. If we get married, that'll be harder."

"Hmm." Missy looked at me, something in her eyes I couldn't quite read. Disappointment? Concern? My brain was running on fumes and didn't have the energy to figure it out.

"It's really for the best. I'm just worried about how it'll affect Renee."

"I'm worried about how it's going to affect *you*." Missy said, staring at the road ahead.

No point in arguing, but I realized at that moment I couldn't bear to talk about it. "So, no waterfall on this trail, huh?"

Missy's mouth puckered and she shook her head slightly. "No, ma'am. The closest horse trail I could find to a waterfall was up in Washington. Probably a little much for a day trip. If you take to horseback riding, maybe we can plan a camping trip in the future,"

I nodded, the ache in my chest deeper. God felt so far away. I needed a waterfall now more than ever.

We headed south on I-5, then east on Highway 58, the truck and trailer moving slowly as it wound through the mountains. The beauty of trees and lakes we saw on the way was like an ointment to my soul, numbing the pain for a moment.

An hour into the drive, Missy said, "You never told me

exactly why you're scared of horses."

"I'm not afraid of horses. I think they're great. I'm scared of falling." I gave a little laugh.

"I get that." She turned to me. "You had a bad experience."

"It happened when I was a kid. About eight years old."

"Did you get bucked off?"

"Yes." The memory was fresh in my mind now.

"And you didn't get back on? What, were you at a summer camp or something?"

I shook my head. "No. The horse belonged to a friend of my grandpa's." I stared out the window, admiring the beauty of the scenery despite the sadness the memory elicited from my heart. "He loved horses, but didn't have the land to keep them, so he kept a horse at his friend's place. After I went to live with my grandparents, my grandpa thought it would be good for me to be on a horse, learn to ride."

Missy nodded. "That makes sense. They are even used in therapy for kids who have been through tough things."

"I know, but let's just say, it didn't work for me."

"What happened?"

I twisted a strand of hair nervously around my finger. "Fred's horse was kind of young, I think, and not accustomed to inexperienced riders. My grandpa felt really bad later."

How I missed Grandpa and wished he could be riding with us today. I swallowed the lump forming in my throat. "Anyway, I got nervous, and it was like the horse picked up on it or something. He got skittish, which scared me, and I screamed. I probably yanked on the reins at the same time. Whatever happened, he bucked, and I flew off. Landed on a rock. My back hurt for days."

Missy let out a slow whistle. "Yikes. Landing on a rock sounds painful."

I nodded. "It was—and my grandma kind of freaked out.

She said I could've been paralyzed. Looking back now, I realize she was an emotional wreck over my mom, and probably afraid of losing me, like she'd essentially lost her only daughter."

"Makes sense. Is she the reason you didn't go riding again?" Missy flipped the turn signal and slowed, getting ready to turn off the highway and onto another road.

"Yes, I guess so. She was afraid of it happening again, and so was I. Grandpa was disappointed, but he didn't push me."

Missy was quiet. The rumble of the truck's diesel engine was the only sounds now that we no longer had a radio signal. Finally, she spoke. "I'm having you ride Scout today. He's a Pinto. The older, gentle horse I told you about. The one my mom calls The Babysitter. He won't buck on you." She turned to me, her eyes holding a seriousness I wasn't accustomed to seeing. "But you have to follow my directions. Okay?"

I nodded, but my heart galloped like a runaway horse. Even with Missy's expert guidance, I wasn't sure I could trust the horse to not let me fall.

Missy pulled the trailer into a Campground called Quinn Meadows Horse Camp.

I turned to her. "Wait, we aren't camping. Can we park here?"

"The campsites are cheap. I reserved one so we'd have a home base for the day."

Missy maneuvered the truck and then backed into a large camping site between groves of tall trees. Looking out the passenger window, I saw a stall for horses. My stomach clenched, fighting against butterflies.

After we used the vault toilet, which was about as

pleasant as getting teeth pulled—and smellier—Missy opened the back of the trailer and began leading the horses out. "Just hang tight, and I'll get the amigos ready."

I stood aside and watched Missy expertly handle the horses. She led them individually into the corral located on the campsite and tied them. After that, she lifted the tack out of the bed of the truck, then saddled and bridled the horses. She was dressed the part herself, in Wrangler jeans, cowboy boots, and a flannel shirt. I was very much the newbie, with old hiking boots and worn jeans. At least I had a coat and a ballcap. The chill in the air announced the onset of fall at the higher elevation, despite the bright sun and powder blue sky.

When the horses were ready and the trailer closed, Missy motioned me toward her. "This is Scout." I approached slowly. Scout was handsome, a tricolored coat of brown, black and white. Missy held his reins and mane in one hand and offered me the other. "Here, put your foot in the stirrup, then lean against the saddle while you mount. I'll help you get your other leg over and then hand you the reins."

I did as Missy said, putting my hands on the scratchy horsehair. Scout nickered. Beads of perspiration formed on my chest and forehead, even though the air was cool. With a heave and a little push from Missy, I swung my other leg over and mounted the horse. Once I was steady, she handed me the reins.

"Okay, I'm going to lead with Beau." Missy nodded her head toward the other horse, which was brown with white stockings, and a white streak down his face. "Your job is to hold the reins loosely. Hang on to the horn, right here, to help you balance." She patted the horn at the front of the saddle. "Keep your toes in the stirrups, but your weight in your heels. Sit straight, don't lean, even if you feel Scout lean because he's maneuvering."

"Okay, got it." Sitting on the horse I felt tall, and way higher up than the horse had looked. Scout felt solid under me.

Missy gave a quick nod. She left me with the reins in my hands and went to Beau. True to her word, Missy and Beau led the way and Scout followed closely behind with little prompting from me. The smell of pine trees and the dust the horses kicked up filled my senses as we found our way to the trail.

The trees were tall. Missy said we'd see a lot of lava rocks on this ride. As long as we watched for them along the path, the trail was wide enough that we could ride side-by-side. Though we were going slow, I focused more on balancing on Scout than on the scenery. It didn't help that my pulse was pounding in my ears.

Between the steady plopping of the hooves on the path, the vistas of the coned peaks of the Sisters mountain range, and the whisper of the breeze through the pine trees, my heartrate eventually slowed. I became accustomed to Scout's gentle, rocking gait, and felt more comfortable in the saddle.

I was doing this.

I missed seeing a waterfall, but we did traverse along a meadow and wide creek with clear shallow water. We stopped to let the horses take a drink.

"We're going to head into a rockier area with a slope. Just let Scout do his job and hold on to the horn if you need to. Remember to sit straight." Missy said, as we left the creek and continued on the trail.

It wasn't long before we reached the area Missy warned me about. My stomach clenched, seeing the black, hole-filled lava rocks shooting up from the path. We made our way down a slight slope. I could feel Scout's body lean forward as he found his footing. I bent over too, Missy's admonition to sit straight not only feeling unnatural, but dangerous to Scout's balance.

"Sit straight! Don't lean!" I heard Missy admonish me as she looked over her shoulder.

But it was too late. Scout shifted suddenly under me, like he was losing his balance. My heart thundered as I countered his move, and I felt my left toes lose their place in the stirrup. Before I could get them back in, I was sliding down the side of the saddle, heading straight toward the ground. I hit the dirt trail and small bits of gravel with a thud. Scout stopped and neighed.

My side ached where I'd landed. Tears came to my eyes, not from the physical pain, but from the humiliation of failing, once again, at riding a horse.

The next thing I knew Missy had dismounted Beau and sat beside me. "Just breathe."

"I don't think I'm cut out for this." I tried to laugh, pushing myself up with shaking hands. "Horses hate me."

"It's not the horse. It's your fear." Missy reached down, offering me a hand up. "You *have* to trust the horse and remember what I told you."

Remember what I told you. The words from the recurring dream of my grandpa echoed in my mind. The dream had guided me through fleeing my marriage and fighting for custody of Renee. Grandpa had stood on a trail then, telling me I must go, and to remember what he told me. It was later that I realized God was talking, to me, in a way I could understand, through the only man who had been there for me and loved me unconditionally.

Was he speaking to me now through Missy, even though she wasn't a believer? I looked into her eyes. Hazel eyes that held fire and strength and were looking at me with devoted love.

"Cassie, your fear is getting in the way. Scout can sense it, too. He's a good, mature horse, so it's not messing him up, but it's keeping you from riding the way you should."

My fear. A shiver went through my body, despite the warmth of the autumn sun. How much did fear control me? I thought I'd conquered it when I first stood up to Derrick. But it was more than fear. The memory of my childhood fall played again in my mind. I had been afraid. The fear had come from more than not knowing what to do. It had come from me not feeling as though I was good enough. I hadn't been enough to keep my mom sober. I hadn't been enough to control the horse.

I hadn't been enough to keep Derrick from drinking.

I wasn't worthy of Matt.

I stared at Scout. He looked back at me with gentle, wise eyes. I reached up and stroked his face, and he leaned into my hand.

Was I enough?

"You can do this." Missy urged. "The only thing standing in your way is *you*. You have what it takes to ride him. You just need to decide to get back on and do what I tell you, even when you feel afraid."

I bit my bottom lip, keeping my eyes on Scout's gentle brown eyes. Something in his face told me he was ready to go.

I remembered Grandpa's other admonition from my dream. *I've already given you everything you need.* I turned to Missy, my wise friend, and nodded slowly. "Maybe you're right."

Missy helped me mount Scout again and we continued our ride. At one point we came to a signed junction. One part of the sign was labeled as the "Pacific Crest Trail." My chest burned, remembering Emily's proclamation of my waterfall hikes being 'cute', as if they were child's play compared to her hiking the PCT.

The sign mobilized me. Maybe I didn't backpack through the PCT up and down the western states, but God had spoken to me at those waterfalls. I had people who believed in me. Some of them may not have impressive church backgrounds, but they had love and faithfulness in abundance. And I had a God that didn't give up on me, even when I had trouble trusting Him.

I may not be perfect, but I was enough.

As we ended our horse-riding adventure, my heart was convicted. When I got home, I knew what I had to do. I needed to pray like I never had before about my future with Matt.

Chapter Thirty-Two

Sharon

I SNUGGLED WITH RENEE ON THE couch, watching Snow White and the Seven Dwarves and waiting for Cassie to get home, doing my best not to worry.

Matt had called me earlier in the day and asked if I knew when Cassie would be home.

"I don't really know for sure," I'd told him, wondering why he was calling me to ask, "but she was hoping to get back before Renee's bedtime."

He sighed. "Sorry for bothering you, but I've tried calling and texting her, and she hasn't responded."

"She's probably out of cell phone range." Based on what Cassie was debating, I guessed it was more than that.

"I'm concerned. She left a message this morning that was," he paused, "so unlike her." The sadness in his voice came through the line loud and clear.

Oh, Cassie. What had she said? I didn't pry but wanted to offer him some reassurance. "I'm sure she'll call you when she's back in cell reception. If it's late, though, she might wait until tomorrow. Don't worry." Though Cassie and Matt weren't married yet, in many ways, he already felt like the son I never had.

He gave a soft laugh. "I'm trying. If you talk to her, let her know I really need to see her. Soon."

I'd agreed, my heart breaking for the poor guy. I wanted to tell him more, give him advice, but it wasn't my place.

I held Renee close, watching as Prince Charming searched for Snow White, and hoped Matt would be as determined not to give up on Cassie. About the time the prince found a sleeping Snow White, my phone dinged. Was Cassie letting me know she was almost home? I looked at my screen, but it wasn't Cassie. It was Johnny. Though I wanted to hear from my daughter, my chest felt lighter seeing Johnny's name on my screen.

Looking forward to dinner Tuesday, the text read, with a smiley face.

I pursed my lips together. Johnny had asked me out to dinner when I'd found myself at his place on Friday. I'd said yes but told him the soonest I could commit to was Tuesday evening. I still needed to run it by Cassie—she might need me to watch Renee while she studied, but I hadn't really found the opportunity to do so between then and now. With the whole Matt thing looming, I wasn't even sure how to bring it up, but I would.

It still amazed me how much Johnny had changed. All in a good way. Maybe it took some of us longer to grow up. I could testify to that. Him having enough equity in a house to make a down payment on the farm showed that he had found some measure of financial responsibility. I'd outright asked him if he was still drinking, and he'd said he gave up the binge drinking when he returned home to help with his dad. "I had to keep my head clear to really be here for my family." He'd said. I understood. The similarity of our paths was crazy, almost too unlikely to have happened without some kind of divine intervention.

Me too. I texted back to him. After a moment of hesitation and fighting off the circus of butterflies in my stomach, I added a heart. If Johnny knew me at all, he'd know that little emoticon spoke a thousand words.

Chapter Thirty-Three

Cassie

MOM AND RENEE WERE WAITING UP for me when I got home. The way Mom looked at me, I knew something was wrong. After she asked about my ride, and I told her and Renee all about my adventure, including the fall and getting back on, Mom said, "Matt called me."

I froze. He'd left me a voicemail and texted me. I'd listened to his message, which said he wanted to talk no matter how late I got home. But I knew I wasn't ready. I needed to pray, and so that's what I'd texted him in return. He had simply replied. "Ok."

"What did he say?" I asked Mom.

"He was just wondering if I knew when you'd be home. He sounded concerned." Mom's eyes searched my face, looking for information she knew I wouldn't divulge in front of Renee.

I gave her a nod. "I'm hoping to meet with him tomorrow after church." I ruffled Renee's hair as she yawned. "It's way past your bedtime. Why don't you go brush your teeth and then I'll tuck you in?"

Renee ambled down the hallway. Once she was in the bathroom and brushing, I whispered to Mom. "I left him a voicemail this morning. I was torn up and felt like I just had to get everything out in the open."

Mom's eyes widened. "You didn't break up with him by voicemail, did you?"

I grimaced. "Kind of? I didn't say those exact words." I rubbed the sides of my jaw, which had tightened. "I feel horrible."

Mom put her hand on my shoulder. "He's reaching out to you. That's a good sign. Many men would get angry, not seeing past their own hurt, and walk away."

I nodded. "I know. He's a truly good guy. Which is why I need to pray." I slid a wary gaze to Mom. "I realized today that I hadn't really prayed about what to do with my feelings about Matt and our future. I'd acted out of fear . . . and feeling unworthy."

Mom shook her head, her eyes glimmering with tears. "I understand those feelings, Baby Girl, but you are far from unworthy."

How I wanted to believe that was true.

After tucking Renee in, I grabbed my Bible, went to my room, and prayed.

Lord, I need you. I want to be with Matt. I love him so much. But I need to know that this is what you want for me, and for him. If you want me to be a pastor's wife, then I'll walk that out, whatever it looks like. The Fergusons... this church... I feel like I'm dying under their leadership. Shrinking, not to make you bigger, but to get out of their way. If I stay there, I'm afraid the only thing left of me will be a bitter shell. I don't know what to do. Please minister to Matt. Reassure him that I love him and only want what's best for him.

Tears streamed down my face. I waited for peace to come, but angst seized my insides, my heart seeking an answer. I opened my Bible and flipped through the pages. I found myself in Ephesians, reading over the familiar verses about the armor of God, but this time a verse stood out to me like it never had before:

"Therefore, take up the full armor of God, so that you will be able to resist in the evil day, and having done everything, to stand firm."

Having done everything, to stand firm.
Stand firm.
Don't run away. Don't charge forward. Stand.
Sit straight! Don't lean.
Sitting straight was a lot like standing.
Cassie, your fear is getting in the way.
Fear made me want to run, caused me to lean when I should sit straight. But what was I afraid of?

On the horse I was afraid of falling because it was both painful and humiliating.

With Matt, I was afraid of. . . failing. My first marriage ended in divorce. As though that were a prophecy of our future success, that divorce was a thorn some were trying to use against Matt. Against us. It was like my fear had come true and I was both humiliated and hurt. Now I was afraid my past failure would follow Matt, hindering him from being what God called him to be. I remembered Mom's words to me, what she believed Nannie would tell me if she were here—*hold your chin up and remember, God loves you and already knew what was going to happen. He has a purpose for you, and sometimes people can't see it, but that doesn't mean it's not going to happen. But also anyone who can't see your worth deserves a good, swift, kick in the pants.*

Stand firm.
Lord, I hear you.
I sent Matt a text.

I'm not going to make it to church in the morning, can we meet tomorrow, early evening after Mom gets off work?

He responded almost immediately.
Yes. How about Buddy's Diner at 5:00 p.m.?

I looked at the time. Almost midnight. He was up late, obviously waiting to hear from me. Guilt washed over me, but I had a plan. No more running.

I'll see you then.

I love you, Cassie.

Through bleary eyes, I tapped out the truth. I love you, too.

I woke in the morning to Renee at my bedside. It was unusual for us to miss church and for me to sleep in.

"Grammy told me to wake you up, because she's going to work."

I patted her arm. "I'm awake. You can let her know."

I hoped she got off in the early afternoon and didn't have plans. I would need her to watch Renee when I met with Matt.

Renee hurried out of the room. The more I awakened, the more anxiety and uncertainty bit at my chest, like tiny fire ants. I took a deep breath. *Lord, I need a sign.* I heard my door open again, and the patter of little feet as Renee hurried to my bed.

"Mommy, look at the picture I drew last night."

I turned my head to look at the piece of drawing paper Renee proudly held up. On it were three figures. A man with short blond hair, a woman with wavy brown hair, and a little girl with curly brown hair. All three were smiling and holding ice cream cones. In the background were cone mountains, like the Three Sisters range that had been my view the day before, and a big, bright yellow sun.

"This is when we eat ice cream on Thursday." Renee beamed, her eyes lit with anticipation.

I bit down on my bottom lip. I could almost hear God laughing. *Well, you wanted a sign.* "It's a beautiful picture, Renee. You did very well."

I'd expected my insides to twist into a knot as the time approached to meet with Matt, but instead, a strange calm came over me. A peace. The one thing I didn't get as the time approached was an appetite. I doubted I'd order anything at the restaurant.

Was Matt angry with me? I wouldn't blame him. If he wanted to vent about being hurt, I understood. Maybe he would agree we should call off our engagement. The thought twisted my insides. Then I thought of Renee's picture.

Stand firm.

When I walked into the restaurant, Matt was already seated at a booth, but noticed me and stood, waving me over.

My heart pitter-pattered at the sight of him. No matter what my future held, I couldn't imagine anyone else who could be more appealing to me. The softness of his blue eyes, the light lines around them a confirmation that he spent much time smiling. The way he wore his blonde hair spiked at the top, regardless of whether it was in style. His easy-going, friendly nature, which was apparent from the way he held himself to the way he talked to people. The dimples that appeared when he smiled big, and the heart-warming sound of his laughter. Whatever happened from this point, though, I was letting God lead.

"Cassie." His voice held nothing but tenderness, and he motioned me toward him.

I stopped with enough distance between us to be out of his hand's reach. "Hi, Matt."

We looked at each other a moment, not saying anything. Matt nodded toward the table. "Want to have a seat?"

I slid into the booth wordlessly.

Matt sat across from me and handed me a menu. "The waitress already brought these by. I've been here a few minutes."

"Did I get the time wrong?"

Matt shook his head. "No, I just wanted to sit here and pray silently for a few minutes before you arrived."

"Oh." I gulped. What was he praying about? My heart hammered in my chest. I feigned interest in the menu.

"I have to say, your call hit me hard on Saturday." Matt wasn't looking at his menu. Hopefully the waitress didn't expect us to order anytime soon.

"I'm so sorry." I managed to both make eye contact and hold back my own tears. I'd cried enough.

"But I understood why you chose to break it off. I just wish you would have talked to me sooner. Answered my calls." He gave me a small smile, the slightest dimpling of his cheeks.

I exhaled. "I know. I shouldn't have left that voicemail, either." I shook my head. "I just wanted to get it over with." I looked back at the menu. "But I've been praying, thinking."

"Me, too."

I looked up at him and garnered the courage to say what was on my heart. "I love you, Matt. I want nothing more than to be your wife. But I can't keep going to a church where there are people in leadership that, well, look down on me. Judge me. At the same time, I can't keep you from fulfilling the purpose God has for your life. You were called to be a pastor." I took a deep breath. "The whole time we've dated, I worried if I had what it took to be a pastor's wife." I grimaced. "The Fergusons made me believe I did not."

"Cassie, you know they are wrong, not only in my opinion, but in the eyes of many others."

I swallowed. "Yes, but there will be others like them. So, what I want to say is this." I took a deep breath. "If you still want to marry me, I'm in. I'll do everything I can to live up to the duties and expectations of being a pastor's wife, not in my own strength, but God's. But I can't do it at Cascade Christian Church. I'm afraid that limits your options so much that it extinguishes them altogether."

"Want to hear a funny story?"

Hear a funny story? Now? I'd just poured my heart out, leaving our entire future on the table. A tinge of annoyance rankled my insides, but I ignored it. It was good that Matt could tell funny stories. I wanted him to be happy. "Sure."

The waitress arrived. "Ready to order?"

I wasn't. I looked at Matt. He turned to the waitress. "Can we have five more minutes?"

"Sure thing."

The waitress scurried off to the next table.

"Anyway." Matt took a deep breath. "There was something I was planning on telling you last week, but you kind of stole my thunder, so to speak, by avoiding me and then breaking up with me."

I was surprised Matt was still laying the guilt heavily on me. It wasn't like him. Except . . . he was smiling. Did he not even care? Did he not see *my* heart was broken?

"Well, you can tell me now, can't you?" I held open my hands.

"Cassie . . . I found another job and put in my two weeks notice with the church."

My head swam, trying to take in the news. "You found a job at another church? Where?"

Matt straightened his shoulders and looked away for a moment, his mouth puckered. When he turned back to me, there was a combination of empathy and heartbreak in his eyes. "It's for the police department, believe it or not. But don't worry, I won't be carrying a gun or chasing down robbers. It's called a community resource officer." A tiny ray of light shown in his eyes. "I'll be helping people."

I grabbed the edge of the table, disbelief making me dizzy. "But why? You're called to be a pastor!"

Matt reached across the table and put his hand on mine. There was a peaceful reassurance in his touch. "Yes, but pastoring involves more than clocking in and out of duty at church." Matt sighed. "I didn't like what the pressure from the new leadership was doing to me. I became more focused on the youth group being successful than on reaching the hearts of the kids who went there. More on numbers and approval than on lives changed." He frowned. "That's not what I signed up for." He paused, then squeezed my hand. "And I could see what it was doing to you."

I shook my head. "You can't give up pastoring."

Matt's eyes met mine with intensity. He leaned against the table, getting as close to me as he could. "I can't imagine any other woman besides you being my wife. God gave me you. I'm not letting you go."

I blinked several times, willing my eyes to be dry. "Wouldn't God want you to continue being a pastor?"

Matt nodded. "Yes, but there are many ways to do that. When I read the job description of a community resource officer, it was like God was opening a door, showing me how to reach people who would probably never step foot in the church. It's another way to pastor, at least for now."

The waitress returned, took one look at us, and kept going. Matt chuckled. "I guess she knows when not to interrupt."

I didn't know what to say. What to do. Matt was giving up his pastor position. "Matt, are you sure? I want you to be happy. I don't want you to feel like you gave up your calling for me."

"It's already done. My resignation has been accepted. I start training for my new job in a little over a week. But there's one thing I need you to understand." Matt took on the tone of someone who would not be argued with.

"What?"

"There could come a day when I have the opportunity to return to pastoring a church. If or when that day happens, it's going to be a decision *we* make together, because God will be calling *us*, not just me."

I opened my mouth, closed it. I didn't know what to say. Yesterday, God had confirmed my worthiness, had shown me

I could conquer my fears. To not let people like the Fergusons tell me my worth. Matt was asking me to live like I really believed it. Could I do it?

I thought of Renee's trusting emerald eyes, filled with hope, showing me the picture she'd drawn of the three of us. An answer to the sign I'd prayed for only moments before she walked in the room.

A promise of the future. I only needed to have faith and stand firm.

"Yes." I said, reaching for Matt's hand. "Yes."

Chapter Thirty-Four

Sharon

I FRETTED WITH MY HAIR, UNABLE to smooth away the stubborn frizz along my temples. Giving up on getting my wavy hair to do exactly what I wanted, I picked up a tube of lipstick and applied it carefully, doing my best to keep the color within the lip line. Once I was done, I stood back and assessed my work. I supposed I didn't look half bad for a woman in her fifties. Now, if I could stop feeling like a teenage girl on her first date, that would be something.

Except, truth be told, that mixture of butterflies, anticipation, and longing felt kind of nice. Something I didn't think I'd experience again. Yet here I was. I heard a knock at the front door. Johnny was here. It was time for him to meet the girls.

I rushed out of the bathroom to open the front door, heading off Cassie as she made her way from the kitchen. "I've got it!"

Behind me, Cassie's laughter was music to my ears. My heart lightened. The light was back in her eyes. A spark of hope.

I opened the front door and was greeted by a smartly dressed Johnny, standing close to the door and just out of the rain, holding three bouquets of flowers. Though he was smiling, there was a nervousness about him I'd never seen before. Behind me, I could feel Cassie and Renee staring, waiting.

"Come on in." I said, stepping aside.

Johnny entered, handing me one of the bouquets. It was red and white roses. Romantic. Classic.

"Thank you. These are beautiful."

"I'm Cassie." My daughter held out her hand, not waiting for an introduction.

Johnny took her hand. "Nice to meet you." After a polite handshake, he handed her a bouquet of gladiolus. "These are for you."

"Thanks." Cassie smiled and looked down at Renee by her side. Today had been Cassie and Derrick's meeting with the counselor, and Thursday Renee would be seeing her father for the first time in almost two years. Cassie's hand fell on Renee's shoulder, a sense of protection emanating from her. "This is my daughter, Renee."

Johnny beamed at Renee. "I've sure heard a lot about you. I'm glad I get to finally put a face to all those stories." He handed her a small bouquet of daisies. "These are for you, young lady."

Renee looked flustered for a moment, her eyes darting between Cassie and me, seeking reassurance.

I nodded at her. "Go ahead, sweetie."

She reached out and took the bouquet, seeming enthralled by the flowers. It was, as far as I knew, the first time she'd been given flowers. "Thank you. I never heard about you until tonight, but my mommy said you were probably nice."

Soft laughter erupted in the room, breaking the tension. Renee puckered her cheeks, obviously unsure if she should smile or feel embarrassed.

"That's my fault, Sugar Bug. I kept Johnny a secret for far too long." Though I was looking at my granddaughter, I could feel Johnny's eyes on me. I handed my flowers to Cassie, "Could you put these in some water?"

She nodded, smiling with her eyes as much as her mouth.

I turned to Johnny. "Are we ready to go?"

He gave me a quick nod, then looked at Cassie and Renee one last time. "It was a pleasure meeting you ladies. I hope your mom . . . grandma . . . let's me stay and visit with you a little longer next time." He gave Renee a wink and shook Cassie's hand again, then opened the door. "After you," he said.

Once we were in the car, I complimented Johnny on the flowers. "It seems you put some thought into getting each of us a unique bouquet."

"I'm glad you noticed." A hint of playfulness laced his tone, matching the smile lines that deepened around his eyes.

"How did you choose the flowers?"

"Well, I sought advice from the florist." He glanced toward me for a moment, then back to the road. "I told her this was an important night, so I wanted the flowers to not just be pretty but have meaning. She helped me pick based on what I wanted the flowers to say." He shrugged one shoulder.

"That's really deep, Johnny Beckett. And very thoughtful."

Johnny's hearty laughter filled the car. "Thanks."

Silence followed, broken up only by the sound of windshield wipers pushing away the falling rain. I sighed. Apparently, he wasn't going to tell me more unless I asked.

"So, what were the meanings of the flowers?"

We came to a stop sign and Johnny looked both ways, peering through the rainy darkness, before proceeding.

"Well, the daisies stand for purity, innocence and loyal love. I thought that fit Renee, based on her age and what you've told me about her."

I sucked on my bottom lip, the image of my sweet granddaughter's face filling my mind. "Yes, I agree."

"The gladiolus represents character and honor. I think that fits Cassie well, from what I've heard."

I smiled. Character and honor. What people like the

Fergusons were apparently unable to see when they looked at my daughter. "Yep. Sounds right."

Silence filled the car again for a moment, and I wondered if Johnny was going to tell me what my flowers were supposed to mean. Red roses, I knew, stood for love, or something like that.

Johnny cleared his throat and glanced at me again, his blue eyes intense. "The red roses represent love—and longing."

My heart quickened.

"The white roses represent a new beginning."

I looked down at my hands. My ringless fingers. Johnny had given me a ring last year, but I'd never worn it. It was a ring with a promise, but no commitment to the future. I remembered his proclamation at the time—he wasn't a marrying man. "Didn't we have a chance for a new beginning a year ago?"

"We could have, but I don't think either one of us was ready."

I studied my hands. The hands of a middle-aged hotel maid. The hands of a grandmother. The hands of someone who had made mistakes and been forgiven. I straightened my neck and leaned back against the head rest, then looked at Johnny. "Are we ready now?"

Johnny turned to me with a lopsided grin. "I know I am. I'm just waiting on you, Angel Eyes."

I returned his smile, but couldn't speak around the lump in my throat

We had dinner at a quiet place on the west side of Eugene, where we began catching up over the last year. Johnny told me more about his plans for the farm, and I couldn't help but smile at his enthusiasm. After dinner he put his napkin on his empty plate and then studied me. "What do you think

about helping me with the you-pick stuff and holiday fairs, once we get them going?"

"I'm kind of busy with my job and family, but I might be able to help out here and there." Maybe I could take Renee with me. She'd have fun.

Johnny leaned back in his seat. "I'm not saying volunteer. I'm talking about a paying job. You can quit the hotel."

Quit the hotel? It was the longest, most stable job I'd held since . . . well, ever. I couldn't imagine quitting. "I don't know Johnny, that's a bit risky. I need a steady, secure income."

Johnny frowned. "I understand." He tapped the table with his fingers, seeming lost in thought. "How's the custody thing going with Cassie? How are things with her and Matt?"

Talk about a change of subject. I took a sip of water. "Cassie and Derrick met with the counselor for the first time today. From what Cassie said, it went pretty well." I pushed a stray strand of hair behind my ear. "Personally, I still don't trust him. I think Cassie's trying to be optimistic because she's been forced into this situation and there's no way out."

Johnny grunted and shook his head. "Man, I feel for her, and for Renee."

I nodded. "Tell me about it. As for the situation with Matt," I smiled. "They are doing good. The wedding is still on the schedule."

Johnny grinned. "I'm glad to hear that. Are they having it at the church?"

I frowned. "I think the location is yet to be determined. Next Sunday will be Matt's last day as the youth pastor at Cascade Christian. They are looking for a new church."

"Whoa, that sounds like a big change. What happened? The last I heard Cassie was having second thoughts about Matt. I didn't know he was changing careers."

"It's a long story." I sighed. Might as well tell Johnny the whole ugly truth of what happened. I gave him the Reader's

Digest version but threw in the overheard bathroom conversation for good measure, so he could have a better picture of what Myrtle was like.

"That sounds like a pile of manure hit the fan on a hot day."

I chuckled at Johnny's analogy. "You could say that."

His brows came together. "Is it hard for you to go to church there now?"

Boy, wasn't that a good question. "Yes, but I'm committed to help lead that recovery group I told you about, so I'm kind of stuck."

"That's during the week, though, right?"

I nodded a yes.

"You're free on Sundays to go where you want?"

I lifted a shoulder. "I guess. When I'm not working."

"Then come to church with me this Sunday."

I straightened in my seat. "What?"

Johnny gave a short laugh and rubbed the back of his neck. "I guess I should say, would you like to come to church with me this Sunday?"

Go to church with Johnny? In Junction City? To the church Christy, who toted casseroles but didn't steal hearts, took him?

"I know it's kind of a long drive for you." Johnny's voice held a hint of disappointment, "I understand if---"

"I don't mind the thirty-minute drive, but I wouldn't want to leave Cassie alone if she decides to go to Cascade Christian one last Sunday."

"Cassie and Renee can come, too." Johnny gave me an impossible-to-argue-with grin.

I inhaled, and before I could overthink, gave my answer. "Then it's a deal."

Chapter Thirty-Five

Cassie

MATT WENT WITH ME TO PICK Renee up from her first counseling session with Derrick. The counselor's office was inside a suite of office buildings with a wall of vertical windows, most of which had blinds that kept others from seeing in. Each office had its own entry door. We sat in my Explorer, watching the time. The counselor said she would send Derrick out of her office first, and then we could come in to get Renee.

"I hope she's okay."

Matt squeezed my hand. "She'll be fine." But even he sounded unsure.

A few moments later Derrick walked out of the building, looking annoyed. Once he was in his vehicle, now a small red Toyota truck, Matt and I got out and went to the counselor's office. I opened the door to the small office and peeked in. Renee was sitting at a children's table when we walked in, coloring a drawing.

"Hello." The counselor, Elizabeth, sat at a desk and peered at us over the rim of her silver rimmed glasses. "Come on in."

Matt and I entered. Renee looked up from her coloring but didn't say anything.

"How'd it go?" I asked.

"Everything went well, all things considered." Elizabeth got up and approached us. She nodded toward Matt. "You must be, Matt, am I correct?"

Matt held out his hand. "Yes, nice to meet you."

Elizabeth turned back to me. "Will this time next week work for you to bring Renee back?"

"Yes, I can make that work."

"She didn't have much to say today, but I expect we will make progress over the coming weeks." Elizabeth smiled. "Patience is key. That's what I let her dad know, as well."

"Hey, Renee, are you ready to get some dinner?" Matt approached Renee, who was still engrossed in her coloring. She raised her gaze at his question but didn't smile.

"I thought we were getting ice cream?"

Matt leaned his ear toward his shoulder. "We are, but I'm thinking we should have dinner first, don't you? Otherwise, we'll get a stomachache."

Renee slowly put the crayons back in the box. "Okay." There was no enthusiasm in her voice.

I looked to Elizabeth, my eyebrows raised, a silent question I hoped she'd answer. Why was Renee acting this way? Had something happened?

"This is all new." Elizabeth said quietly, a small smile wrinkling her aged skin from chin to ear. "Like I said, patience."

I nodded and reached for Renee's hand, but she walked straight to the door without looking at me.

Elizabeth gave a sympathetic nod. "See you next week."

Matt took my hand, gently rubbing the back of it with his thumb. "Let's go."

We tried asking Renee how her visit with Derrick went, but she stonewalled us. Based on what the counselor had told me when I met with her earlier in the week, I knew not to push for information.

After a quick spaghetti dinner, which, thankfully, my mom had made before going to her group, Matt and I took Renee to the ice cream shop she requested. It was newer, in a nice part of town and had exotic flavors I had never heard of.

"What second grader wants lavender and honey ice cream?" I asked Matt, as we perused the menu. "I'm surprised this is the talk of eight-year-olds."

"You'd be surprised. With social media and all the pressure, kids are growing up way too fast these days."

"I guess so." My heart sank a little. It seemed I missed so much time with Renee between work and my studies. Now I could be looking at her spending every other weekend with Derrick, too. Time, it seemed, was a thief.

When we got to the counter, instead of ordering any exotic flavors, Renee requested their version of her old standby, mint chocolate chip. Matt and I exchanged a look, both of us smiling. Maybe she was staying little, despite the pressure. We found a small table and sat with our cones. We had discussed how to talk to Renee about the changes coming up with church. She had a steady friend there in Isabella, but I knew we would stay in contact with Samantha and arrange playdates. Matt and I still didn't know where we'd go to church after this Sunday, and he'd even given me an out for this time, saying I didn't have to go. But the words in the Bible that stood out to me over the past weekend were still there. Stand firm. No running.

"Hey, kiddo, I have exciting news." Matt lifted an eyebrow as he leaned ever so slightly toward Renee.

"What?" She licked her green, chocolate chip speckled ice cream.

"I got a new job!" Matt genuinely sounded enthusiastic.

For the first time all day, I felt a sense of excitement about the future.

"Job?" Renee asked, pausing on her ice cream consumption. "What job?"

"I'm going to be working for the police department."

"You're going to be a policeman?" Renee's eyes grew wide.

Matt took a bite of his ice cream. "Kind of. I won't have

a gun though. I'll be helping people, maybe directing traffic, stuff like that."

"Will you have stickers? Police officers who visit our school bring stickers."

Matt made a frown, as if thinking. "Maybe. If I do, want me to bring some home for you?"

Renee nodded and licked her cone again. "Does that mean you won't be my pastor when I'm a teenager?"

"I'm afraid not, kiddo, but I'll make sure you have a good one."

Renee's eyebrows came together, and she stopped eating. "Are you still going to be my daddy?"

Matt smiled, and we exchanged a look that spoke a thousand words. Then he bent toward Renee. "Absolutely. Always and forever."

Renee smiled.

I cleared my throat. "But we are going to try something new, since Matt isn't going to be working at our church anymore, we're going to go visit some other churches and see what they're like."

"Will Grammy come with us?"

I sighed. "Maybe. It sounds like this Sunday she's going to church with her friend Johnny."

Renee beamed, green ice cream lining her mouth. "I like Johnny."

"He brought you flowers."

"He makes Grammy really happy." Renee took another lick of her cone. "Can I go to church with Grammy? At Johnny's church?"

"This Sunday?"

Renee's head bobbed up and down. I looked at Matt. He shrugged and held up the palm of his hand.

"I guess so. I'll talk to Grammy." I knew my mom would

say yes, but best not to assume.

Renee's statement stuck with me. *He makes Grammy really happy.* I agreed. Where would their relationship lead? Mom might have wedding bells in her future, too.

Sunday arrived. Mom and Renee were heading out the door. I hugged them good-bye.

"Keep your chin up, Baby Girl." Mom looked at me with a fierce love.

I nodded, but inside I was a hurricane of emotion. It seemed appropriate that I would be going to Cascade Christian Church alone on my last Sunday there. I'd gone alone on my first Sunday, when I began my search for a church. Church shopping, as they called it, was not a fun experience. As a single-mom, I'd found it especially difficult to find a place where I felt like I belonged. I found it at Cascade Christian Church. Their group for single parents made me feel like there was a place that recognized and cared for me. I'd grown in my walk with the Lord during Bible studies, and my time in the Adult Children of Alcoholics group. I somehow even managed to get Mom to go, even after her run-in with Samantha.

And Matt had ended up there. If not for Cascade Christian, we'd likely never would have crossed paths again.

As I drove, I was overwhelmed with gratefulness. I didn't like how things were ending at the church. I didn't like what had become of the leadership. But if I had to go back, I wouldn't change it. Doing so would erase everything I currently loved about my life, about myself. I might never understand the bad that happened, but God had brought me to Cascade Christian Church. For a purpose, and for a time.

Now he was setting me free, into a new beginning.

"Cassie! Good to see you." Samantha looked to the left and right. "Where's your mom? Renee?"

Mom must not have told Samantha she was going to church with Johnny this Sunday. I hedged, not wanting to lie. "They went to church with a friend of Mom's today."

"Oh." Samantha's face fell slightly, then she tilted her head. "You're on your own for Matt's last Sunday as the youth pastor?"

I inhaled. Everyone knew. At least all of the leadership. I'd undoubtedly face more questions than I was ready to answer. "Yes, but it's fine. It's kind of nice."

Samantha studied me, her dark eyes slightly squinted. "Will you and Matt continue coming here?" Her voice was low, almost a whisper.

There were only a few people I'd feel comfortable telling the truth to this morning. Samantha was one of them. "Probably not." I met her eyes. "It's too hard."

She nodded. "I completely understand." She squeezed my arm. "Tell your mom I said hello and to give me a call when she has a chance."

I nodded. "I will."

I continued toward the sanctuary, having no appetite for a donut. Matt was standing at the youth room entrance. Emily stood on the other side of the entrance, chatting with a parent. Matt's posture was stiffer than usual, guarded, but smiling. He was probably dealing with a whole host of questions himself, plus he had to tell the youth goodbye. I knew the good-byes would be hard for him. He truly cared about the kids. I held up my hand to give him a wave. He raised his hand in return. Emily saw me and waved back enthusiastically. I gave her a weak smile and continued walking, but from the corner of my eye I saw her rushing toward me.

Great. I tried to turn toward the pastries, looking for someone to talk to so she would, hopefully, not interrupt.

Stand firm.

I sighed, feeling a new strength. I turned toward Emily just as she reached me.

"Cassie! How are you? We missed you at church last Sunday."

She noticed I wasn't at church. Interesting. "Oh, I wasn't feeling great that morning. Over-tired, I think."

Emily's face scrunched to a look of exaggerated concern. "You poor thing. It's hard being a single mom, I'm sure."

I pasted on a smile. "It's worth it. Plus, I have a lot of support."

"Oh, well that's good. I was so surprised to hear that Matt handed in his resignation, and that it was for a non-pastoring job." Emily shrugged one shoulder. "I'm sure it's for the best."

"For the best?" I kept smiling.

Emily waved her hand at me, the scrunch returning to her face. "Oh, you know, with your upcoming wedding and everything. Taking on fatherhood with a blended family, all of that."

I gritted my teeth. "Yes, it's definitely for the best."

"My dad said I should apply for the position, but I don't know. I mean, I'm new here and all, and I haven't been to seminary or anything." She laughed lightly. "Daddy always likes to point out how worthless my interior design degree is." Emily inhaled, lifting her chin. "Regardless, he thinks I have enough experience for the youth position."

I nodded, a chord wrapping around my stomach. Those poor kids if they ended up with Emily as their youth pastor. Also . . . Emily . . . it was like there was something she was telling me that went far deeper than what was on the surface.

"I think you should pray about it." It was the truth,

though it sounded cliché and inadequate. "Sometimes we need to block out all the other voices, know what I mean?"

Something shifted in Emily's features, like a mask being dropped. I saw pain in her eyes. Sadness etched around her small smile. Then, in a flash, it was gone.

"Oh, you are so right. Prayer is everything." She beamed, touching her heart. "Well, I better get back to the youth room. Worship will be starting soon." Emily beamed and then sauntered off.

Before service began, several other people approached me who were in the know, and gave me best wishes on Matt's new career, as if it were my own. I didn't tell any of them that I most likely would not be coming back to Cascade Christian, until Kathy approached me. Her knowing, wise eyes were impossible to lie to.

"Will you guys keep coming to church here?" She asked.

"I don't think so." I frowned, feeling sad. I'd miss Kathy's genuine warmth and care for people.

She nodded. "You have my number?"

"Yes."

"Good. Stay in touch. I expect one of those wedding invitations." She wrapped me in a big hug. "I'm going to miss you."

"I'll miss you, too." It was true. Saying good-bye was hard. How I wished life never required them.

Chapter Thirty-Six

Sharon

"Grammy, does this church have donuts?"

I turned back to look at Renee, who was trying to undo the seat belt of her booster seat in the back. We'd pulled into the Grace Community Church parking lot. The parking was in the back of the church and people were walking down a walkway to the front of the brick building. The church looked more like a large, single-story house than a place of worship.

"I don't know Sugar Bug, I guess we'll find out."

I got out of the car and opened the back door for Renee, who had chosen to wear one of her spring dresses, even though the temperature was hovering near forty degrees. The sky was clear, though, with only a few scattered clouds. Altogether a beautiful fall day. I took Renee's hand. "Ready?"

She nodded and clasped my hand, holding tight. I followed the stream of people going toward the front of the church, keeping my eyes peeled for Johnny. I spotted him at the peaked entrance, standing in front of the double doors and looking the other way. When he turned toward me, I waved.

Johnny spotted me and beamed. He was dressed nicely, in dark jeans and a button up shirt. I was glad I'd chosen to wear one of my few dresses today, along with a long cardigan. When Johnny approached me, his mouth dropped open ever so slightly. "You look beautiful."

Despite my best efforts, I felt heat run up my neck. "Thanks."

He looked at Renee. "Hi, Renee. I like your dress, very pretty. Makes me miss summer."

She giggled. "Do they have donuts here?"

Johnny's brow wrinkled, as if in thought. "I'm afraid not, but if it's okay with your grandma, I'd love to take you to brunch after service. I think the diner I like has donuts." Johnny gave me a sly smile.

Renee's eyes lit up and she looked at me, the question evident in her expression.

"We can probably do that," I agreed.

Johnny gently took my elbow. "Let's go inside. Christy's been telling everyone you're coming today."

Great. Talk about showing up low key. But part of me warmed at the idea that my appearance was anticipated and talked about. When we walked through the entrance, we were welcomed by the greeter, an older gentleman who wore a checkered suit. A younger lady, who looked like she might be about Cassie's age, handed us a bulletin once we were in the entryway. Worn carpet lined a wide, long hall. A set of double doors opened to the sanctuary, which was filled with chairs in a C shape around a stage. This church was far smaller than Cascade Christian but felt homey, even if it didn't have donuts.

"Hello, there." Christy walked up to us. I almost didn't recognize her with makeup on and a nice dress.. "I'm so glad you're here."

I introduced her to Renee, and Christy told me about the children's services. "We have children dismissed after worship for their own time of teaching."

"That's nice, that they stay during worship." I liked that idea, and hoped Cassie and Matt would consider coming here, even though it was a bit of a drive from Springfield. "I'm thinking Renee will probably sit with me during the whole service this time, though."

Christy smiled. "Of course." She looked at Renee. "I could

get you a coloring sheet and some crayons if you like?"

Renee nodded. "Yes, please."

Christy excused herself. I turned to Johnny and smiled. "Who would've thought, back when we met, you and I in church together?"

Johnny gave me a dimpled smile. "I guess sometimes broken roads lead to the best destinations."

I nodded my agreement. *You got that right.*

The warmth of Sunday made going to the Higher Focus meeting on Thursday night even more difficult. I needed to talk to Frank. He had been pretty quiet himself, and I wondered how he was doing with the church and the uncertain future of our group. After the meeting, I asked him if we could chat before we headed out the door.

"Of course." He said, stuffing a stack of pamphlets in his bag. "What's up?"

I pulled a chair from one of the tables and sat in it, indicating Frank to do the same. This wasn't a conversation I wanted to rush. "Last time we talked about the group, you said you weren't sure if you would continue doing it, at least here."

Frank let out a sigh and nodded. "Yes, that's correct."

"I don't know how you're feeling now, but I know I can't continue." Though I was relieved to be letting Higher Focus go, I was sad about all the missed opportunities for those who needed the group—and I was sad for Frank.

"I understand." Frank nodded. "I heard about Matt, and I wondered if your family would continue coming to church here, given everything that's happened."

I leaned back in my chair. "It's been tough. I went to another church with a friend this last weekend. I think I may continue there." In all honesty, I was almost one-hundred percent certain I would. On top of enjoying going to church with Johnny, his church kind of reminded me of the one I'd grown up in. Not too big. Warm and friendly, like a big family meeting. "I'm not sure what Cassie and Matt will do."

Frank studied me with eyes that held a touch of sadness. "I'm glad you found a friend to go to church with."

I chewed the inside of my cheek, considering if I should tell Frank more about my "friend." The way he said friend, though, hinted that he knew. Plus, it wasn't like Frank and I had dated. We'd been partners in ministry.

Before I could decide what to say, Frank continued. "We're almost wrapped up with the core course for Higher Focus, and then the participants are supposed to break into small groups." Frank shrugged. "I'm not sure what to do. Without support from the leadership, this group won't grow. There's not enough attendance and commitment in the group right now to support having even one small group."

"I'm so sorry this hasn't worked out the way you hoped." I tried to find words to encourage Frank. The look of defeat in his eyes was disheartening. "But it's not because of you. I think you should keep trying. Find another place."

"I agree." Frank nodded and lifted his chin. "I've already reached out to a group that's Christian based but not connected to any church." Frank blew out his cheeks. "I admit, this has been tough, but I guess if we look at what all the disciples went through, we have it pretty easy." He picked up his bag and stood, then held out his hand. "It's been a pleasure working with you, Sharon. Thank you for taking this on with me, despite everything."

I rose to my feet and shook his hand. I looked in his eyes and tried to find the little spark I thought I'd caught glimpses of before, but it was gone. Whether it had never been there, or had been chased off by the circumstances, I didn't know. Either way, it was for the best. "Thank you, Frank, for believing in me. I'll never forget that."

He smiled. "It was an easy thing to do. Remember, God has a plan, even when we can't see it."

I knew Frank was right. Now, I was starting to see the beginning of His plan. With just enough light for me to take the first step.

Chapter Thirty-Seven

Cassie
Two months later . . .

I OPENED THE EMAIL FROM ELIZABETH during my lunch hour. She had called earlier in the morning, so I knew it was coming, but dreaded reading it.

It'd been a little over two months since Renee and Derrick had started the counseling with Elizabeth. The counseling-centered visits extended far longer than Derrick had anticipated, and what we agreed to in mediation, due to Renee's lack of communication during their sessions with Elizabeth. The counselor had managed to convince Derrick that more visits were vital to the future success of unsupervised visits. Over the weeks, though, Renee had slowly warmed up. Elizabeth said she saw positive signs in their relationship, and Derrick seemed fully capable of unsupervised parenting time. The extra weeks of counseling had been a gift to my anxious mother heart. Now, that time was up.

I clicked on the document and scanned its pages. A weight grew on my chest with each word I read. The proposal called for unsupervised visitation every Saturday for six hours. Through Elizabeth, Derrick had requested that I give up the protective order I had against him. After much thought and prayer, I refused his request. Now, to avoid violating the protective order, Elizabeth's proposal said I would drop Renee off at the entrance of our local mall, and then wait in the parking lot for Derrick to arrive and pick her up. Once he had arrived, I would leave. We'd repeat the same process in reverse for Renee's return to me those afternoons. After eight weeks of unsupervised daytime visits, Renee would begin overnight stays with Derrick.

My mind whirled, trying to take it all in. Two things made me nervous, like when driving and coming up to a blind spot on a winding mountain road. I didn't like the idea of dropping my eight-year-old daughter at the mall entrance and having her stand there waiting for Derrick. What I hated even more was her riding in a vehicle with Derrick behind the wheel. The last time she'd been in his truck, he'd been drunk, ran off the road and into a fire hydrant. Luckily, Renee wasn't physically hurt, but she was emotionally scarred. In my opinion, he hadn't yet gained enough trust to have that much freedom with her.

"This is nuts." I spoke my thought out loud, my blood boiling over.

"Work drives me nuts, too." Missy's voice came from behind me.

I swiveled my chair and looked at my friend. "I can't even see straight right now, my heart is beating so fast."

The look on Missy's face shifted from bright-eyed good humor to the furrowed look of concern. She leaned against my desk, a Snapple tea in her hand. "What's up?"

I pointed my thumb over my shoulder, toward my computer screen. "The counselor sent over the recommendations for unsupervised parenting time."

"I take it you don't like her recommendations." Missy gave me a wry smile. "What has Mr. Bossy Pants conned her into?"

Missy didn't hold back her opinions, including that of my ex, though she'd never actually met him. Some would call it judgmental, but I knew Missy. She had good intuition. I told her a summary of the plan, and why it didn't sit well with me.

Missy took a sip of her tea and gave a nod. "Yep, he's got her fooled. I say you tell her your concerns. If you end up not agreeing with her recommendations, you guys can still go to court over this, right?"

"Yes . . . it's not that cut and dried, but yes, there are options. The thing is a judge will look at this and probably give Derrick what he's asking for here."

Missy gave a little laugh, shaking her head. "When I listen to this plan, I wonder how much Derrick influenced it. I mean, he tried to get you to drop the protective order, saying it would make parenting time exchanges easier on Renee, right?"

I nodded. "I can't drop it. I don't trust him."

"You have valid reasons not to. It seems like this *proposal* puts you in a place where you're desperate. I mean, he's got to know you're not going to be happy with him driving her around after what happened." She gave a shrug. "I don't know, but I say you tell this counselor you're not comfortable with that and why."

I stared at the floor, digesting Missy's words. Could the counselor have been swayed by Derrick's pleas? Missy was right. I needed to call her and make my case. Do all I could, within my power, to protect my daughter, and pray.

Then stand firm.

"I'm going to call her." I turned around and picked up my phone.

Missy waited patiently, sipping her tea.

Elizabeth didn't answer, which wasn't surprising given it was the lunch hour, so I left a message.

"You go girl." Missy slapped me on the back. "By the way, I found some wedding decorations that are perfect for the barn. I'll send you the link."

I gave her a smile, thankful she had come up with something to distract me. "Thank you."

Matt and I had set the wedding for a week after school got out in June. After much discussion, and some coaxing from Johnny, we'd agreed to have our wedding outside at

Johnny's place, with the reception in the barn. "I work better on a deadline," Johnny said. "Knowing I need to get it done before June will motivate me." I was thankful for his offer, but knew it was just as much for Mom as it was for Matt and me. Matt and I both wondered when Johnny was going to pop the question. The flustered way Mom acted sometimes, I think she wondered, too.

Pastor Reynolds had agreed to officiate our wedding. Matt and James Reynolds had stayed in touch after we left Cascade Christian Church, and they played golf almost every week. Our church shopping expedition had been cut short by Matt's variable hours, and by the fact that we were quickly finding ourselves feeling right at home at Grace Community Church with Mom and Johnny. We both agreed, though, that we hadn't been there long enough to ask the pastor to officiate our wedding.

Mom stayed in touch with Samantha, and I regularly talked to Kathy and occasionally to Trish. From everything we heard, the tension at Cascade Christian Church had not let up. I heard from Mom that Frank, the guy who had led the Higher Focus group, left the church and was going elsewhere.

I sent Matt a text before my lunch break was over, letting him know about the counselor's recommendations, my fears, and that I had a call in to her. I knew he would pray, even if he didn't have the chance to reply to the text or call right away.

Toward the end of the afternoon, Elizabeth called. I laid out my concerns.

"What do you propose be done for transportation for his visits?" Elizabeth asked. "He's made it very clear that he is not okay with you dropping her off at his place, given his fear of violating the protective order."

I was thankful we were on the phone, so Elizabeth couldn't see me roll my eyes. Perhaps Derrick had changed so much that he truly was fearful of any kind of violation of the order, but I also knew he was smart enough to know what a prosecutable violation would take. "My mom or fiancé can drive Renee to and from his place on Saturdays," I offered. I hadn't talked to Matt or Mom about that plan, but I knew both would do whatever they could to help. Between the two of them, we could make sure their schedules lined up.

Elizabeth was quiet. I could hear the clacking of a keyboard on her end. "I think your concerns are valid, at least for now, and that's a reasonable solution. I'll present it to Mr. Peterson."

"Thank you," I breathed, speaking as much to God as Elizabeth.

"I'll let you know. We have almost a week before our next meeting. That should be more than enough time to fine tune any details."

I spent the next several days focusing on schoolwork, the wedding plans, and my family. Staying busy helped me not think about the fact that Elizabeth wasn't getting back to me right away.

Monday morning Cynthia gave me another distraction of sorts. She called me into her office, then told me to shut the door and take a seat.

"I'm pregnant." Typical Cynthia. No preamble or emotion. Just the facts.

"I kind of suspected as much." I smiled. Missy had been right from the beginning. Over the last month or so, I'd noticed Cynthia's clothing getting a little tighter around the middle.

"I'm due in May." She took a deep breath, held her shoulders back. "I've decided to take an extended leave."

Extended leave? I was expecting a couple of months, maybe three, and that the attorneys would fill my time with overflow work from their assistants. "How long is extended?"

"A year." A smidge of sympathy showed in her brown eyes. "I'm afraid that means your position here will end when I take leave."

I opened my mouth but didn't have words. I wouldn't have a job as of May. The month before I was to marry Matt. I'd need to find another job, one I could still somehow manage to work around my school schedule, and one that had comparable pay. I took a deep breath. "Thank you for letting me know."

"Of course. I completely understand if you want to look for another job sooner rather than later." Cynthia glanced at the clock. "Though, I'd prefer you'd stay, of course." She picked up a file from her desk. "Now would *not* be a fun time to train another assistant."

I stared at her, unsure of how to respond.

"Besides," she extended the hand that held the file, obviously wanting me to take it. "You do good work."

In Cynthia speak, I'd just been handed a huge compliment, at least by the terms of our relationship. "Thank you. I'm going to talk it over with my fiancé, but I don't see a reason to jump ship quite yet." I took the file from Cynthia's hand, noting the piece of legal paper with barely readable handwritten notes she'd pinned to the cover.

"I'm glad to hear that." She turned in her chair and picked up an apple that was sitting on a plate by her computer. "I need to get dictating."

I smiled, took a calming breath, and exited her office.

Tuesday night, my phone rang with an unknown number. I almost didn't answer it, but a nudge in my spirit made me change my mind.

"Hello?"

"Cassie? This is Elizabeth."

The counselor. She must've been calling from her personal cell phone since it was after hours. "Hi, Elizabeth."

I gently sat in one of the dining chairs. Mom and I had just finished cleaning the kitchen. When she heard my greeting, she stopped drying the last dish and sat in the chair beside me. Renee had gone to her room to play before bath time.

"I'm calling to give you an update on the parenting time proposal." Elizabeth's voice had a slight quiver to it. "I called your attorney and left a voicemail."

I blinked. She'd called my attorney? "I'm listening."

"Well. Okay. To put it simply, Mr. Peterson did not take well to the amended proposal that didn't allow him to transport Renee."

I wanted to say, "I'm sure he didn't." But I held my tongue.

Elizabeth continued. "He became quite livid and verbally vulgar when I spoke to him on the phone about it, after you and I talked last week. I was taken aback, to be frank. After we hung up, I emailed him that going to unsupervised visits at this time was clearly not a good idea, given his explosive temper. I said that he needed to seek counseling individually, outside our sessions with Renee. He didn't take well to that, apparently."

I looked at Mom and mouthed the words. "Derrick," and shook my head. "I'm sorry he was like that with you." I told Elizabeth. I knew what it was like to be the subject of Derrick's scary outbursts.

"I was waiting to hear back from him before I finalized my decision and let you know what had occurred." Elizabeth sighed. "He emailed me back last night, making some vague but also . . . chilling threats. I've forwarded that to the police."

My mouth gaped. Derrick had, once again, shown his

true colors. At the last hour, when all I had to hang onto was hope. When all I could do was stand and have faith that God would protect my daughter.

"What happens now?" I asked, after finding my voice.

"That's up to your attorney, and the judge. After seeking some advice from my own attorney and the board that licenses counselors, I need to remove myself from this case. At this point, unfortunately, it's a conflict of interest for me to even continue seeing Renee. If you feel that she could benefit from counseling, I can send you a few recommendations."

I thanked Elizabeth, and told her, again, how sorry I was for what Derrick did, then hung up the phone.

"Well?" Mom asked, sitting on the edge of her seat.

I filled Mom in on the details. "I need to call my attorney tomorrow." I concluded. "I'm not sure what will happen from here."

Mom lifted her eyebrows. "Whatever it is, it won't be good for Derrick, I can tell you that."

Mom was right. It took some phone calls and the scheduling of a hearing before the judge, but the result took us back to square one. Supervised only parenting time, until decided otherwise by the judge. From what Zane told me, it meant Derrick needed to seek counseling and to show that in addition to overcoming his alcoholism, he had learned to manage his anger. It wasn't even a week after the Judge's order when I got a call from Zane.

"Derrick called. He has a proposition."

I braced myself. What was he up to now? "What is it?"

I heard a smile in Zane's voice as he continued. "He will sign away his parenting rights in exchange for you dropping all future claims to child support."

That was it? Derrick was giving up Renee. There would

be no more battles.

It was good news, but my heart pinched, thinking of Renee. Derrick was walking away from his daughter. For all appearances, it was for money. Or maybe it was simply because he wasn't getting his way. But what could I do? It wasn't in my power to change Derrick. That was up to God. Perhaps someday Derrick would look in the mirror and realize the damage he'd done. Maybe someday he would seek help from the One who could restore his heart, his mind, and his soul. Until then, my duty as Renee's mother was simple. To love and protect her, any way I could. To seek God in all things as her parent, and then to stand firm.

"How do we get the process going?" I asked Zane.

Chapter Thirty-Eight

Sharon

TIME MOVED FASTER AS YOU GOT older. It might not be a scientific fact, but from what I'd been experiencing, it was true.

Matt and Cassie's wedding date approached quicker than a race car on its last lap. Here it was early May, and it seemed there was so much to do. Of course, the whirlwind life we'd been riding didn't help with the ticking of the clock. The final order—ever—in Derrick and Cassie's case had been issued. Once Matt and Cassie were married, he would officially adopt her as his own. Listening to the adoption process made me teary-eyed. It wouldn't only be Renee's name changing. Her new birth certificate would list Matt as the father, like he had been there from the moment she was born. Watching Renee with him, I knew in her heart, he already had the title. I was certain that relationship helped her bounce back quickly and without any apparent harm from Derrick's antics.

For Cassie to find out her job was coming to an end was a turn of events I didn't expect. Matt and she had discussed it, and much to my surprise—given Cassie's stubbornness— they decided it would be best for her to focus on school and not find a new job right away. They'd have Matt's income, which would be just enough for them to get by. Cassie could finally breathe a little after she was married and enjoy her role as a wife and mom without all the added stress of a full-time job.

Matt and Cassie had found a small home, a house just big enough for their family of three. After much prayer, I'd passed on Matt's offer to continue living with the family after their marriage. A wise mother knows when she's needed, and when she needs to step back. I thanked God for giving me the wisdom to tell me when to let go, even though it was hard.

Now I had to find a place to live. Janice offered a room in her home. I thanked her for it, and had it in mind as a backup option, but still I searched for a studio apartment I could afford. I was making a little extra money on the side, helping Johnny on the farm. Truth be told, watching him diligently labor away on the barn was pay enough. His heart, soul, and sweat went into that project. I'd be lying if I said I didn't like to stand back and watch him, his burly arms working a saw, lifting a two-by-four. We'd been dating for five months, and at times he still made me feel like a silly teenage girl with a crush. I'd even pulled the ring he gave me last summer from my mom's music box and put it on my right finger. When I agreed to meet him for dinner Friday night, after I'd put in a fifty-hour-week between my job and helping him, it was a testament to my feelings.

Driving up the gravel road to his house, I laughed, thinking back to the day I showed up unannounced. Thank God I had done one last crazy thing in my life. Turning the bend in the drive, I admired Johnny's work on his mom and dad's manufactured home. He had their little deck completed, and Mr. and Mrs. Beckett were sitting out on it as I drove by. I waved and they waved back, looking especially cheerful. With spring in the air, who could blame them?

I parked my car in the drive of the house . . . Johnny's house. It'd take me some time to retrain my brain on that one. When I got out, Christy signaled me through the open living room window. "Johnny's in the barn." She bellowed, waving with gusto.

What was she doing in Johnny's house? I shrugged away the thought. Probably making something for his folks and didn't want to make a mess in their new kitchen. Of course, she could have made it at home and brought it over, but Christy, as sweet as she was, didn't always do things that made sense to me.

I headed to the barn, surveying all the changes in progress on the property as I went. The barn was repaired, cleaned up, and painted. An arbor was in the process of being built in the field to the side of the barn, and gravel walkways had been made from the barn to that field, allowing easy access from a wedding there to a reception in the rehabilitated barn. Johnny had been working on putting a concrete floor in the barn all week. He was probably at it still, and in a spot where he couldn't stop.

When I walked in the barn, the first thing I noticed were the string lights hanging in the beams along the sides. I'd assumed those wouldn't go up until after the floor was done—which was the next thing I noticed. The floor. Johnny had been working on it in sections, and it appeared he had one section left to go. I guess I was so impressed it took a moment for my eyes to land on the white clothed table along the wall, with two chairs, candles, and service ware. I tilted my head, suppressing a smile. Johnny.

Where was he?

"What do you think?"

I jumped, startled by Johnny's voice behind me. Before I could turn around, he wrapped his arms around me, and nuzzled my neck. "No hobo stew for you this time, Angel Eyes."

I laughed, remembering the dinner he'd cooked over the fire the last time he'd surprised me. I craned my head over my shoulder, meeting his eyes. "I'm impressed—and I think I'm underdressed." I'd shown up in jeans and t-shirt, expecting grilled burgers and maybe some chips.

Johnny gave me a squeeze, "You look perfect, and we make a good match." He came to my side. He was dressed casually as well, wearing jeans and a t-shirt with flannel over the top. It felt too warm out for flannel to me, but I didn't question his attire. He motioned toward the table. "After you. I hope you're hungry."

I walked over the new concrete floor, admiring Johnny's handiwork. The table was on the right side of the barn. As I got closer, I heard soft music playing, and then noticed the speaker plugged into the wall. "You've outdone yourself, Johnny." I scanned the table, noticing the nice dinner plates, utensils, cloth napkins, and even champagne glasses. One hurricane candle glowed in the middle of the table. Red and white rose petals were scattered around it.

My heart soared. This was the kind of stuff you read about or saw on the Hallmark channel. It wasn't my life, was it? The emotion built in me, and I took a deep breath to stuff it down, keep it at bay. I needed to say something but couldn't find words. The only thing I could think to ask was, "Where's the food?" I wanted to hit myself in the middle of the forehead for blurting that out, but luckily, Johnny grabbed my right hand before I could.

"It's coming." With his other hand, he pulled out a chair. "Take a seat."

I did as he said, noticing that the chairs were the nice wooden kind and not metal folding chairs. Johnny took the seat across from me, and a satisfied grin spread from ear to ear.

"Christy volunteered to serve us dinner tonight," he said, the familiar twinkle appearing in his eyes.

So that's what she was doing in his house.

"That's awfully nice of her." I put my hands on the table and smoothed the tablecloth that didn't need smoothing. Talk about nerves.

"It sure is. It gives a us a chance to talk."

I met his gaze. The glow of the candle in the semi-darkness of the barn brought out the blue in his eyes, making them more intense. "Is there something we need to talk about?"

Johnny chuckled and looked at his plate, then his gaze shifted to my hands. He gave a little nod toward my right hand, the one with the opal ring he'd given me. "You like that ring?"

I considered the ring on my hand, as if seeing it for the first time. "It's pretty. And unique. Yes, I like it."

Johnny gave another little nod, his eyes still on my hand. "I think you need one for the other hand. Something with a diamond." He lifted his gaze, meeting my eyes. "Something to wear for life."

I swallowed, my heart fluttering in my chest.

Johnny reached into the pocket of his flannel shirt and pulled out something small, something I couldn't quite see. Reaching across the table, he took my left hand in his. Then he opened his other hand, which held a simple white gold, solitaire diamond ring.

"Sharon, will you marry me?"

I stared at the ring, gleaming in the candlelight. A promise of commitment. Of forever.

"I thought you weren't the marrying kind?" I croaked.

I expected Johnny to laugh, but instead he spoke with the kind of emotion he had that day in the orchard, when he'd told me about finding God. "That was the old me. This is the new." His gaze met mine, unwavering. "I love you, Sharon." Johnny's periwinkle blue eyes shimmered in the candlelight. "I want you to be part of my new life. Now and forever."

I sucked on my lips, willing the tears not to come, but it was no use. "I love you too."

"Is that a yes?" The corner of Johnny's mouth lifted in a playful grin.

My head bobbed up and down.

Johnny slipped the ring on my finger.

Epilogue

Cassie

THE WEATHER TURNED OUT PERFECT FOR our wedding day, despite a rain storm the day before. Blue skies, not a cloud in sight. The temperature was warm but cool enough that I was comfortable in my simple white dress.

I stood alone behind the tool shed, waiting for the song to play that would signal my time to walk to the altar. It was the perfect waiting place for a bride with the setup Johnny had made for the wedding. I was able to slip out of the back door of the house, where Missy, my mom, Renee, and I had all gotten ready for the wedding. As my maid of honor, Missy had already walked around the tool shed and down the aisle in the outdoor venue. Christy had then come and guided Renee to the beginning of the aisle. Any moment now it would be my turn.

Finally, the strum of the guitar sounded, the beginning of the song Mom had found to play for this day. A song she had modified for me and Matt, and one that my famous, country-singer uncle, who I'd only met once, was helping her perform.

Clutching my bouquet of mixed flowers, I began my walk toward the arbor where I would stand with Matt and say the vows that would join us for life. As I walked, I didn't feel alone. In my heart, Grandpa walked beside me. My smile broadened, thinking of how Grandpa would approve of Matt . . . and of how God had used Grandpa's image and my trust in him to reach me when I was lost.

When I turned the corner of the tool shed, I saw Renee reaching the end of the aisle. My heart swelled. My daughter looked like a true princess in a pink dress and with her hair pinned up, tiny flowers running through it like a crown. I couldn't see her face, but by the smiles of the guests, I could tell she was beaming. She'd been looking forward to this day almost as much as I had. The day she could start calling Matt, Daddy.

I continued down the aisle, lined on each side by rows of white wooden chairs. The closely trimmed grass of the field squished under my feet. Familiar faces smiled at me as I walked toward the arbor. Faces from work, like Cynthia, who held her newborn baby in her arms. Faces of people from Cascade Christian, like Samantha and Kathy, who had stayed in my life even though we didn't spend Sundays together anymore. Faces of people from our new church, who were quickly becoming good friends. My smile broke into an excited "O" when I saw Bonnie, the woman who had been my daycare provider right after the divorce. I had invited her, but not expected her to come. Yet, here she was, sharing in my joy.

I blinked back tears. All these people God had put in my life. In one way or another, they had been part of His plan. Some guided me, some challenged me.

Many loved me when I was unlovable.

Just like Jesus.

Now, I stared straight ahead, focused on the altar. Missy stood on the left of the arbor, tan and beautiful in her summer dress, giving me her spunky smile. I'd hoped my wedding day would finally get her in a church building. Our outdoor wedding nixed that idea, and I'd worried that my experience at Cascade Christian might deter her from ever stepping in a church building. It took me by surprise when, just a few weeks ago, she told me she wanted to know more about "this Jesus guy." When I asked her why she now was curious, she said it was seeing Matt and me not give up on church after everything that happened. "I figured this Jesus thing must be something good, to not run away from the whole shebang after that."

On the other side of the arbor and next to Matt was his best man, the friend from Silverton I'd only recently met. A friend, it turned out, who had connections to a church in Medford that was looking for a pastor. After Matt and I prayed about it, we agreed he would reach out to them after our honeymoon. It meant another change for Renee, and moving three hours from Mom, but we agreed it was worth looking into further.

Mom. Because she and my uncle were the band, she wasn't able to fill her traditional spot as the mother of the bride during the ceremony. A few years ago, I wouldn't have wanted her at my wedding. Now I couldn't imagine life without her.

The chair Mom should occupy in the front aisle was empty. When I looked that way, I could almost see Nannie sitting there. The woman who had been a mom to me as much as she was a grandma. The one who had prayed for her family, no matter how hopeless our situations seemed.

In perfect timing to the song's end, I reached the altar. Matt stood with his hands crossed in front of him, smiling ear to ear. In only a few moments, he would be my husband. The man I thought myself unworthy to stand beside. The man who hadn't given up on me even when I tried to run away.

Just like Jesus.

Pastor Reynolds held a Bible in his hands, ready to begin the ceremony. We were doing things in a slightly untraditional way, including not having him ask who was giving the bride away. There was no one here, other than perhaps my mom, who could give an answer to that question.

Renee stood beside Missy, the flower basket still in hand. She wore a smile so big, it would put any flowers to shame.

"Who gives this woman to be married to this man?"

Pastor Reynolds asked, his voice carrying across the field.

My shoulders tensed. Oh, no. Had he forgotten our plan?

"Me and Jesus do!" Renee shouted, rising on her toes.

My gaze shifted to my daughter. Her smile was brighter than the gold heart necklace around her neck. The one Matt had given her when he asked me to marry him. Two promises made in one day. Three lives woven together by a loving, eternal God.

Soft laughter, mixed with many "ahhs" came from behind me. Laughter rose in me, too, mixed with joy unlike any other I'd ever felt. My focus shifted to Matt. The glimmer in his eyes told me that he and Renee had planned this moment. A perfect way for our family to begin.

Matt reached his hand out to me, and I took it, taking my place beside him. A place where I would stand, forever.

Author Note

Finishing this book was bittersweet for me because it wraps up the *Whispers of Grace* series. When I wrote *One Woman Falling*, I had no idea a series of books would come out of it and the journey that would mean for me as a writer.

I have three daughters, and I can tell you with certainty that I do not have a favorite. I love and have a special relationship with each of them. I now have three books, and while I can say I love each one, I *do* have a favorite, and it's the book you just read: *One Last Stand.*

I loved being able to share the viewpoints of both Cassie and Sharon in one book. I wasn't sure how the story would end, exactly, and I cried happy tears as I wrote the last chapters and epilogue. After all the struggles they faced in the previous books, having Cassie and Sharon both finding their "Happily Ever After," was the perfect way to end Whispers of Grace.

Thank you for taking this journey with me, dear reader. I hope you have enjoyed this series, and that your own story has its happy moments, filled with the hope that comes from above.

BOOK DISCUSSION QUESTIONS

1. When the story opens, Cassie feels unsure how she will juggle her responsibilities at work, her role as a mother, and the extra pressure and time commitment brought on by school. Her mother, Sharon, helps by taking some of the childcare and housework load off Cassie. Who have you known in similar circumstances? How did you find ways to help?

2. What do you think of Sharon's "fleece prayer" in her decision on whether to co-lead the Higher Focus group? Why did she equate Johnny not accepting her Facebook request as a sign to say yes to co-leading the class? Have you ever asked God for a sign in this manner? What was the outcome?

3. What does Renee's reactions to the letter from Derrick and her response to seeing him at the park tell you about her memories of him? How could you reassure a child in the same circumstance and help them feel safe?

4. "Every good and perfect gift is from above, coming down from the Father of the heavenly lights, who does not change like shifting shadows." (James 1:17 NIV). Matt and Cassie are good gifts to each other. Yet, Cassie struggles with accepting this good gift. Why do you think she struggles with accepting Matt's love and devotion? Have you ever struggled to see and accept the good God gives you?

5. In this story, Samantha seems to have forgiven Sharon for things in the past, and the two have become unlikely friends. Have you ever had an enemy become a friend? What initiated

the change? If there is someone you currently harbor resentment toward, how can you let that go and move to a place of forgiveness and restoration?

6. Cassie questions her worthiness of Matt. Her feelings of inadequacy become a wedge in their relationship. Have your negative feelings about yourself ever caused harm to a relationship? Were you able to mend the damage? If so, how? If not, is there something you realize now that would have made a difference?

7. Sharon and Cassie are both angry and hurt by the leadership at Cascade Christian Church. Have you experienced leadership failures in a church or bias and shunning by church members? How did you handle the situation? How did church leaders respond? If the situation ended in hard feelings, how can you move past those? How could the situation have been better handled? How did you stay strong in your faith despite the failures of a church body?

8. Throughout the story, Frank seems undeterred by the situation at the church when it comes to doing ministry through the Higher Focus group. Have you ever felt like you did not have the full support of church leadership when involved in a ministry that was important to you? How did you handle the situation?

9. Do you think Matt and Cassie communicated well as a couple? Why or why not? Could Matt and Cassie's problems have been less serious or even avoided if they had been more upfront about their feelings? Do you find it easy to share your feelings with your partner?

10. Johnny returns to Junction City without a word to Sharon. Why do you think that is? What kinds of reservations do you have about him at that point in the story?

11. During the wedding scene at the end of the story, Cassie reflects on how the people she sees there, including her husband-to-be, have been "just like Jesus." Who has shown you the unconditional love of Jesus? Is there someone in your life you can be "just like Jesus" to today?